BANGKOK
WET

SIMON ROYLE

Also by Simon Royle

Bangkok Burn
Tag

About the author

Simon Royle was born in Manchester, England in 1963. He has been variously a yachtsman, advertising executive, and a senior management executive in software companies. He lives in Bangkok, with his wife and two children.

BANGKOK
WET

SIMON ROYLE

PRESS

First published in Thailand by I & I Press 2013

This I&I Press trade paperback edition 2013

This is a work of fiction. Any similarities to people
or places, living or dead, is purely coincidental.

ISBN 978-616-90769-2-6

A CIP catalogue record for this title is available from the
National Library of Thailand.

Typeset in Adobe Garamond Pro and
Franchise for Chapter Headings.

I&I Press
249/17 Lat Phrao 122,
Lat Phrao Road,
Wang Thonglang,
Bangkok 10310

WWW.SIMON-ROYLE.COM

For Kae and Neo
the *real* Godmother and Godfather

naam theung nai bplaa theung nan – Wherever there's water, there're fish

A Shitty Job

Por sat in his motorized wheelchair in the sala looking out at the river. A ramp had been built alongside the steps. The sound of the rain beating a soft persistent rhythm on the roof of the sala mingled with the urgent whisper of the river. I walked around in a wide circle so as to come into his peripheral vision from a respectful distance. His hearing had been getting worse, and I also didn't want to startle him. The sawn-off shotgun he always kept loaded by his side, a deterrent to such stupidity.

Beckham was sitting cross-legged at Por's feet, mixing a whiskey soda. When he saw me, he smiled and raised his hands in a wai, the tongs for the ice held in the palms of his hands. Por turned to face me and smiled, indicating with a wave the chair next to his right hand. I waied Por

1

and sat down. A Mac Air was open on his blanket-covered lap. He pointed at it.

"Pim sent me a list of prosthetic limb manufacturers. I will need to go to New York soon. I thought we might go together, like old times."

Beckham put a whiskey soda in front of Por and started mixing a glass for me. Por really did mean old times. The last time we'd been to New York together was when I was sixteen or seventeen, something like that.

"Yes, Khun Por, I will look forward to that."

"Perhaps when you come back from your honeymoon?"

"Yes, Khun Por."

Beckham put a tall glass in front of me. Por raised his, and we touched glasses. The heavy crystal made a satisfying ping. His hand steady as rock, Por took a long swallow and let out a satisfied sigh. "Ah, there's nothing like a long, cool drink while the sun's going down."

I waited patiently, Por never wasted anyone's time, especially mine. He'd get to what he wanted to say, in his own way, at his own pace. He closed the notebook with his free hand, and Beckham unobtrusively slipped it off his lap. He leaned forward a little, his voice barely above a whisper. This was his gangster voice. A voice that had delivered a thousand secrets, shared hundreds of plots, and more than a few threats. A quiet voice gravelly with harsh use, certain in its power, words carefully, distinctly delivered.

"I'm hearing rumors out of Here Leng's patch. Bad stuff about his son, Goong. They've been around for a while, but it looks like things are coming to a head. Have you heard anything?"

"Nothing new, Por. Just the usual. There was the incident with the Kamnan's teenage son last year, but Leng paid out. Kept it quiet, and since then I've heard nothing." 'Here Leng', Big Brother Dragon to you farang, controlled Phra Pradaeng, a district bordering our district of Muang Samut Prakarn and also Phra Samut Chedi District.

"I heard the boy did it again, but this time the father is not interested in money. The father wants justice or Goong's head."

"Who is the father?"

"A farang."

Now it was clear why I was here. As 'Dek Farang', the nickname given me by Por when he adopted me, it was my job to deal with everything related to farang.

"I see."

"Leng asks if you could have a chat with this farang and see if you can work something out."

My personal preference for dealing with this would be to put a bullet, of a large caliber, in Goong's head, but I kept those thoughts to myself.

"I know you'd prefer to put a bullet in Goong's head..." with Por I was an open book, "but Leng has been our friend for many years. He has also given permission for you to talk to his son. After you've talked with the farang, I want you to tell Goong that if he does this again, we will turn him into a woman before we feed him to the crocs in 51. The crocs like shrimp."

"Yes, Khun Por." I took a sip of the whiskey, a sour taste, to be washed away.

He looked me in the eyes, holding me in his stare. I

nodded. His round eyes narrowed slightly, then relaxed, satisfied I'd got the message. He was due to retire in six months. Till then he was still boss of bosses, and even if I was 'acting boss of bosses' – he was still my boss and always would be. Of course, he had admitted to me a long time ago that Mere Joom was the real 'Big Boss' – although you'd never hear Por admit that in public.

He continued, his voice like the river, a quiet murmur but powerful. "There's something brewing over in Virote's district. The second wife of his youngest son, I think her name is Som, something like that anyway, she's taken out a couple of contracts on the eldest son and the first wife of her husband. The gunman is a friend, so he passed it on, but if she doesn't see some action soon, she may take the contract somewhere else."

Virote had three sons and one territory. The eldest son, Khemkaeng, a forty-year-old with a reputation for being a cold-hearted bastard, hated the youngest son, who had exactly the same reputation and reciprocal hate. The feud had been simmering below the surface for years. As the old man's day of reckoning got closer, it looked like it was about to reach the boiling point. I didn't need Por to tell me what would happen if either of the two sons was killed prematurely. There'd be a free-for-all grab for the territory, and a shooting war would erupt. Every guy with a gun and a couple of buddies would think they had a shot. Bad for business.

"The middle son is the reasonable one. He's a good-hearted boy, but he's a little weak. Doesn't want to rock the boat. When Virote goes, and I understand that's going to be any day now, we're going to have a war on our hands.

When the old man passes, we should step in. Declare our support for... what is his name?"

"Supot."

"Yes, that's it, Supot, but we'll need to deal with the other two at the same time. They'll move fast, so we must be ready first."

"I'll put someone on it, Khun Por."

He nodded and settled back in his seat, reaching down to scratch the stump of what remained of his right leg. I still had a score to settle with Pim's father over that missing leg, but it was one of those things you had to let go. The evidence I had, I couldn't share, and the desire to kill Sankit I definitely couldn't share with Pim. Por and Mother had taught me there are many ways to deal with a threat. The surest and best is to destroy its source. I wasn't taught to forgive and forget. I was taught to seek and destroy. Was Sankit still a threat? I doubted it, but I hadn't forgotten nor forgiven.

I'd put a team on watching Virote's sons. Learn their movements and habits. When we needed the information, we'd have it at hand. It wouldn't be long now; Por was right. Virote hadn't left his home in over a year except for visits to chemo. His radiologist told us "not long now", the cancer had spread too far to control. The chemo sessions had stopped a month ago. I took a sip of the whiskey and looked at the swollen river running by.

It wasn't just that I was a dutiful son, that I followed Por's 'suggestions'. I'd learned by experience his words always meant something. At times obtuse, vague, variously direct, and indirect, his timely advice was always apparent when whatever had happened was looked at in hindsight.

Of course, the fact that I was his son meant that I would do whatever he asked me to, whenever he asked.

The ice cubes in the glass floated free of the remaining whisky, sliding down the glass and bumping my upper lip. Beckham raised his eyebrows and made a 'do you want another one' face. I shook my head, put the glass down, and gave Por a wai.

"Khun Por, I have to get going. Tomorrow's going to be a busy day, and Saturday I'll be traveling. I must see the farang this evening."

Por nodded, I rose, Beckham handed me an iPhone. The farang's details would be inside it.

Walking up the path, I heard one of my phones beep. An SMS from Chai – 'Meet u at hospital, Starbucks'. The bamboo network at work. I SMS'd him back – 'K'.

With Pichit driving, I had time to read the information we had on Michael Sullivan, the father of the boy Goong had beaten and raped. The more I read, of what little we had, the more pissed off I got. The police report: boy found naked, sobbing beside the road, bleeding from mouth, nose and anus. I felt sick. The fastest flicker of a thought: I could disobey Por and kill Goong; do it right now. Quickly dismissed, the thought banished, I breathed out. The moment over, I had to do this Por's way.

Michael Sullivan, British, worked for a multi-national. He was an accountant, married to an Aussie woman, Susan, and they had one son, David. The son was now recovering in Bumrungrad Hospital, the most expensive hospital in Thailand, having come out of ICU the previous day. The cops were sitting on it, waiting for direction from the powers-that-be, in this case, me. Or rather through me to Por and then to a couple of friendly cops and the whole thing would vanish. At least that was the idea. We had to see what Mr. Sullivan had to say first, a conversation I wasn't looking forward to.

At Sukhumvit Highway Route 3, the river had burst its banks, and parts of the road were under water. It was still navigable, but Pichit took it easy, the roads busy at six p.m. on a Thursday evening near the end of the month. When we reached the ramp to the expressway, it was reduced to a single lane with cars parked either side up the ramp by those who lived in low-lying areas. I sympathized, nothing worse than a flooded car, you'll never get rid of the smell. All the parking lots in Bangkok were full. Office buildings, the airport, every piece of high ground occupied by the cars of the people of Bangkok. The official population of Bangkok is nine million or thereabouts, the actual population, on any given day, is closer to eighteen million.

It took us an hour and a half, good going for a rainy rush-hour commute, to get to the hospital. I got out next to the Starbucks and looked through the window. Chai was sitting at a corner table, his back to the wall. The left side of his face was swollen to the size of a small watermelon. He'd been to the dentist. I tapped on the window. He didn't smile. Chai is my bodyguard; we grew up together. I went inside.

"Bad day?" I asked him.

He still didn't smile. Just stood up and made a 'follow me' gesture with his head. We turned right out of Starbucks, in the corner of the lobby, toward an elevator hidden away. Chai pressed the up button, and we waited. Bumrungrad is like a cross between a five-star hotel and a hospital. The hospital's signs in Thai, Arabic, and English – a sign of where most of the customers come from. High society and middle-class Thai, wealthy Arabs, and then farang. Despite the marble flooring, it still smelled like a hospital. I had a flashback to the conversation I'd had with Pim a couple of weeks ago.

"It's easy. You walk in, make a deposit, and walk out. Nothing to it," Pim had said. She was lying on her stomach, a pillow under her hips, reading a baby magazine, post sperm extraction. She had studiously avoided looking at me when she spoke. Her first line, "You should go see that specialist recommended by Dr. Tom," had been delivered the same way. I shuddered.

The elevator stopped at the sixth floor, and we walked out. A nursing station and a seating area in front of us, I went straight to the nursing station.

"Hi, I've come to see a friend, Khun Michael Sullivan?" The nurse tapped at the keys on the keyboard in front of her. One advantage to looking like a farang is that Thai people in Bangkok will automatically assume all farang know all other farang. If Chai had asked for Sullivan, she'd have asked Chai for his name. She picked up a phone and punched nine, followed by six, four, and one. She looked at me while she waited for Sullivan to pick up. She smiled. Without reading too much into it, I would have put money down that had I asked her what time her shift finished, I would have got an accurate answer. I'm not a gambling man, and I didn't ask. The tiniest pique of annoyance disappeared with a frown as she spoke into the phone.

"Mr. Sullivan, a friend has come to visit you. He

is waiting at the nurse station." Her English was pretty good. I smiled at her in thanks and sat down on one of the sofas in the seating area. Being early evening, the area was quite busy with a mix of patients and the relatives visiting them. An old man in a wheelchair, IV drip attached, sat a couple of meters away from me, watching the news on CNN. The angle of the television screen, hanging from the ceiling, had caused his eyes to roll up, his mouth open and slack. I wondered if he was still alive.

Sullivan walked to the nursing station. I recognized him from the photos in the file. He looked disheveled, as if he'd been sleeping, a shirt tail hanging out. He was wearing flip-flops, black suit trousers and a white short-sleeved shirt. The nurse pointed at me. I rose and walked over. His eyes were red, swollen, I guessed, from crying and lack of sleep. Your worst nightmare will do that to you.

I held out my hand. He looked at it and then slowly, gingerly raised his to shake mine. His grip was weak.

"Mr. Sullivan, my name is Chance Paknam. I'd like to have a talk with you, if I may."

"Are you with the press?" Bucketfuls of hurt in his eyes.

"No, I'm not with the press. Mr. Sullivan, you don't know it, and maybe never will, but I'm a friend, and I'm here to help. Can we talk?" I noticed he had a pack of Marlboro in his top pocket.

"Perhaps we could take a walk outside where it's more private and you can have a smoke?"

He looked at the doors to the balcony with a smoker's hunger and nodded. I led the way. Chai moved ahead of us, strolling through the doors, an eye on me. I shook my head slightly. No need for backup.

It was still raining outside on the verandah. I walked over to a covered area, a smoking sign stuck to its wooden pillar. The little sala offered protection from the rain. It'd be cozy if you ignored what we were here to talk about.

We sat down, and Sullivan pulled out his smokes. He offered me one. I quit last year, really I did, but I took one to keep him company. Pim would shoot me if she found out. The first lungful was pure guilty pleasure.

A Promise Made

naam ning lai leuk – Still waters run deep

Bangkok, Thursday, 27 October 2011, 8:05PM

On the drive to the hospital, I'd thought about how I was going to approach Sullivan. I tried to think about it from his perspective. That of a man whose only son had just been beaten and raped. I struggled with that. Hard to imagine wanting to do anything except burn the world down around the ears of whoever had done it. He was staring at his feet, forearms on his thighs, cigarette dangling from his fingers.

"Mr. Sullivan, I can't begin to imagine how you must feel right now, but please do accept my heartfelt condolences for what has happened."

He took a drag of the cigarette. I waited.

"Who are you, and what do you want?" He didn't look up when he spoke and took another long drag on his

11

SIMON ROYLE

BANGKOK WET

cigarette when he finished.

"Like I said, I'm a friend, and I'm here to tell you the best way to sort this out." That got a reaction.

His head came up sharply, his mouth tight around the edges, gritting his teeth. He swallowed, his Adam's apple bobbing up and down a few times. "Mr. Paknam, I don't know you. So I don't see how you could be my friend. If I don't know you, how can I know that you know the best way to sort this out? Who sent you?" He glared at me.

"Mr. Sullivan, I'm the guy who is going to kill the man that did this thing to your son. That's a promise." I looked him in the eye and enjoyed another illicit drag.

His eyes widened, and he looked around to see if anyone had heard what I just said. "What did you say? Who are you?" He looked confused, a little frightened.

I leaned forward, hands clasped in front of me, getting my head close to his. "I said I'm the man who is going to kill the beast that did this thing to your son. It's better you don't know who I am, but if you insist, I will tell you. Let's just say I represent powerful interests who understand your situation but also want a certain outcome."

"What do you mean?"

"I mean that if you make a noise about this, nothing will be achieved except more harm to your family. The alternative is to take a long paid holiday. Move to Australia for a few years. Take your son away from this place, somewhere where you can spend time together and help him heal his wounds. And when the time is right, I will send you evidence that the man who did this terrible thing to your son is dead. That's exactly what I mean. By the way, the threat to your family will not come from me or those I represent. It will come from the man who did this to your boy. If you accept my proposition, my protection, I'll put the wheels in motion right now. If you don't, then I'll finish this smoke and you won't see me again." Just in case you were wondering, farang, I don't make idle promises.

Sullivan looked at me, his eyes round with surprise. A little of the tiredness fell away from his face, and something that might be called hope crept into his eyes. He looked wary. He had taken a beating in the last couple of days.

"My job…?"

"That's a minor detail. Money is not a problem. The man's father, and the reason we have to wait, will pay. Not blood money, nor a pay-off. We'll take it because it will hurt him. To make it hurt, we'll take a lot, maybe half a million Aussie dollars."

"… but I can't just leave…"

I held up my hand and raised my eyebrows. He stopped speaking.

"Your boy is the only thing that matters now. Believe me when I say that the best treatment right now is to get him away from here, be on a nice beach somewhere, and lavish love and attention on him. That's it. You take care of that, and I'll take care of everything else. Deal?" I held my hand out to him.

He looked at it warily and then looked in my eyes. I guess he saw enough, as he took my hand. His grip was still weak. I squeezed his hand firmly, not letting go as he started to pull his hand away. I kept it in my grip. His eyes, a startled look in them, found mine again, his gaze having shifted away when he took my hand. I wanted to give him strength, not scare him. I smiled with my eyes. His grip strengthened; I squeezed back and released his hand. He had tears in his eyes. I nodded and grasped his shoulder, giving it a hard squeeze.

"I want you to go back to your wife and boy now. Stay in the room until I call you. If there's anything you need, anything, in the meantime, you can call me twenty-four seven on this number." I wrote a number on a card and gave it to him. He held the card in one hand and took a beaten-up brown leather wallet out of his back pocket with the other. He carefully placed the card in the wallet after he'd read the number a few times – I saw his lips moving silently as he'd read.

"We'll move you to a suite later this evening, and as soon as David is well enough to travel, we'll escort you to the plane. In the meantime, I'll have my men guarding you and your family. You can travel freely around your business, but I think it'd be smarter to lay low for a few days and spend the time with your family. Got it?"

He looked at me, a more determined man now that he had a way out. "Got it."

I stubbed the cigarette out in the little bucket of sand provided and stood up. Sullivan stood.

"Be well, Michael. I'll be in touch soon." I left him there. I knew he'd need another smoke.

Chai joined me at the elevators.

"Did you bring a car?"

Chai nodded.

"Car got a trunk?"

Chai nodded again.

"Okay, let's go pick up Goong."

Chai's eyes took on a slightly feral gleam.

"No killing. Not yet."

Chai led the way. Past the food court, McDonald's, the Au Bon Pain, and the little merit-catching cluster of clear Perspex donation boxes, crammed with green and red, mostly twenties and hundreds. If you're sick and in Bumrungrad, there's only so much charity you can afford.

Chai was exaggerating when he said the car had a trunk. He was driving a brand new Ferrari 599 GTB Fiorano. I could have picked better cars for the night's work but not many more expensive. Landed in Bangkok, a Fiorano would set you back in the region of seventy-three million baht, or about two and half million United States dollars. I looked across at Chai over the roof of the car and looked pointedly at the rear of the car. He shrugged and got in.

Goong owned a gay club and massage joint out on Lat Phrao Road in a small sub-soi off Soi 43. He was there now. Our guys had been following him since yesterday when Por first received word of what had happened. Goong's father had provided the first location, knowing what would happen if he didn't.

Normally we would have just taken the Din Daeng Expressway and dropped straight down onto the beginning of Lat Phrao Road, but Lat Phrao intersection was flooded under a meter and a half of water. Instead, we could ride the expressways until we reached the middle of Lat Phrao and put in a U-turn. Odd-numbered sois are always on the left-hand side of the road if you're looking from the beginning of that road.

The on-ramp at Sukhumvit up to the expressway had

the now familiar parked cars running down both sides of the ramp. Motorcycle taxi boys had a new market: delivering car owners to and from parking spaces on the elevated expressway. We're an enterprising people. Always ready to turn a disaster into a profit.

The roads were emptier than earlier in the day. A lot of Bangkok's people had left – those that could. Those that couldn't leave were looking for high ground, and those that didn't have it were waiting to get wet. In typical Thai style, the government had decided not to charge for expressway use, generous of them, given that some parts were under a meter of water and others you couldn't descend from unless you wanted to go swimming.

Chai only knows one speed when he's driving, and I suspect he chose the Fiorano because he knew the roads would be empty. I thought we'd lose traction at any moment as he held a steady 120 kph coming around the loop from Din Daeng to the expressway leading out to the turn-off for Lat Phrao and the airport. We didn't crash, and with the toll gates up, Chai punched us up through fourth and then fifth gear, a glance at the speedometer showed the needle climbing to 240. A little fishtail skid and a heart-thumping correction as he over-braked for the corner, Chai got us on the Chalong Rat Expressway without a wipeout. The road straight, he wound us up again until, I looked at the time on the cell, six minutes after leaving the hospital we were on Lat Phrao Road heading north. I wondered how many mentally scarred drivers Chai had left in his wake, but it's an excellent way of getting the adrenalin going.

At Soi 41 we made a U-turn, and Chai put us in the

left lane and turned slowly into Lat Phrao 43/Soi Santi Kham. We took the first right, cruising slowly up the road, saw the sign, and took another left and then another right. Directly in front of us, Goong's Club. Plus one for Google Maps.

I recognized one of our boys, Dan, sitting in a taxi, engine idling, window open, having a smoke. Chai slowed to a stop next to him and lowered the windows. Dan tossed the cigarette and gave us a wai.

Chai mumbled something. I couldn't make out what he'd said. I didn't laugh.

"He's still inside. A few customers, mostly his rent boys, and it looks like he's got some muscle boy for a bodyguard," Dan said, his face eager for praise.

"How many?" I asked.

"About ten, not counting the customers, boss."

"Okay, stay here, no one in or out until you see us again."

"Yes, boss."

We pulled away at a crawl, Chai turning the lights off. I watched in the rear-view mirror as Dan blocked the entrance to the small soi with his taxi. I pulled on my DSI sharpshooter's cap and put on my Ray-Bans. Chai handed me a Glock 17, one of my favorite weapons. I checked the load and racked the slide, putting one in the spout. Better to be safe than dead.

The club was in a typical seventies-style, single-storey Thai house. Chai parked next to the front door. I got out, and we walked to the door. A dark-skinned young guy wearing very short white shorts and a tank top opened the door for us. He smiled at me. I smiled back, then he saw

Chai, the wrong end of Chai's Uzi, and his face went pale.

Chai pushed him ahead of us into the dim interior of the club. I stood still, my eyes adjusting to the gloom, looking around the room. Low-slung black chairs on a black carpet. Blue light, a fish tank, a TV screen and a curtained-off door with a VIP sign above it. Chai moved in front of me. Neither the rent boys nor the customers moved. It was as if it was a tableau frozen in time. Chai pushed aside the curtain and stepped into the room. Two sofas faced each other with a low table in between. A huge hairy testicle was on the large screen set in the wall. Goong on one sofa, his muscle boy had just got up from the other and stepped towards us. Big mistake.

Chai skipped forward, ramming the suppressor on his Uzi into muscle boy's crotch. He folded like an obedient beach chair, writhing on the ground at Chai's feet. Chai put his foot on muscle boy's head, pinning him to the ground, and pointed the Uzi at Goong. Goong put his hands in the air. Smart. You could see why he was the leader.

"What the fuck is this? Who the fuck are you? Do you know who I am?"

Chai reversed the Uzi and lightly rapped the butt into Goong's mouth for an answer. He screamed, eyes wide with terror, now that the usual bullying shit hadn't worked, spitting teeth into his hand, blood streaming from his open mouth, glaring at us with scared eyes. Chai took out a stun gun and pressed it against Goong's chest, pushing the little red button set in its center. Goong shuddered, his eyes rolled up, and he went slack against the sofa. Chai shouldered the Uzi and took a black cloth hood with a drawstring out, putting it over Goong's head, and double cable-tied his wrists behind his back. Chai stooped and pulled Goong up onto his shoulder, unslinging the Uzi at the same time. Muscle boy had started to retch; it was messy. We got out of there.

I closed the door of the club. Dan saw us and jumped in the cab, reversing towards us and popping the trunk. Chai looked at me, I nodded, and he, not too gently, dropped Goong into the trunk of the taxi. It was a tight fit with the LPG gas tank that our taxis run on. Chai slammed the trunk shut. No one came out of the club.

"Take him to the farm. We'll follow you," I told Dan, and we walked back to the car. Rainfall slashed white in the light of a street lamp. I flashed on the dyke at the farm. It had rained steadily since I had left it before noon.

bplaa nao dtuaa diaao men moht thang khaawng — One rotten fish, everything stinks over a wide area

NO HARM NO FOUL

Bangkok, Thursday, 27 October 2011, 8:45PM

We made good time. The expressway empty of traffic, we stayed on the tail of Dan's yellow and green taxi, dropping down onto Sukhumvit Road by BITEC convention center. Even Sukhumvit, normally jam-packed at this early hour, was mostly empty. It reminded me of last year when riots had gripped Bangkok. This time the enemy was water not each other. Don't get me wrong, we're still at each other's throats politically, just that the imminent problem was the twelve billion cubic meters of water that were upon us.

As we passed Soi 113, an eighteen-wheel truck roared past us in the inside lane and swung out in front of us. Chai braked to avoid hitting him. The rear of the truck slewed right to left as the driver braked hard to avoid

Dan's taxi, but he was too late and rammed into the back of the taxi. In slow motion, the truck and the cab, welded together by the impact, slid across the road, hitting the bridge of the canal and smashing through the wall, and plunged over the edge into the canal below.

Chai pulled over sharply, and I jumped out, running to where the truck and cab had gone over. The truck and cab had separated. I saw with relief the taxi floating, the trunk open, Goong clearly visible lying next to the gas tank. I could just see Dan's head. He was slumped over the steering wheel. There was a soft whoomph sound, and the canal burst into flame around the eighteen-wheeler. I watched as a thin finger of flame spread on the water towards the taxi. I thought, "Shit," and a bright flash and an orange fireball lit up the gray walls of the buildings on either side of the canal as the taxi's LPG gas tank blew up.

My first thought was for Dan; he was a good kid. My second was that I'd have a tough time sending Sullivan a photo of what remained of Goong. My third thought was that I'd just started a war. Shit.

Time to call in the cavalry. Chai handed me a phone. I called Mother.

"Yes, Chance."

"We've got a problem. We're at Samrong Canal. Dan was driving a taxi and got hit by an eighteen-wheel truck."

"Is Dan all right?"

"Dan's dead, and Here Leng's son, Goong, was killed with him. Goong was in the trunk and immobilized when the taxi blew up. We need to tidy up."

"Understood. I'll take care of it. You should leave. There's nothing to be done for Dan. I'll handle the police.

Is Chai with you?"

"Chai's right here," I said.

She cut the connection without saying goodbye. A habit of hers with those she loves.

Sullivan. As soon as Here Leng heard of Goong's death, he'd be after Sullivan.

"Chai, let's get back to the hospital." Back in the Fiorano, I got on a new mobile. A quick word about our use of mobile phones and a tip if you're a criminal – don't use a mobile phone. Use lots of them. We circulate new numbers through five new phones every day for key family members: all color coded and pre-programmed with the day's contacts. Our communication strategy supports a micro industry of retail phone shops, phone thieves, programmers, couriers, operators, and SIM Card purchasers. For those who're up on their crypto, sort of a mobilized one-time pad; unless you can do this, do not use a mobile phone.

"You awake?" I said as soon as I saw 'connected' come up.

"Yes. Just finished a shift…"

"Good. I need you in the back of an ambulance outside Starbucks at Bumrungrad in thirty minutes. Have you got a visa for Australia in your passport?"

"I wish I could say no."

"Good. Don't forget to bring it. See you there."

I had seriously fucked up. The whole reason I had to pick up Goong was so that nothing untoward would happen. We couldn't guarantee Goong's safety with anyone else; he was too hated. Many a glass would be raised to his death in the coming days, most to lips with a smile on them. Goong wouldn't be missed by anyone, except perhaps his father and muscle boy. And maybe not even muscle boy, but blood is blood, and blood would be wanted for blood. What Shylock missed, 'Brother Dragon' wouldn't.

With Here Leng out for blood, which was inevitable, Sullivan, and most likely his son, would be an obvious choice. Next on the list would be me. The simple logic of 'face'. From there it would escalate into revenge and retribution, which could last decades. I had just driven a bulldozer, blindfolded, through a warehouse full of crystal. The whole delicate balance of interests maintaining the façade of civility in our districts smashed by a wayward eighteen-wheel truck.

The logical way, looking at a map, to get to Bumrungrad from where we were was straight down Sukhumvit Road. Logic and our traffic. Usually it would be packed with traffic, and a faster route would be to hit the expressway and loop around. It wasn't busy, though, and Chai went through it like we were running on fiber optic. Just after Asoke intersection, we cut across to the back sois running on the odd side of Sukhumvit Road. PB Hotel flashed past on the right as Chai punched the Fiorano down the narrow soi, tapping the brakes as we poked our nose onto Nana Soi 3 and shooting us past a guard, his mouth hanging open, into Bumrungrad's entrance.

Chai stopped at the pedestrian crossing in front of Emergency. An old woman supported by a male porter waited to cross. The porter smiled his thanks. As we waited for the old woman taking a count of three to make a step, five guys walked onto the other side of the crossing, near the lobby. I didn't recognize any of them, but they had the look – moving with purpose, a little swagger, and not a smile among them. I took out the Glock and racked a round into the chamber, keeping it hidden from view. I glanced around, not too many people around. Good. Cap and Ray-Bans donned, I felt my heart begin to thump.

The group of guys reached the island in the middle of the road and split around the old woman. The guy closest to us looked in our car. I watched his eyes take in first Chai, me, and then he looked straight ahead, cool. They were all carrying concealed weapons. They walked into the Emergency room. Probably just here to see a colleague. Not unusual for gangsters to be hospitalized: karmic hazard of the job.

And then the guy who had looked in our car stopped and turned around to look at us again. His face changed. Recognition. Ignition. His hand going for the gun at his back.

The old woman still in front of us, Chai looked over his shoulder, threw the car into reverse, and stomped on the gas. Twisting the wheel violently, Chai spun the car through a one-eighty-degree turn, and we were facing the wrong way on the one-way road out of the hospital. Chai clipped the front end of a taxi as he drove us the wrong way around the roundabout and onto the correct lane leaving the hospital. The guy who'd looked at us was running hard, followed by the rest of them. Chai slammed us over the speed bumps, the Fiorano airborne with its front wing hanging off. Mother wasn't going to be pleased. Another glance in the mirror. Most of the guys chasing us stopped and ran back towards the car park. The guy who'd recognized us kept coming, sprinting hard, and he was fast.

We turned right onto Nana. Chai stopped the car, and we jumped out. We were about five meters from the entrance. The guard took one look and started running away up the road towards Petchaburi, he could run too. Speedy Gonzalez came round the corner, leaning into it, and then he saw us. He tried to stop, a look of panic on his face, but Chai shot him with the Taser before he could. He crashed into the hospital's entry sign face first and bounced back, smacking his head hard on the edge of the pavement. He twitched violently and then lay still. Chai walked over to him and knelt down. He looked back at me and shook his head slightly.

I ran around to the driver's side and popped the trunk. Chai lifted now 'not-so-Speedy Gonzalez' in a fireman's lift, getting him over his shoulder. We folded him in the trunk. No body, no trial. We had to get out of there, though, and fast. The whole area is littered with CCTV, I was glad of the DSI cap and glasses, but I'd be ditching both before the night was out.

Back in the Fiorano covered in Speedy's bloody DNA, Chai stomped on the gas and threw a U-turn. Driving the wrong way up Nana Soi 3, we took off as we cleared the bridge and hit another taxi, this time with the left fender. We reached the intersection. I glanced at the police box; it was empty. Luckily the cops had decided to call it quits for the night. Chai drove us against light traffic through the red light and into the intersection. Another taxi hit us rear side right. We spun, Chai's foot on the clutch, revving the engine, until we got traction, and then we shot forward into Makkasan and cut through the parking lot of the Plaza Entertainment Complex. Anything named 'entertainment complex' is code for massage parlor. We have some of the largest brothels on the planet.

A left and a left later, we were slipping through the entrance to the expressway, free of charge thanks to the floods, and apart from the cars parked along its edges, empty. As soon as we cleared the toll gate's cameras, Chai floored it. I sat back and exhaled. There's nothing in Thailand that can catch Chai on an open road in a Ferrari. Nothing short of spikes and our cops don't have those. I retrieved the red phone from the 'phone' bag on the back seat.

"Yes, Chance?"

"Mother, we're on the way to the farm, making a special delivery. We also need valet service…" I glanced at the speedometer, two hundred and forty kilometers per hour.

"We should be there in about twenty minutes." I hung up and called Tum.

"Yes, boss."

"Double the security on Sullivan's room, and get ready to move him. Get some guys down to the entrance next to Starbucks, and make sure the way to the expressway is clear. We should be moving the kid and his parents in about thirty minutes. Dr. Tom will be in an ambulance waiting at the main entrance lobby next to Starbucks in about that time. I'll tell him to call you when he's ready. Got it?"

"Got it, boss."

I dialed Tom.

"Tom, I won't be able to meet you at the hospital. Tum is driving the play. Call him when you get there. I'm sending you his number now. Stay with the kid until I call you." Rain pelted down on the windscreen. I dialed another number, trying not to think about the folded-up body in the trunk.

After ten more calls, the Sullivans' passage to Singapore, Brunei, and then Darwin had been arranged. Medical evacuation flight clearance had been granted, and immigration was waiting by the charter jet.

The Ferrari slowed and stopped. Chai punched in the security code at the staff gate to the farm. It had been eighteen minutes since Speedy had died.

Standing next to the open doors of the warehouse, Pichit and Somboon looked like a pair of aliens. Chai drove us in and stopped on the plastic sheet laid out on the floor in the middle of the warehouse. I got out, squinting my eyes in the brightly lit, whitewashed interior. The warehouse doors closed behind us. Pichit walked over to me, holding out a bag, wearing a protective suit, helmet on. We have procedures; it's why we're the best at what we do.

I stripped, placing each piece of clothing in the bag along with the mobile phones, gun, everything I'd touched except the amulets around my neck. Pichit placed the bag on the sheet beside him and grabbed the handle of the extraction tube, basically a huge vacuum cleaner, above my head. The mouth was large enough to fit over my shoulders. Pichit flipped a switch, and a sound like a jet taking off filled the room. Powerful enough that I felt as if I'd be lifted off my feet, I held on to my amulets. The warehouse was sealed for sound; you would hear a pin drop outside the main door.

Pichit turned the fan off, the sound immediately winding down, and swung it over to Somboon. Another jet took off as I headed for the showers. The shower drainage ended up in the same place as whatever was sucked up by the vacuum: the furnace room. The Fiorano was a goner, too much DNA. 'Valet service' – code for vacuum-sealing a car in plastic. The car and engine block would be crushed, compacted, melted down, and on sale as scrap iron in Klong Toey before midnight.

The scalding hot water felt great. I turned up the pressure, the water pounding into the back of my neck, hands against the wall, tracking back over everything that had happened. Was I recognizable on a camera somewhere? Was Chai? Would any of what had happened be reported? I was sure the crash and explosion would have been reported already, but had they identified the victims? I turned the heat off and turned the cold tap on full, gasping with the shock, feeling each inch of me. I breathed out heavily, waiting for my body to adjust. Clearing my mind.

"Rough day, boss?" Pichit came into the changing rooms. Helmet off now that they'd wrapped the car and sent Speedy to processing. He placed big fluffy white towels on the bench, Mother's touch, and had a smile on his face.

"Yeah, not a good day," I said, ever the witty conversationalist.

Chai came out of a shower stall. The gentlemen's locker room could fit a football team comfortably. Green velvet and burgundy leather abounded. My locker was number 9. Nine for the tattoo on my chest, courtesy of last year's bombing of me and Por. He lost a leg. I got a permanent tattoo from the elevator button.

Somboon came in.

"Car will be on its way soon. Guy who was in the trunk has been dealt with." He grinned at Chai. "Mother is going to give you hell for that one. Bad choice." He chuckled.

"Wrong. Mother will agree with my choice of vehicle. Anything else and we might not have made it out of there."

Good approach. I thought it had merit.

Nobody had died around me for over a year. In one day, I was involved in three deaths. One day. My 'duang', karmic harmony flow, to you farang, must have been way off balance. I'd have to talk with Aunt Dao about that. I should have stayed in bed with Pim. The day had not gone well. But I was still free and clear, at least, of the law. No car, no body, no evidence, no crime. No harm, no foul.

wuaa gaae gin yaa aawn – Old bulls eat soft grass

THE BIG DAY

Grand Hyatt Erawan Hotel, Grand Ballroom, Friday, 28 October 2011, 10:05PM

The speeches were done, the photos taken, we were onto what we do best, eating and drinking, mostly drinking. The wedding reception provided a good chance to look in people's eyes and see the sincerity or the hate. Khun Suchada, Colonel Sankit's wife and Pim's mother, had demurred to Mere Joom's organizational skills. I didn't blame her for that decision; it was a smart one. Seating arrangements are a nightmare when the guest list has to include a very broad section of Thai society: from minor royalty to Jor Por, 'Godfathers' to you farang; rising and falling politicians of every color (we color-code our politics, makes it easier to follow); gangsters, cops and gunmen; even a few farang. Although farang are perhaps the easiest, you just put them all together at one table.

Two of the tables, set aside for the district heads, were left empty as a sign of respect. Here Leng had called Por in the morning to say he couldn't make it because of Goong's death. Por told Here Leng what had happened and how Goong had died. Here Leng had accepted his word, and war had been averted, we hoped. Por and Mother were planning to return Goong's body to him on Sunday morning.

The other empty table was Loong Virotes. He achieved something few godfathers do, dying in bed surrounded by his family at two in the afternoon today. Khemkaeng sent his apology on behalf of the family and hoped for our understanding – in the return envelope, the one we had sent the invitation in, a check for ninety-nine thousand, nine hundred and ninety-nine baht, and ninety-nine salung. A nice gesture.

Just before lunchtime, an over-excited minister had burst out of the FROC meeting and announced to the press that Bangkok had to be evacuated immediately – "Twelve billion cubic meters of water in a great tsunami is about to enter the city," he had shouted, waving his hands in the air. Thus, through Mother's influence, traffic had been non-existent in Bangkok, and our guests had the opportunity to drive on empty roads. Sorry about that if you were inconvenienced. I saw the minister and Mother having a good chuckle about it over a glass of wine earlier in the evening. He was laughing all the way to the bank; we got fast roads and less risk of a hit.

Most of the nine hundred and ninety-nine invited guests had left now. No expense had been spared, and why would you, when the whole point of the exercise was branding. Our wedding receptions typically entail the bride and groom talking about how they met, funny incidents together, that sort of thing. Of course, you also have a 'sponsor' or super 'phu yai' – big shot – in our case, the Deputy Minister of Culture. Then all the parents get to make a speech. Then the bride and groom cut the cake and circulate around the room, getting their photo taken with every guest, and some individual phu yai. After a few 'Chai Yo' cheers and toasts being given by various friends and phu yai, everyone tucks into the grub and alcohol. That's the formula. We were now down to the hardcore drinkers draining the Hyatt's alcohol supply.

Aroon the shopkeeper and Chainarong, otherwise known as 'Chang Noi', which translates to 'Little Elephant', hadn't had a death in the family, and therefore had no excuse not to show up. They were sitting together, alone at the table, talking. Arms crossed, elbows on the table, heads down staring at their drinks kind of talking. I ambled over.

"Jor Por Aroon, Jor Por Chang Noi," I said, Chainarong didn't mind being called 'Little Elephant'; he was proud of his size. Had once killed a man by sitting on him. They both looked up from their drinks and smiled. They looked like a couple of old crocs, one fat, one round, both tricky and mean as hell.

"Nong Oh, sit down, sit down, we were just talking about you," Aroon said, waving me down into the seat next to him. Neither had called me 'Nong', literally 'younger brother Oh', for many years, but it was my wedding day.

"Good or bad?"

"Good, good, only good, of course, Nong Oh. How

can we talk bad about you on your wedding day?" Aroon said. "Only good. No, we were talking about the trouble Here Leng's had with Goong and how lucky Por and Mere Joom are to have a son like you."

"You're lucky you only have daughters. My boys are both 'up-country'. Not going to see them free for another fifteen years or so," Chang Noi said and downed the rest of his whiskey. Before his glass hit the table, a fresh one was in its place. Both of the 'old-fellas' were smashed. Aroon glowed like a red traffic light.

"Lucky to have daughters, hah, you have no idea. I could open a department store on what they throw away, and none of them have the slightest interest in getting married and giving me grandsons. Hey, Nong Oh, how's that coming along?"

"Giving you grandsons?" I said. Chang Noi slapped his hand on the table, laughing and choking on his drink, deep racking coughs, his face turning an ugly shade of deep purple. Aroon patted him on the back, Chang Noi nodding his thanks as he got back to normal.

"No, I mean you producing a grandson for Por and Mere Joom?" It is the prerogative of our elders to ask personal and blunt questions of us and expect an answer.

"Going well, a few more practice runs and I should have it all figured out." That set Chang Noi off again. I noticed a lady a couple of tables over glancing with disgust at Chang Noi as he hacked up into the tablecloth in his lap.

"Chance," a female voice said. I swiveled in the seat, and Chang Noi's little sister, all grown up, was standing there.

"Nong Mai, you're looking well. I missed you earlier."

"Sorry, Khun Oh, I had to go to the Wat, Loong Virote…"

"Yes, sure, bad timing, but at least the old guy is in peace now," I said.

"Hell more likely," Chang Noi said, Aroon laughing and little sister getting a pout on.

"Pi Noi, that's not nice, and you've had enough to drink. It's time for us to go before you make a fool of yourself," Mai said and went around the table to stand next to her brother's seat.

"Khun Oh, sawasdee ka," she said and gave me a wai. I waied the two old guys and moved over to Steve the Yak.

"Steve, thanks for coming. Sorry I couldn't get away any sooner."

"She is a most beautiful and charming lady. You are a lucky man, Chance san," Yakuza Steve said.

"Yes, she is, and yes, I am," I said, looking at Pim sitting with her parents across the floor of the ballroom.

I drank some more Pellegrino sparkling mineral water, with a slice of lime. I prefer it that way.

"Chance San, the board in Tokyo wanted me to give you this wedding gift, a small token of our affection." Steve took a bulky envelope out of his jacket and handed it to me, one hand supported by the other, bowing his head slightly at the same time, polite, Thai style. Flawlessly executed, you had to hand it to the Yaks, their in-country localization cultural training is top notch.

I opened the envelope. A bunch of stiff-papered documents written in Japanese. I looked at Steve.

"The papers are the deed to an apartment in Moto

Azabu. It is the most prestigious area to live in Tokyo. The board also wishes me to thank you for your family's selfless assistance after the Tohoku earthquake and Fukashima; it will not be forgotten. Their exact words that I was asked to convey to you: 'It is during crisis and danger that we learn the nature of our friends.' In my own words, Khun Chance, I am honored to call you my friend."

"Steve, I am honored that you consider me a friend, means more to me than an apartment in Tokyo, seriously," I reached out and, squeezing his shoulder, gave him a smile. "However, please do thank the board on my family's behalf. Their gift means much to me, and I will visit soon. I am looking forward to meeting the board in person."

Pim's parents were leaving.

"Steve, if you will excuse me, my in-laws are about to leave, and I must pay my respects. Again, please tell the board how pleased I am with their generous gift." I got up and walked between the tables, watching as Sankit stumbled after getting up. He had had a skin-full, drowning his sorrows, no doubt. His only daughter getting married to the gangster son of a gangster and being blamed as the guy responsible for not taking care of people's welfare and happiness during the floods, Sankit was having a rough time of it – the thought put a smile on my lips.

"Hi, baby, how you holding up?" I asked Pim. She'd been up since five in the morning, getting the war paint on.

"Tired but happy," she said, squeezing my hand.

I leaned in and kissed her ear, whispering, "I'm the luckiest guy in the world."

Sankit turned and saw me kissing Pim's ear. His face

went a little darker shade of red.

"Let's walk my mother and father out of here; then we can head up to the suite," Pim said, giving me a look that put a bigger smile on my face and a bounce in my step as she took her mother by the arm. Pim and her mother led off, and a tottering Sankit sidled up to me. Chai rose from where he was sitting with Beckham and the boys and moved ahead of us towards the doors of the ballroom.

Sankit slowed his pace, allowing Pim and Khun Suchada to move out of earshot. He placed his hand on my arm and, at my flicked stony glance, removed it speedily.

"She's your responsibility now. I've given the best I had to her, now it's your turn." His voice had the blunt edge of one too many whiskeys.

"Don't worry, Khun Sankit, I plan to give her the best I've got right after I've seen you off." I couldn't resist it. He stumbled sideways and glared at me, but I kept a straight face and kept walking. It was one of those moments you'll remember forever. He'd put up with it; he was lucky to be alive. No Pim and I'd have killed him a long time ago. Shoot him in the chest so he could see who was killing him.

His car, a black BMW 7 Series, a gift from Mother, was waiting in the forecourt. His driver was in full dress police uniform, standing by his door. Khun Suchada's door was opened by the Hyatt's doorman. Our cops know which side of the bread the promotion butter lies. A flurry of polite wais later, another glare at me from Sankit, and they headed off down the ramp.

Pim grabbed my arm, pulling me towards the entrance.

"Come on, let's head up to the suite, I want to fuck your brains out." A farang standing by the doors having a smoke dropped his cigarette as his mouth fell open. Pim has her way with the English language.

"I was thinking exactly the same thing," I said and smiled. She looked gorgeous, and better than that, I knew her inside was even more beautiful. Love. Deep as an ocean, wide as a sky, countless as the stars, however many lives I have, I want to spend them with you kind of love. Yeah.

We made it to the elevators, and Chai was holding one open for us. A farang with his Spasso's score for the night stood nearby with a hurt expression, "Welcome to Thailand." Chai gave me the biggest smile of the evening.

Farang, you know what? I'm not going to tell you what happened in the elevator. It's private. We got the CCTV back from the hotel the next day; no copies, guaranteed by the hotel manager. We took a long, hot, cold, hot shower, and exhausted, collapsed on the king-size bed of the President's Suite. I held my beautiful wife in my arms and fell into the most satisfied sleep I'd ever had.

From way down deep, I felt someone shaking my arm. I opened my eyes. Chai handed me a mobile phone. Pim was asleep in the crook of my arm, her cheek on my heart. I looked at the time on the cell. 1:45am. '26 Missed Calls', I thumbed the call list – all from Sankit. Chai leaned close; he didn't want to wake Pim.

"I took one call, but he insists on talking to you and you alone. Keeps calling, insists I wake you up. Sorry, Chance."

"It's okay," I said, and Chai slipped out of the master

bedroom. I went into the ensuite bathroom and called Sankit. The second it connected, he came on the line.

"You fucking farang, bastard lizard." Understand, farang, that this is a literal translation of what he said, and calling someone a lizard ranks highly in the personal insult stakes.

"You steal my daughter and my money. You are fucking dead, and I don't care what she will think. What you did was stupid, you hear me, fucking stupid."

I could hear his spittle hitting the phone as he ranted, and I heard Khun Suchada say, "Give me that phone, you old fool."

"Chance, this is your mother."

I thought, lady, you have no idea how far from the truth you are, and said, "Yes, Khun Suchada, what can I do for you?"

"Chance, the Minister is a little upset, you see, he believes that you might be involved in a robbery at our house tonight."

"I wasn't." I thought the truth was the best path to take, be brief and succinct.

"I see, um, well, you see, thieves broke in and stole the dowry money that your parents sent over earlier today."

"Yesterday, you mean?"

"Yes, sorry, yesterday."

"No, I had nothing to do with it. I'll get the guys to look into it tomorrow. Was that all?" You might, farang, consider me to be impolite to my in-laws, and you'd be right. I tolerated them for Pim's sake, but the one thing I'd never forgive either of them for was the pain they'd inflicted on their daughter. In our quieter moments, Pim had told me things that made me wonder and think about things I'd rather not.

"Chance, son, perhaps you could come and see the Minister now, it would be of great help to me. You see, the problem is not the dowry, that's only a small part of the problem."

My mind spun out sideways on that one. "Khun Suchada, perhaps you could tell me what the major problem is or are?"

"Well, the dowry is only ten percent of the problem." Okay, so she was talking about the money, stupidly, I had thought she might be talking about her daughter.

"All right. I'll be there in about forty minutes." They lived out in Puttamonton Sai 3, which was a hike from where we were. I went back into the bedroom, wrote a note for Pim, and got dressed. The only clothes I had were the ones I'd chosen for traveling. Pim and I were on an early morning flight to London, staying there a few days before flying to Santiago, Chile, where we planned to disappear for a few weeks. Drink wine, eat food, make love, repeat – that was the plan. I joined Chai in the hallway of the suite. Chai handed me a baseball cap and a pair of Ray-Bans.

"Let's go."

We cut through the lobby. Empty now, with that late-shift feel, owned by the night people as Bangkok slept. We went down to the car park below the hotel. Mother had given me a Mazerati Quattroporte Sport GS for one of my wedding presents. It was my favorite car. Understated with plenty of guts.

beep naam dtaa – Squeeze out tears

BERLIN WALL

Khun Suchada sat on one of her extremely uncomfortable Louis XIV chairs, hands in her lap. I flicked my hands up in a barely civil wai, even when alone we maintain civility and social order; it lends a pace to our interactions with each other.

"Chance, thank you for coming. The Minister," she'd stopped calling him the Colonel when Mother got him his current job, "is beside himself with worry." Suchada nearly always spoke to me in English. In one part it was to show that she could speak English well; she, like Pim, said she had been to school in England. Another part was her showing she didn't consider me a Thai. No matter how long I'd been here, nor that I had been brought up by Mere Joom and Por, to her my blood was farang blood.

"Good," I replied. That jerked her head around.

"Sorry?"

"Good that the Minister is by himself, give him some time to think."

"Yes, yes, well, I am sorry for those dreadful things he said to you. Of course, neither of us think that you're involved…"

"But you still asked me, right?"

A dark piece of slate, perhaps granite, slid behind her eyes and then was gone. The twisting of the handkerchief signaled her deployment of the number one tool in the Thai Women's Manual of Man Management. Tears. In her case, a little tiny tear edged out of the corner of her eye. She let it run long enough to reach her well-defined cheekbone, and then the hand with the handkerchief stopped its twisting and daintily dabbed at the tear.

"Chance, we're so confused. I was wrong to ask you if you were involved. Please forgive me, Pim has."

A flash of satisfaction, well-hidden, but there, amber in the granite. I've watched Mere Joom spar enough with the aunts to know a verbal kidney punch when I've taken one.

"Pim's forgiven you for what?"

"For disturbing her honeymoon and her wedding night. I just spoke with her, and I told her how sorry I was to have doubted you and how thankful I and the Minister are for your help. She said she understood entirely and not to worry, family is family."

Game, set, and match, Khun Suchada. Give me guns and hand grenades any day, a lot less scarring. The only thing to do now was retreat.

"Yes, well, you better show me the room where the money was stolen."

"It's up the stairs, third floor, turn left, room is at the far end of the corridor." She pointed her chin at me and dropped the social façade for a brief second, showing the true balance of our relationship in her eyes. Flat, cold, uncompromising, hard eyes. The old, dead-eye, 'you mean nothing to me' and 'I hold all the cards' look. Been there, done that.

I gave her a wai, a very polite wai. "Excuse me, Khun Suchada, I must go wash my hands." That would make her think.

At that moment I decided I was there for form's sake and form alone. As soon as we got done here, we were done with Sankit, Suchada and his missing money. But first I had to play to form. I got up and walked out. Chai followed me up the thick-carpeted stairs. I turned left; the corridor was dark. Chai edged around me. At the end of the corridor, a thin shaft of light and a clicking sound came from the partially open door. Chai took his gun out and held it behind his back. He opened the door slowly. I squinted, protecting my eyes against the light.

Sankit sat, shirtless, on a Lazyboy facing the door. The clicking sound came from the revolver in his lap cocking and un-cocking. A Smith & Wesson thirty-eight Model 15, if I wasn't mistaken. Apart from this ugly sight, the room was empty except for a large amount of cardboard boxes strewn about on the right side of the room.

Black scuffmarks on the wall below an open window showed where the thieves had made their entrance. I walked over to it. If Sankit decided to shoot me, which frankly had been on my mind, he'd have to turn. He hadn't moved nor said a thing; he just sat there cocking and un-cocking the thirty-eight. Distraught would be a light version of how he looked – completely fucking deranged far closer to the truth. His eyes had wildness in them, like a trapped bull, all white with blood-red veins bulging. I've seen him a fair bit over the time I'd been with Pim, always reluctantly; now I wished I was anywhere but in this room with him. Some things feel wrong right at the start. This had wrong, in bold, capital letters, in red, bloody as the veins in his eyes, written all over it.

Outside, rain still falling glittered in the light from the spotlights on each of the corners of the wall that ran around the property. It was still dark. I glanced at the cell, 3:45am, and saw five missed calls from Pim. Now wasn't a good time to return the call.

Two parallel track marks ran from about two meters away from the house directly to the opposite wall. Beyond that was about ten rai across, five acres to you, farang, of rice paddy and beyond that houses and a road. The rice paddy reflected the street lamplight along the road. Frogs, their chorus increasing in intensity and pitch, warned each other of my presence to the metronome-like sound of the thirty-eight coming from behind me.

Where the twin tracks met the wall, there was a gap in the steel spikes on top of the wall. Underneath this gap, someone had spray-painted 'the finger' in black, stretching from the top of the wall to the bottom. Just underneath the single finger, the number 9 written in Thai in red spray paint. Now I understood why Sankit thought it was me. I had a 9 tattooed on my chest, courtesy of an elevator button, and caused by the bomb with which Sankit had tried to kill Por and me. I smiled. Whoever did this had an appropriate sense of humor regarding our politicians. Insult to injury in very graphic form. I was tempted to ask Sankit if I could keep it, like Berlin Wall art.

Lugging a billion baht over a lawn, across a wall, and then across a flooded rice paddy to a road about seven hundred meters away wasn't easy to pull off; to do it without being seen, almost impossible. A billion baht weighs about a ton, give or take. To move the money would have taken a team, breaking it down, moving small lots to boats on the other side of the wall.

This room had nothing. They were good enough to handle the logistics of this crime. They hadn't left anything here for us to know. I walked back past Sankit, my eyes on Chai's face. Chai closed the door behind me. With a quick look at each other, we silently fled to the safety of the stairs.

"I'm too young for this shit."

"No shit," Chai said, deadpanning it. I grinned. An oldie but a goody, we'd been sharing that line since I was eleven.

I called Pim, but she didn't pick up. At the bottom of the stairs, I looked right. Khun Suchada was still sitting in the living room. I turned left towards the kitchen and the maid's rooms.

Khun Suchada's maid was about as round as she was short and the color of shiny teakwood. Early forties at a guess. She was quivering with fear.

"Aunty, please relax. I'd like to ask you some questions. Please be honest in your replies and don't worry about your job. If Khun Suchada decides to fire you, then we have plenty of need for staff over at the Crocodile Farm."

She paled a little. I smiled, realizing that my choice of words might have been a bit off the mark.

"Okay, are you ready?"

She nodded. "Yes, sir."

"Good. Now first thing. Do you have any hot water in the house?"

"Yes, sir."

"Good. Second. Do you have any coffee?"

"Yes, sir."

"Excellent. Third. Could you please make me a cup of coffee?"

She smiled, a row of white teeth and cheeks like coconuts. Our Isaan girls have a sense of humor.

"Aunty, what is your name? Mine's 'Oh'."

"My name's Noi," she said and, waddling over to the counter, took down a mug. I noticed that all the essentials were kept low in the kitchen, her domain. She got the coffee sorted. I sat down at the table and indicated the seat opposite me. Khun Suchada appeared in the doorway. I flicked a glance at Chai and he, smiling politely, gently closed the door in Suchada's face.

Noi smiled nervously at me, how someone could shut a door in the homeowner's face in their own home rattling around behind her eyes. I dropped a couple of lumps of sugar into the coffee and started stirring.

"Aunty Noi, can you tell me what happened tonight? Did you see or hear anything? Like I said, don't worry, just tell me everything that happened from when Khun Sankit and Suchada left the house this evening."

A thought occurred to me. "Do you have any whiskey around? I could use a drink to go with this coffee?"

Noi smiled and headed over to the sink. Underneath, a bottle of Sang Som – Thai rum. She got a short glass from the cupboard over the sink.

"Noi, bring two glasses. I reckon we could both use a drink; it's been a long night. I got married tonight, you know. I'd like to get this over with and away on my honeymoon."

I saw a little smile, and she got another glass. She put the rum and the glasses on the table between us. I reached over, taking the bottle, and poured us each a good slug.

"I know, Khun Oh, I heard the Minister talking about it tonight. I've only just arrived here, and this happens. Khun Suchada thinks I am involved because I only just came here, but I swear I'm not, I swear on my babies' lives I'm not involved."

"And I believe you, Ba Noi, relax, like I said, if you need a place to work after this, then just give me a call, okay? Relax, though, I'm sure Khun Suchada was just shocked and upset, and when people are that way they say wrong things. So let's stay calm, and tell me what happened."

"After Minister Sankit and his wife left the house, that was about 6pm, I tidied up their rooms and then came downstairs. I had my dinner; then I went to my room. I had a shower, watched La Kohn (soap operas) for a while, and then I went to sleep."

"What time was that?"

"After nine because I watched some of the news, and it made me sleepy."

"And then?"

"I was woken up by Minister Sankit shooting his gun and shouting."

"Where was he doing this?"

"The room upstairs."

"What do you know about the room upstairs? The one Sankit was shooting from."

She caught my lack of deference and took a healthy slug of the rum. "I was told never to go in it. The first day I came to work. It's locked, and I don't have a key."

"Did you ever see anyone coming or going from the room?"

"Only Minister Sankit. He would go in there after dinner. He told me it was national secrets, and I was never to mention the room to anyone. I never did. I believed him. But tonight he was screaming about money. His money was stolen. Screaming, spit flying everywhere and waving that gun of his about. It scared me, so I hid in my room. Then Khun Suchada came to see me. She told me she knew I was involved and to confess to her and nothing would happen. I'm not clever, but I'm not stupid, Khun Oh. I wasn't involved. So I asked Khun Suchada to call the police, and I would tell them I didn't do it. Then she went to make phone calls, and I stayed here until you arrived."

"What about the guard?"

"'Old Nung', oh, he's useless, apart from trying to chat me up." Ba Noi smiled coyly and took another smaller sip of the rum. "He's usually asleep or drunk, most times both, before the Sankit's car has reached the front of the soi."

Sankit had left the reception at about 11pm. He

would have been home no later than 11:30pm, and the first unanswered call to me was 11:40pm. So sometime between 9:15pm and 11:40pm, someone had made off with Sankit's state secrets – a billion baht worth of unlaundered cash. If it wasn't for the fact that I was sitting here, I'd be enjoying this.

I downed the rest of the rum in my glass.

"Ba Noi, I'm going to have another little chat with Khun Suchada. I'll tell her that I don't think you're involved, but Chai will give you a number to call just in case you need my help, okay?"

Noi smiled and gave me a wai. I returned her wai with my first genuine one since entering the house. I got up and went back out to the living room, where Khun Suchada had reinstalled herself on the same uncomfortable chairs we'd been sitting on earlier. I didn't sit down. I didn't plan on being here that much longer.

"Khun Suchada, who did you call apart from Pim and me?"

"No one. I only called you, and then, later, when I'd thought of how terrible it was for me to disturb your wedding night, I called Pim." She was lying through her evenly proportioned, very white back teeth. Now wasn't the time to find out why.

"Can you supply me with a list of all of the people who knew about that money?"

"That would be a very dangerous list to have, Chance."

"Someone on the list stole the money, or ordered it, anyway. The robbery was done with military precision. It wasn't opportunistic, it was planned."

"You mean you think the military is involved?"

"No, I don't mean that – I mean the people who did this knew exactly where the money was and chose a time, well known in advance, when you wouldn't be here to steal it. So can you send me the list, and leave no one out, no matter how sure you might be that they wouldn't do this?"

She nodded, no doubt already thinking who she'd have to leave off the list.

waan ohm khohm gleuun — If it is sweet, savor it, if bitter, swallow it

YOU CAN'T ALWAYS GET
WHAT YOU WANT

Bangkok, Saturday, 29 October 2011, 5:35AM

Pim wasn't in the room when I returned. Her clothes and toiletries were gone, mine remained, as did my note to her, except it was on the floor under the bed. Chai and I had just finished watching the hotel's CCTV with the manager, and there was nothing on them. I took the tapes with me, and we left.

I told Chai to drive around the block. I needed time to think and feel like I knew how I was going to get her back.

I called Suchada. Didn't get an answer; called Sankit, same thing. I called a cop we knew at the airport to personally verify that Pim wasn't on the flight manifest. She wasn't. Chai kept us within the speed limit, cruising the area, eyes on the street. Finally, I called Mother.

She answered before the second ring.

"Yes, Chance."

"Mother, Pim has disappeared from the Hyatt. The dowry you sent over to Sankit's was stolen last night, along with some other valuables. Khun Suchada called and asked for my help. When I got back, Pim was gone from the room."

"Did she call you, was she upset about anything?"

"She called me twice, but it was when I was with Suchada, and I had the phone on silent. No, she wasn't upset. We were both looking forward to the honeymoon. Can you get me the CCTV for Ratchaprasong intersection and anything on Chidlom for the time between 1am to 5:15am today?"

"Yes, no problem. Have you called Suchada?"

"Yes, she and Sankit are off-line. I'm planning to send someone around to wake them up. If they're still there, I want to talk to them. Is Somboon there?"

"No, and that may be another problem. Somboon and Pichit haven't been seen since Thursday night. They haven't been home, and no one's seen them."

"The car?"

"It wasn't delivered."

My two biggest fears are my family being hurt and being put in a prison. In that order, very close together. I breathed out slowly, emptying my lungs, a trick Uncle Mike taught me.

"Chance, are you still there?"

"Yes, Mother, sorry, I was thinking."

"Good, Chance, act with your head, more than ever now. If they wanted Pim dead, she'd still be in that room.

They want her for leverage, and we'll know why soon. Come home, we'll work it out." She rang off.

"Head back home, no hurry," I said. I needed time to get my emotions under control.

Chai pulled a lazy U-turn on Sarasin Road. The hawkers around the bottom corner of Lumpini Park were getting ready for the morning joggers and weightlifters. Through the tinted glass of the passenger window, I saw an old man unloading tables from a pickup look at the Maserati as it passed him. He said something to the woman near him, standing in front of the samlor she was cooking kuai tiao on. She looked at us and laughed with him, continuing to stir the soup in her cauldron. He's doing better than I am, I thought.

We turned right onto Rachadamri, driving past the weightlifters, heading towards Silom. The roads were empty, nothing like usual. Even during last year's riots, there had been more traffic on the street and a lot more noise. I opened the window. The morning air strangely fresh for downtown, the street was as quiet as a library. We were supposed to be on a flight, but I'd lost her. 'Fight or Flight' I think they call it. The body's response to danger, or in the modern office-workers' world, stress. No one to fight, nowhere to run.

"Chance?"

"Yes, Chai."

"We'll get her back, and whoever did this to us dies a bad death."

"Agreed. Hit it, we need to get to work."

Chai dropped his foot on the pedal, and I was punched back into the seat.

"There's something else I've been thinking," Chai said. He swerved to avoid a motorcycle taxi rider, missing him by a hair.

"What?"

"I think the reason we couldn't make any phone calls from the car was because someone put a jammer on us. They must have removed it when we got back to the hotel."

"You might be right. And they, either alone, or working with someone, turned the CCTV off at just the right moments. I couldn't tell from watching it, but I'd bet there's time missing."

"I'll get a list of staff on duty from the manager once I've dropped you off, and then I'll join you back at the house. Please don't go anywhere without me once you reach home."

"I won't." We were just about to go up onto the expressway. Dawn, gray and wet, broke over the City of Angels, darkness giving way to shadows. "Chai, turn us around, get us back to the Hyatt." There weren't any cops around to catch Chai's U-turn on Rama IV, and within minutes, we were back on Rachadamri heading towards Pratunam.

As we turned into the car park of the Hyatt, a guy on a motorbike passed us coming out. Chai looked at me; I nodded. I looked in the side mirror and put my seatbelt on. The guy on the bike turned around. Chai put the car in reverse, and the guy on the bike, dressed in the uniform of a Hyatt doorman, took off. Chai pulled the steering wheel down hard, and the rear end of the car whipped out of the exit going left. Chai got us in drive just as I saw the number 514 bus fill the side mirror. It hit us square on, the air bag inflating hitting me hard in the face.

Chai stamped on the gas as the bags deflated. The white uniform easy to spot; the rider had stayed on Ratchadamri, blue smoke jetting out of the exhaust of his bike as he gunned it for all it was worth. If I wasn't sure before, now I was a hundred percent certain.

A 125cc motorbike or even a 250cc motorbike is no match for a Maserati unless there's traffic. The road was empty except for us and the bus that had stopped behind us. I could see the rear end of the car through the rear window, not a good sight. The rear fender dragged along the road, creating an arc of sparks. At the intersection with Sarasin, the bike swerved into Lumpini Park. A good choice. Chai slammed on the brakes, and we skidded to a stop just before the metal bollards.

The white uniform was heading diagonally across the park.

"You go around. I'll go after him on foot," I said and jumped out of the car. I knocked over a table and a few chairs. The old man I'd seen putting them out earlier shouted at me.

"What, are you crazy?"

I didn't stop to answer, sprinting after the white uniform. He'd slowed down, dodging the few joggers that were braving the rain. Running around the lake, I slipped on some wet leaves and went down hard, ripping my trousers and grazing my knees. I picked myself up and went at it again, ignoring the pain in my legs. Adrenalin pumping hard, I saw the guy on the bike had just crossed onto the bridge that divides the park's lake in two. He looked my way and took off again.

Breathing hard, my thighs screaming pain, I turned onto the bridge. Couldn't see the white uniform. The bridge expands into an area of grass, trees and shady areas and then narrows again. I guessed he was headed for the Rama IV Road side of the park, where he could easily disappear into the back streets of Silom area or further up into Klong Toey slum. If he reached either, he'd be gone.

I slowed down, had to, I was out of breath. It had been a while since I'd run that far. I flashed on Speedy Gonzales, wondering if his dead body was going to show up. I kept up a slow jog, keeping an eye out for white in front. I saw something flash out of the corner of my eye.

***

I was dreaming about chasing someone down a dry riverbed. Rocks and boulders made it difficult to keep up, but I could just see them ahead of me. I was also being chased, and they were using a tracker. I needed to catch the person in front before those behind got me, but the beeping was getting closer and louder.

"He's waking up. Chance, can you hear me?"

I recognized the décor and the voice. I started to answer, but my face hurt too much to speak. I nodded and learned that more of me was hurting. I could see large swathes of white gauze padding just below my eyes.

"Don't try to talk. It'll hurt for a few days yet."

"Wha hap…?" I managed to get out.

"I got the Sullivans to Darwin, and then they just up and left. Without even a thank you. One minute they were there, and then they were gone. So I flew home."

I shook my head.

"He means what happened to him, Thomas," Mother

said.

"Oh. Yes, of course, well, you were hit by a blunt object. Judging by the shape of the bruising around your nose, I speculate that you were hit by a motorcycle helmet. Your nose is broken, and your upper lip lacerated. I put three stitches in. It should heal up nicely. Apparently, you have good reflexes because you saved your front teeth from being broken. Unfortunately, at the expense of breaking and cutting the little finger of your right hand."

I tried to sit up and discovered yet more bits of me that were in pain.

"You should try to lie still as much as possible. You've also got a couple of broken ribs and a swollen knee with not much skin on it. But apart from that, you're in good shape." Tom smiled at me. Cambridge doctors develop a very strange sense of humor. If I'd had a gun, I might have shot him in the foot.

"Tie, tie..." I said. I couldn't close my mouth, hurt too much.

"It's eight thirty in the evening, same day, Saturday," Mother said. She gave Tom a look, and he quickly stepped backwards. I might be his patient, but I was her son. He swallowed his Adam's apple and slightly bowed his head, hands clasped in front of him.

I grimaced from the pain, 'only when I laugh' springing into my mind. I breathed out slowly; it still hurt. Then I remembered Pim was missing, and it hurt more. A deep, dark void I didn't want to face.

Por pulled up a chair. Swinging his artificial limb straight out in front of him, he sat down. Mother cast another glance towards Tom, and he sidestepped his way towards the hallway. I was in a suite at Bumrungrad. Full circle, last time I'd been in here as a patient was when Sankit had tried to blow me and Por up.

Por leaned in close to my ear; I could hear and feel his breathing. "We've got his name. Lek, from Ubon. We've got his cell number. He hasn't called anyone yet, but he will. His type always does. No, don't say anything, just listen. The invisible hand is at play here. We don't know who it belongs to yet, but we will. Your ribs aren't broken, only cracked. Tomorrow we have to take Goong back to Here Leng. You need to stay here tonight, get some rest. Tomorrow we'll work on getting Pim back to us, safe." His large eyes turned hard. "Whoever did this will regret the day they were born."

I nodded.

Por used his cane to stand up. I saw his favorites, a Colt .45 and a sawn-off shotgun, underneath the Armani jacket he was wearing. He held my look for a second and nodded, smiling down at me. We were at war. We just didn't know who with.

Mother leaned down, kissed my cheek, and Dr. Tom appeared over her right shoulder. I watched him insert a needle into one of the tubes coming from the IV drip. They filed out. Beckham holding the door for Dr. Tom, then he followed, then Mother and Por. Chai grabbed one of the chairs from the kitchen counter and placed it in the middle of the corridor. He told Tum to sit in the chair and then took up position cross-legged on the floor, behind the wall next to the hallway, Uzi on the floor in front of him.

I thought about what Por had said, the invisible hand,

ever present in our lives, and fell asleep.

luaang khaaw nguu hao – Stroke the throat of a cobra

OLD SCHOOL

Bangkok, Sunday, 30 October 2011, 6:25AM

The Bertam's engines throbbed as we crossed to left bank of the Chao Phraya, heading upriver to Phra Padaeng. My nose throbbed in concert. I was finding it hard to breathe, and sight had been reduced to a world seen through my eyelashes as my face had swollen overnight. Chai had used an old Thai boxing trick, liberal doses of sprayed local anesthetic. It kept me moving and relatively pain free. Still, I was doing better than Goong in a black body bag in the cabin.

Por sat on the bench seat at the stern, Mother beside him, Beckham and Chai standing either side of them. It was a show of respect and solidarity. We were on our way to see Here Leng, delivering his son back to him. It was the least we could do.

SIMON ROYLE

I wasn't sorry about Goong. He was dangerous, vile-natured, black-hearted scum, and the world was a better place for his absence, but apart from that, I didn't really have an opinion. I was sorry about Dan. He'd joined us straight out of the army. A poor kid from the provinces, Dan had just finished his national service. With no skills other than the ability to drive a car and shoot a gun reasonably straight, he was a willing and ready new recruit to our ranks. Was that moment, when the eighteen-wheeler hit the back of his taxi, fated the day Dan was born? Or did I put him there? Or did Goong put him there?

On the fly bridge, Tum opened up the throttles. The Bertram nosed up a touch and then settled as we cruised under the King Bhumiphol Bridge. Nat directed the searchlight into the dark in front of us as the sun's light foreshadowed its arrival over the city on the right bank. An island of 'old' Thailand set, in the midst of a city of 20 million, created by the ox-bow meandering of the Chao Phraya.

Resting up was good, it had given me a chance to think.

There were three options for Pim being kidnapped. That word and its relation to her made me furious, but I bottled it up. I needed more than ever to have a clear mind. The first option was the money. Whoever had it, or lost it, wanted Pim as insurance against me finding or not finding it. The second option was Here Leng, but this seemed the least likely. Here Leng would come at me, not Pim, his style. Still, he couldn't be discounted. The third option? It was something else entirely, something new that we couldn't see. The invisible hand, the x factor, possible, but given the timing, it seemed unlikely.

Tum dropped the speed to about three knots as we turned into an ancient world. No roads, just jungle and narrow canals overhung with bamboo and the leaves of coconut trees. Illegally tapped electricity lines carefully lifted out of the way by Nat using a bamboo staff designed for the job. Birdsong heard over the throb of the engines. It was almost sunrise, but not quite, our searchlight confusing the birds.

We inched our way up the narrow klong, canal to you farang, the hint of dawn escaping the black skyscrapers behind us enough to cast a pale light into the space left open by the branches and leaves above our heads. The water was a dark muddy brown, black where leaves threw it into shadow. About a kilometer in, the jungle gave way to a clearing and a floating dock. The oil drums at the limit of their tether with the height of the water.

The steady drizzle that had been our companion stopped. Steam rose from the lawn that sloped up to the two-storey Thai house set back from the river about a hundred meters. On the balcony Here Leng stood, arms by his sides. Huge brown belly resting on the rail, he looked down at us; then he turned slowly and entered the house.

This was a risk, but it was also our custom. Our culture provides the guidelines for all sorts of situations, this one included. It was possible Here Leng would come back on that balcony and open up with an AK-47, possible, but highly unlikely. Here Leng, Por, Mother, all 'old school'. Traditional values of respect, loyalty, and honor ingrained in every cell.

Here Leng and his family had lived on this piece of land for over eight generations. He was the last man standing. We followed Por as he made his way slowly up the wet red brick path, holding Mother's arm with one hand, a wooden walking stick in the other, back straight, head held high, looking straight ahead the whole time. His gait was awkward with the prosthetic leg that he was not yet used to walking on. We were all dressed in black suits, except Mother, who was wearing a body-hugging ankle-length black dress. Behind me, six of our boys carried the body bag, three a side.

This house wouldn't have a problem with the flooding. Built on wooden stilts that had seen the back of a thousand floods, with nothing but earth beneath it and a staircase. Boats, fiberglass and wooden, modern and long-tail were pulled up to the edge of the house and tied off to the mango trees rising taller than the roof. I noticed the electricity was wired correctly, special for this neck of the woods.

Underneath the house was space to walk upright and still have a meter of headroom. The boys lay Goong's body on a long, low table.

Here Leng had donned a traditional Thai shirt, black silk, and a sarong. He came down the stairs with nothing in his hands. He didn't pause or wince when he saw the body bag. He sat down beside it on the low table. His fingers reached for the zip, and I noticed his hands were trembling. Mother had hired a mortician who'd worked overnight to make Goong look as good as possible. He'd done a good job on the face. Apparently the woolen hood had saved his features from being burnt. He'd even managed to craft a peaceful smile on his face. I was impressed. In the photos we'd taken to show Sullivan, Goong had a whole different look about him.

Here Leng sat and stared at Goong's face for a good five minutes. No one said anything or moved. He let out a long sigh, his shoulders slumped, and he zipped up the bag. He patted it lightly with his hand, and turning to face us, he waied Por and then Mother. I gave him a deep wai and was followed by our crew. He stood and walked over to Por.

"Thank you for bringing my son home to me. Please forgive my rudeness and come and sit down." Here Leng led Por and Mother to the side of the house. Under a canvas awning, next to huge ceramic water jars were a cement table and benches. From behind the jars, a young woman appeared, rubbing sleep from her eyes.

"Go get the whiskey and bring water and glasses," Here Leng said softly to the girl. She nodded and, looking big-eyed at us, went up the stairs. Here Leng waited until Por had stretched his leg out and Mother had taken her seat before sitting down. Mother took his hand in hers. His elbows on the table, he held her hand and used his other to hold across his eyes until he rubbed his face vigorously, sniffed and cleared his throat. He sighed. I moved around behind Mother and Por and sat down opposite Here Leng.

Unlike most Chinese Thai, Here Leng was tanned the color of the earth we were sitting on. His eyebrows had turned gray as had his hair, cropped short, military style. He looked at me with tired eyes, the same kind of tired I'd seen in Sullivan's.

"I heard what happened. It wasn't your fault. It was

just an accident. Who knows whose karma it was? Your mother said he was unconscious when he died?"

"Yes, Here Leng. We'd stunned him with a Taser to subdue him. He wouldn't have come around yet. Our intent was to scare him not hurt him. As per your request."

Here Leng turned to Por. "Do you remember old horse-face and his two sons?"

Por nodded.

"Good, strong, smart boys they were. I killed them. His only sons, I thought I'd pay for that someday. No one knew I did it…"

"I knew," Por said.

Here Leng looked surprised and stroked his jaw. "You knew?"

"Who do you think sold you the car bomb. Old horse-face's sons put it under my jeep. I thought it right to return it."

Here Leng nodded and chuckled a little. "I thought only I knew that. Ah well, perhaps it is my karma to be the last one…"

Mother put her other hand on his. "Here Leng, what are you talking about, last one." She looked up and flicked her eyes, first at me and then at Beckham. I waied him again and stood up, leaving them talking at the table. The girl came down the steps, smiled at me, a bottle of Johnny Walker Blue in one hand and a basket with ice, soda and glasses in the other. Out of sight of the table, I glanced at my phone. It was ten minutes past seven in the morning. It looked like war had been averted. I stood under the house, looking down to the river.

It was a wide lawn sloping down to the water. Patches

of bare earth underneath old mango trees that guarded it against the jungle on either side. A soft drizzle started, above us a gray sky. A flock of ravens burst from the jungle to my right and flew low in front of me. Something in the air changed. The hairs on the back of my neck stood up. I scanned the edge of the jungle. I heard a grunt and glass breaking coming from the other side of the house where Por and Mother were sitting.

Shots rang out, and out of the corner of my eye I saw Beckham go down. Firing erupted from both sides of the lawn. The angry wasp's sound of bullets flying around us, we opened fire on the jungle. Couldn't see what I was shooting at, but it felt better than just being shot at. Chai beside me, we ran around the side of the house. Mother, gun in both hands, covering a gut-shot Here Leng moaning loudly on the ground. Por rising from the table, gun in hand; the girl with the whiskey, dead, shot in the chest.

I heaved the concrete table over on its side. Beckham crawled around the ceramic water jars. I ran over and pulled him to his feet. He'd been hit in the shoulder and was bleeding badly. Mother and Por pulled Beckham down with them behind the table. Chai, using the water jars as cover, methodically emptied rounds into measured spaces in the wall of jungle.

From the direction of the river I heard Tum open up with the M249. I peeked around the table. Firing was coming from both sides of the jungle. I could hear the bullets hitting the upper portion of the house. Our guys had run upstairs when the firing started. The stairs were being turned into wood chips by the volume of fire.

"Por, that way," I said, nodding in the direction of the

jungle at the back of the house.

Por nodded, paused, aimed his gun, and shot Here Leng in the head. Helped by Mother, he made a break for the jungle. We covered their retreat, facing the lawn, laying down a curtain of fire while backing our way after Por and Mother. Thick bamboo and low scrub, squelchy underfoot, we penetrated in about ten meters from the edge. The ratta-tat-tat of the M249 stopped. We sat down. Mother tore her dress off at the waist, wearing a pair of black shorts underneath and a holster strapped to each thigh.

The shots behind us tailed off and then started again. We waited, crouching low, Por sitting on the ground, Mother with a Berretta in each hand. Chai stripped off his suit jacket and shirt, stuck his fingers into the mulch we were sitting on, and smeared it over his face and torso. Mother made two compresses out of her torn dress and pressed them on Beckham's wound front and back. I took Chai's shirt and tied the compresses in place. Beckham gritted his teeth and didn't make a sound. He handed me his gun and spare magazines.

"You two go back. I'll take Por and Moo through to the road," Mother said.

"All right, call me when you're at the road."

"Go, be careful."

"Yes, Mother."

There was a loud explosion from the direction of the river. I hoped that didn't mean what I thought it meant. I helped Por up, and Chai got Beckham on his feet. Por and Mother, with Beckham between them, crouched their way into the jungle behind us. Intermittent shooting still coming from the house, Chai got on the phone. I reloaded our weapons.

"How many?" He nodded. "Tum?" He shook his head at me. Shit. "All right we're coming in through the jungle on the right side. Keep your fire low and targeted at the river end. No more than twenty meters in from the river's edge. Got it? Repeat the order." Chai listened and nodded again. "Okay, start in four minutes from now." He turned to me. "Boat's gone. They hit it with an RPG. Tum was on the fly bridge when it went up. You ready?"

I nodded.

"Okay, stick three meters to my right. Let's go." Chai had done jungle warfare training with the Australian SAS and the Thai Navy Seals. Out here, he was boss.

The jungle was wet and, despite the overcast day, was a steamy humid soup of air. Sweat dripping from every pore, mosquitoes buzzing around my ears, following Chai in a wide semi-circle, I crept as silently as I could. Walk a few paces. Stop and listen. Walk again. My upper thighs burned with the effort of walking in a crouch, carefully, slowly, moving branches out of our way.

Chai lifted a foot over a fallen strand of bamboo, easing over it without making a sound. My Bally shoes slipping in the mud, I envied Chai his paratrooper boots. Function over form any day. Firing increased from the house. Chai held his fist up. Ahead of us the brush moved. Chai took out his Ka-Bar and signaled for me to stay put. I squatted down. Chai disappeared into the jungle.

gop yuu nai galaa – A frog in a bowl

An Honest Cop

I waited by the fallen bamboo, eyes strained for movement in the brush ahead of me. Nothing moved. Sweat poured off me in a river. Chai appeared from my right. He plunged the Ka-Bar into the earth and wiped it on his trousers, returning it to its sheath on his belt. He beckoned for me to move to him. Shots fired from the direction of the house picked up again. I followed Chai to where he'd just been.

Just back from the jungle line, a body lay face down, an M16 beside it. I stuck my Glock back in its holster and picked up the M16. I turned the body over to get at the ammo pouches. Eyes staring wide, throat cut enough to show the back of his serrated windpipe. My stomach did a little flip-flop, but I didn't puke. The left flap of the ammo pouches was still closed. I opened it and took a magazine out. Releasing the one in the M16, I cleared the weapon and loaded the fresh magazine. Chai made signals. Fire down the tree line, I'll flush them out. I nodded. He slipped off.

I grabbed the dead body and rolled it over again, giving myself a bit of extra cover. I settled down, barrel pointed over the dead man's body, waiting for the prey to be flushed. Black smoke from the burning remains of the Bertram drifted lazily across the lawn. I emptied the magazine, bursts of three, aimed a meter apart down the tree line.

The shooting had stopped. I aimed down the edge of the jungle. Nothing moved. Off in the distance, the sound of police sirens. Hot salty sweat trickled into my eyes, burning them. I calmed my breathing, trying to be quiet. The buzz of mosquitoes, the sound of my own breathing, and my ears rang from the shots I'd just fired. Still nothing moved. The sirens sounded closer. Chai popped out of the jungle near the river and gave the all clear sign. Nat and Pok, the only two of our guys who'd survived, ran down the stairs of Here Leng's house. Nat stopped at the bottom step, lit a rag sticking out of a bottle, and lobbed it up the stairs into the house.

The island is connected to the mainland by a single road that runs straight down its middle. The odds that it would have a police checkpoint on it were good. The sirens sounded much closer, perhaps only a couple of hundred meters away, both fire and police. Something exploded inside the house, probably a spare LPG tank for cooking.

"We have to cross to the other side," I said and pointed

down to where the Bertram was burning.

The guys looked at each other. I heard Nat whisper. "Did Chance just say we have to get in the water?"

He looked at me. "You mean the canal? I'd rather shoot myself now and just be done with it."

"Police," shouted from the far side of the property got us moving. Our police almost always announce their presence, loudly, and then wait for the bad guys to either shoot or leave. It's a kind of custom, but given how custom had been playing out, I turned and ran for the river. Getting arrested here would be problematic; we'd just broken one of the local police chief's 'rice bowls' – he'd be missing his monthly paycheck from the Dragon. We raced down the side of the lawn and slipped into the canal. The bank dropped off sharply; I was careful not to let any of the water into my mouth or ears. The canal water in this part of Bangkok was toxic, a physical manifestation of the effluent of our corruption.

Using the Bertram as cover, we climbed up the opposite bank and crawled on our bellies into the jungle. Chai kept watch on Here Leng's property behind us. Nat got our position up on GPS and took out a plastic-wrapped iPad with a True Air card attached. Got Google Earth up, and we fixed our position on the satellite image at about five hundred meters from Soi Bang Yo 3. The boys got busy digging a hole. If the cops brought dogs in, which they might do, burying the weapons would be useless. Shooting our way through a bunch of cops wasn't an option. Killing cops on duty is a big no-no; even the most powerful get in trouble for that. They might not get prison, but they do get a lot of bad publicity.

Our cops may be corrupt, but they're not stupid. They'd have all the roads around here sewn up and a police launch cruising up and down the riverbank by now.

I pointed on the map to the far end of Bang Yo 3.

"We move here and wait."

My biggest fear, next to family being hurt or lost, is prison. The image of being caged up made me hesitate, but giving them a final wipe off with my shirt, I put the M16 and the Glock in the hole.

"Let's go," I whispered, and with Chai leading the way, we moved off in single file.

Bang Yo 3 is a small concrete road with occasional widened spaces to allow two vehicles to pass each other. We hid in the jungle ten meters in from the end of the road. We were now about six hundred meters northeast of Here Leng's house. Behind us, I could still hear sirens.

In the distance, I heard dogs barking. That might be bad news, or it might just be dogs barking, too early to tell.

"Cops," Pok said. A black-and-white police pickup truck came into the entrance of the soi. Driving slowly towards us, there were two cops sitting in the cab. About a hundred meters away, it stopped, lights flashing. The steady drizzle kept the cops in the cab of the pickup. I flicked a glance at Chai and nodded towards the cops.

"How long?"

"Give me ten," Chai said.

Chai slipped away into the jungle, I glanced at the time on my cell, 7:35am. Still no SMS or call from Mother, I was worried about her. It was unlike her not to call. I peeled off the bandage covering my nose; it hurt, a lot. I unwrapped the bandage around my torso. Twin black, purple and violet lines ran across my ribcage. As the bandage eased, I breathed out, and the pain spiked. Nat and Pok smiled at the expression on my face. I heard dogs barking again, much closer, they were across the klong now. As I feared, the cops had brought a K-9 unit.

A glance at the cell, 7:40am, somewhere back in the jungle I heard cops yelling at each other.

"Pok, give me your knife."

Pok handed over a very sharp Leatherman. I pulled the blade out and cut my forehead. A cut on the forehead will bleed profusely, and that's what I needed. Another glance at the cell, 7:42, it would have to do, the dogs were sounding as if they would be on us any second.

Blood pouring down my face, I stepped out into the soi, staggering. It wasn't an act; my legs felt like they were made of rubber. I stumbled my way towards the cops, waving my empty hands at them. If they stayed in the cab, we were screwed. I called out, "Help, help," and then fell to the ground. Through barely open eyes, I watched as they got out. The thinner of the two pulled his revolver. The fat one kept his eyes focused on the road behind me, his hand ready on the butt of his gun.

Neither of them saw Chai, who had emerged from the jungle ten meters behind them, Ka-Bar in hand. I groaned loudly as they got nearer and rolled over onto my back. Chai came up behind the older fat cop and put the Ka-Bar to his throat. The younger, skinnier cop still hadn't noticed, until I sat up and pointed at Chai. Chai had relieved the fat cop of his gun and, using his right hand, had it trained on Skinny.

Skinny put his gun on the ground. I got up, Nat and Pok came out behind me, running for the pickup.

They both sweated heavily, the fat, older cop more than the skinny one, but both looked terrified. I walked up to the fat one.

"Here's how it is. You can both be rich men by tonight, or you can be dead. You choose, money or death?"

"Money," they both said in unison – I wasn't surprised by the answer.

"Right, we're all getting out of here. You," I pointed at Skinny, "get in the back of the cab with these two, and you drive," I said to the fat cop. He nodded and moved fast for someone with a belly his size. It looked like he'd swallowed a basketball, the buttons on his sweat-stained uniform at full stretch, a white T-shirt showing in the gaps around them where the cloth couldn't hold the pressure of his belly.

I picked up Skinny's gun and waved him into the back of the pickup with Nat and Pok, Chai sat in the middle, and I sat in the passenger seat by the window.

"Get on the radio and report that you're taking a drunken farang and three Thai guys to the station; anything funny, we'll kill you here and take our chances. Do it well, and you'll have a hundred thousand in cash tonight."

"Only a hundred thousand?"

I waved the gun at the radio via the middle of his forehead.

"All right, all right, I was just asking." He picked up the handset. "Station, station, hello, hello…"

"Station, report?"

"Lance Corporal 1605 report, over."

"Who?"

"Lance Corporal 1605…"

I glanced around, no one was looking, our windows were tinted, and put Skinny's gun to Lance Corporal 1605's head.

"Yeah, yeah, it's Moo. I have a drunken farang and three Thai guys that were disturbing the peace. I'm bringing them in now."

"Okay, bring them in, station out."

"Good. Now drive us slowly out of here, anything funny and…"

"I know, I know, you'll kill me. Do I look stupid, I must do, because you only offered me a hundred thousand, and I know who you are. I recognize that tattoo on your chest. You're Khun Oh, and this is your bodyguard, Chai. I guess too that you have something to do with Here Leng's killing and house burning down. I would have thought such knowledge was worth at least five hundred thousand…"

"Just get us out of here without any trouble, and I'll give you two hundred to split between you and your partner back there," I said, nodding my head towards Skinny in the back. Fatty licked his lips, smiled, and got the pickup turned around on the narrow soi. A few twists and turns and we were on Petchahung Road, the main road that runs up the spine of the island. About a kilometer up the road, two fire trucks were parked in front of the narrow road that led to Here Leng's house with an assortment of police motorbikes and pickups next to them. Fatty leaned out of the window and waved at the cops by the roadblock.

As we passed, I looked out of the passenger-side window and saw Mother, Por, and Beckham sitting on a bench, handcuffs clearly visible. At that moment, Mother looked up and saw me. A slight shake of her head and a smile, we kept on driving. Five minutes later we were off the island and driving across Bhumibol 1 Bridge back into Bangkok. I looked at the time on my cell, 8:00am, the way things were going, I wondered if there would be any of us left by nightfall.

I got to thinking; 'Pig' might come in handy in the days to come.

"What's your name?"

"Adisorn, but most people call me Moo." 'Pig' to you farang. We have no negative connotations regarding our pork, except perhaps in the South. For instance, we never refer to our police as 'pigs'. We call them a lot of other names, but not pigs. In our culture, pigs, while not regarded with the same reverence as in China, are looked upon fondly, especially when flattened, crispy, and steaming on a big plate in front of us.

"The skinny cop in the back, he's going to be okay?"

"Oh sure, he's my wife's younger brother. Our whole family's police, even my wife, she's immigration police, works at the airport. She's a sergeant, never lets me forget it either." He grinned, a tarnished gold tooth winking in the corner of his mouth, looking at me as he drove, confident that none of the cars around were stupid enough to crash into a police vehicle.

"Drop us off at the Crocodile Farm," I said.

His grin disappeared; the corners of his eyes dropped.

"Do I have to?"

"Oh no, it's not like that. Don't worry, we've made a deal, we'll honor it. Just more convenient for me."

He looked nervous and a bit wary, but he nodded and didn't say anything more.

"Moo," I said, smiling at him, "you sound like a smart guy. We can do business with guys like you."

Moo nodded, wariness replaced by avarice.

"Do you like cars? Perhaps a Benz?"

"Nah, not a Benz, the station sergeant would have me up against a wall with a truncheon up my ass wanting to know where the hell I got a Benz from and where his was. But a Toyota Camry, Hybrid, I could explain as my wife's good fortune…" He looked across at me to judge my reaction.

"What color would you like?"

"Black."

"Okay." I liked Pig, he was as corrupt as a Turkish brothel owner, but at least he was honest about it.

khwaam wuaa yang mai haai khwaam khwaai khao maa saaek — Still putting away the cows and here come the buffalo

WHEN IT RAINS
IT POURS

Pak Nam, Sunday, 30 October 2011, 11:15AM

I was in the hot pool of the spa at the farm. Soaking in the bath was good. It took away some of the physical pain. Emotionally I was gutted. Chai, Nat and Pok were outside under strict instructions to leave me alone for a while. I needed time to think.

There was a knock on the door. Strict instructions have a different, interpretable status in Thailand.

"Boss?"

"Yes, Pok."

Pok was a skinny kid from the provinces. He'd been selling ice, the legit kind, not the drug, from the back of a pickup, when he'd seen a chance at wealth in the form of an open till at a 7-Eleven. He'd served his apprenticeship in a medium-security prison in Ayutthaya where he'd met

79

Beckham. Normally he'd be at a distance from me, just one of the boys, but we were fast running out of reliable 'known' men, and times were anything but normal.

"Phone, boss. It's Khun Chompunooch."

"Where's Chai?"

"He said he had to go to the Hyatt."

I nodded, took the phone, and Pok beat a retreat to the door. Chai was following up on whoever had turned the CCTV off.

"Khun Nuch," that's pronounced 'Noot' by the way, farang, in case you had 'much' in mind, "how can I help you?" I said.

"Khun Oh, sorry to bother you, but I tried to call Mere Joom, and I couldn't reach her."

"Yes, Nuch, she's on holiday," I said, regretting it instantly. Mother never took holidays. "Por insisted."

There was a long silence, and then she said, "Yes, well, I wanted to tell her that Khun Vinai called."

"Right… and?" Vinai was in charge of the grounds of the farm.

"And Khun Vinai said the dyke on the west side has started to collapse and crocodiles are escaping into the river…"

I got out of the tub slowly, careful not to slip. Lying in the tub hadn't improved the general spin of the day.

"Okay, thank you, Nuch, and please tell Khun Vinai I'll be there soon."

"Yes, Khun Oh, I'll call Khun Vinai right away," she said and hung up.

Floods and one hundred thousand crocodiles, most of which were bad-tempered and hungry, were a bad combination. All I wanted to do was find Pim and get Por, Mother, and Beckham back. I'd sent our lawyer down to Phra Padaeng Police Station. Por and Mother weren't there, and no one knew anything, or they weren't saying. If they weren't being processed normally, I was sure someone would call. Por hadn't given me the contact of the person who was tracking Lek's cell number, so I couldn't do anything about tracking him. Suchada hadn't sent a list of the names as she'd promised, not much I could do about tracking the stolen money down without it, but in the meantime, preventing a hundred thousand crocs in a flooded downtown Bangkok was something I could deal with.

I dried myself and reached for the anesthetic spray. Gave it a shake, and it was empty. Par for the day.

Dressed in combat boots, jeans, and a waterproof poncho had a sort of Clint Eastwood kind of feel. I drove out to the west side of the farm, Nat and Pok with me. The road was under water, reaching up to the hubcaps of the Land Rover Defender. I managed to hit every pothole and bump in the road. I got out and walked over to Vinai standing on the dyke. Vinai raised his hands in a wai.

"Khun Oh, you see the far end of the dyke?" He pointed down the dyke. We'd built it a couple of weeks ago. It was supposed to hold the rising water back from the river side of the property. We had flood issues on the other side of the farm, but this was the primary weak point, where the water rose fastest.

At the far end, a small section had collapsed. I turned to Nat and Pok. "You two head over to the fishing village at Bang Pu and tell them we need their fishing nets, the heavy ones, as many as they can spare. Offer to pay them double replacement cost."

"Yes, boss."

"Khun Vinai, you better head up to the farm and get a rifle. Get one with a scope. The crocs will know that section has collapsed, and they'll be escaping. Get a bunch of the guys, grab some of the sandbags we stocked by the entrance gate, and come back as quick as you can. Take the Defender. I'm going down to take a look at the break."

"Yes, Khun Oh."

I walked down the dyke to where the Chao Phraya poured into a three meter and rapidly widening gap. The river side water level was less than ten centimeters from the top of the dyke. Not enough. In the pen farm side were about three thousand young saltwater crocs between six months and three years old. These were for export. I watched as a one-meter baby 'salty' swam out to freedom. I sympathized, but all the same, we were losing crocs.

I took a look around and got the feeling that if I stayed on the dyke much longer, we'd be losing me. The determined drizzle turned into stubborn rain, prelude to the daily slashing monsoon deluge that looked like it was about to drop early. I walked back up the dyke, taking it easy. Slippery as a politician called on a promise. It was about three hundred meters to where the dyke met the road.

I heard a loud splash. Ahead of me, a croc had just tried and failed to get over the dyke. It slipped off the top and landed back farm-side of the dyke. This was really bad; we had to move fast. I kept an eye on the croc as he circled. Shit. He aimed at where I was standing, coming back for another go.

The croc launched out of the muddy water and landed in front of me. I glanced to the rear, clear, and backed up, getting out of lunge range. The young male croc was about two meters long and probably weighed two hundred kilos, about five hundred pounds. It squared off to face me. Not good. I backed up a little more and pulled my Glock out.

Now let me tell you something, farang. You might have seen stuff on the Discovery channel where some guy is tooling around with crocodiles? Yes. Good. Forget it. All of it. When a two-meter-long Crocodylus porosus is five meters in front of you, animal rights are the last thing on your mind. Walk in my boots and then judge me. Right now I was wishing I carried a Desert Eagle. Still a 9mm full metal jacket round can do a lot of damage. You have to make sure you get the angle right. A croc's hide is tough, and a bullet can deflect.

Another piece of advice, never fire a warning shot. Make the first shot count. Put it down. Mother taught me that when I was ten. I lined up the sights on the croc's cranium. It opened its jaws and flashed its tail. I held a breath, and he slipped into the river. Smart croc. A quick glance behind, still clear. Fuck it. I ran the rest of the way. I'd rather be undignified than lunch.

An overturned oil barrel made a decent seat as I tried to ease my breathing to something a little less painful. I checked my phone for tweets about the flood. FROC (Flood Relief Operations Center) was useless, most of the information they put out hours old by the time it hit the feeds, but there were at least ten other 'twitterers' that were putting out accurate information. Don Muang Airport had just flooded, and one tweet made me smile – 'FROC now evacuating due to flood'. Irony doesn't even get close.

My black phone, the general line usually handled by Chai, rang.

"Chai, a jet ski gang from Pattaya sunk one of the long tails working down near the market."

"When and who's speaking?"

"About ten minutes ago, this is Uncle Tong, who's this?"

"Hi, Uncle Tong, this is Chance."

"Chance, oh, how are your mother and father – I hope they're well?"

"They're fine, Uncle Tong."

"And how are you, Chance?"

There were a lot of ways I could answer that question. I chose to lie. "I'm okay, Uncle Tong, now what about this jet ski gang?"

"Ah, just some young thugs with jet skis. They have a Pattaya license on the truck they brought the jet skis in, and they beat up a couple of elder local guys that were using a long tail ferrying people across the flooded road down by the market. They sank the long tail."

"Spread the word to leave them alone and not use their service. Get as many of our boys as you can to muster down there, but spread out. I'll meet you outside the 7-Eleven soon."

"Yes, boss."

Khun Vinai with three pickups full of men and women turned off the soi and parked. Vinai handed the rifle to one of the men, and he went down to the edge of the dyke, getting in a prone position. Another man with binoculars squatted beside him as spotter. I thought about taking them to the market with me, but it was overkill, and they were needed here.

"Khun Chance, we can take care of this. I'll sandbag the gap, and we'll string the nets across the whole dyke when Nat and Pok get back."

"Thanks, Khun Vinai, give me a call if you need my help with anything." I walked back to the Defender and got in. Vinai already had everyone in a line passing sandbags down to the edge of the dyke. I got the Defender turned around; driving when you can't see the road is a tricky thing. The black phone rang again.

"Khun Chai, Uncle Virote's sons just came into Big Tiger's restaurant and said they are the new owners."

"Which sons?" I recognized the caller as the manager from the restaurant.

"Khemkaeng and Damrong." So the eldest and youngest had made a truce.

"Did anyone ask for proof?"

"Yes, Khun Oh."

"All right, do nothing for now. We'll be in touch."

"Yes, Khun Oh."

Once I cleared farm property, the road became clear. All five phones I had were laid out on the passenger seat in the belt that Chai had made. It looks like an ammo pouch with the screens of the phones showing. All five phones rang. I pulled over and picked up the blue phone, Pim's line.

"Babe?" Silence, but I could hear breathing. "Pim, if that's you, press a button on the phone." There was a 'beep'.

"Pim, two for yes, one for no."

Two beeps.

"Are you hurt?"

One beep, relief flooded through me.

"Are you in Bangkok?"

One beep.

"Are you in Thailand?"

Two beeps.

"Can you tell me where? Send me an SMS." I realized that was two questions.

Two beeps, a pause and one beep. I heard a shout, "Hey," in the background, and the line cut off.

I picked up the red phone, Mere Joom's line.

"Yes, Mother, sorry I couldn't answer. Pim, at least I think it was her, just called."

"What did she say?"

"She couldn't talk or send SMS for some reason, but we did a kind of Morse code. She's in Thailand, and she's okay."

"That's a relief. We'll find her, Chance, don't worry, she'll be fine. We've resolved the situation from this morning. We're on our way back. Chai's picking us up at the Police Hospital."

"How's Beckham?"

"He'll be fine. The doctor said no permanent damage."

"How's Por?"

"Angry. How are you holding up?"

"I'm good, but I need the contact Por has on Lek."

"I'm sending it now. Have you seen the papers?"

"No."

"Sankit's front page, have a look as soon as you can.

I'm trying to find out who wrote the article, just says 'staff reporters' as usual."

The other phones were still ringing. "Mother, I've got to go. Tell Por that Virote's sons are making a move. Khemkaeng and Damrong have joined up and just taken over Big Tiger's restaurant. I've got to go down to the market and take care of a little problem there; then I'll see you at home."

"Take care, Chance."

"I will, Mother." She hung up.

The green phone was Chai. "I'm picking up Por and Mother. They've been released."

"I know, I just spoke to Mother. I'll see you at the house. Who do we have that can shoot the Barret?"

"Sirote, nickname, Beer."

"Sirote?"

"Bank's sister, daughter's husband."

"Right, I remember. Tell him to pick up the Barret, with suppressor and armor-piercing shells. Find a high point overlooking Pak Nam market and wait for my call."

"What's the problem?"

"Some Pattaya beach thugs muscling in on our territory. We need to find out why they're stupid enough to think that we'd let them get away with this."

"Okay, sending you Beer's number now." He hung up.

I picked up the yellow phone, the 'family line'. "Hello?"

"Chance, this is Aunt Dao. I've been dreaming about you."

"Aunt Dao, I've been meaning to call you, but I'm sorry I'm a little busy right now…"

"Chance, listen to me. Your 'duang' is very, very bad right now. You have to come and see me, and we have to go to the Wat..."

"I understand, Aunt Dao. I'll call you back, okay."

"All right, Chance, but don't forget to call me. It's very important."

"I won't, Aunt Dao." I hung up. I was racing to reach the black phone before they all started ringing again.

"Chai?"

"No, it's Chance, Nat. What's happening?"

"Boss, we went down to Bang Pu pier, and some of Uncle Virote's guys told us this was their pier, and we had to deal with them."

"Did you get the nets?"

"Yes, but not from them, they wanted a million each, laughed at us. We went across to Laem Fa Phra and got them there."

"Okay, good job. Drop the nets off at the farm. Go to the house and get tooled up, and meet Uncle Tong at the 7-Eleven down at Pak Nam market."

"On the way, boss."

I hung up. I watched the phones warily, all quiet.

At Sri Samut Road, I parked the Defender and walked over to the 7-Eleven. Where the road dips, the flood water was about a meter and a half deep. Telephone booths had water up to the phones. On the edge, a group of guys, all dark-skinned, stood around near a bunch of jet skis. On either side of the two-hundred-meter flood, groups of people were stranded.

I took a look around the 7-Eleven. One of the older male staff was looking out of the window at the gang.

"What's happening?" I asked him.

"Some jet ski operators just had a fight down there." He turned around and, despite my beat-up appearance, recognized me. He raised his hands in a wai.

"Sorry, Khu Oh, I didn't realize it was you."

"That's all right. Has anything happened since the fight?"

"They chased off one of the army trucks that came to help and put a chain of spikes across the road on the other side. You can't see it, it's under the water, but my friend on the other side called me and told me about it."

"Okay, thanks," I looked up at the shiny aluminum shelves where cigarettes were hidden from the eyes of minors, "and could you get me a packet of Marlboro reds and a lighter?"

He smiled, opened the shelves, and handed me a packet of reds and a lighter. "On the house, Khun Oh, it is my gift."

"Thanks," I said and left the shop. Pim had forbidden me smoking anything but the occasional joint in her quest to provide Por and Mother with a grandson. I lit one up. It tasted delicious.

naam pheung reuua seuua pheung bpaa – Water floats boats, tigers need the jungle

THE HONK OF A HORN

Pak Nam, Sunday, 30 October 2011, 1:30PM

You might be wondering why, when I had so many serious pressing issues, I was down in Pak Nam market dealing with a bunch of thugs from Pattaya. To be honest, so was I. The thing you have to realize is that our relationship with the people is born of trust. They trust that when shit like this happens, we'll take care of it. Weddings, funerals, business openings, births, labor disputes, contract signings, loans, just about every facet of ordinary life in our community, we get a call. When it comes to thugs, the people don't call the cops, they call us. That trust has to be honored and, more important, maintained.

Uncle Tong, 'Gold' to you farang, had brought a few of the boys with him. He sent them to stand in different

90

places through the market. We waited until Beer had set up position in a five-storey shop-house. He was opposite where the gang from Pattaya stood around. Total distance to the gang, about a hundred and fifty meters. Fish in a small barrel. Every now and then one of them would jump on a jet ski and drive it around at high speed near the group of stranded people, trying to spray them with the wash.

I clipped on my hands-free mike and called Beer.

"Beer, can you hear me?"

"Yes, boss."

"Don't kill anyone, but when I say a color I want you to shoot any jet ski of that color that is nearest to Uncle Tong. Got it?"

"Got it, boss."

I walked with Uncle Tong to his black-tinted window Toyota Vigo. I got in, and he walked down to where the Pattaya gang was standing, stopping about five meters away from them. Our boys fanned out behind him. Numbers were about equal. One of the gang stepped out in front, a belligerent look on his face. I was watching with a pair of Steiner's and listening on the comms masquerading as a pen in Uncle Tong's top breast pocket of his blue safari jacket.

"What do you want – hey, old man, you know who we are?"

I watched as Uncle Tong waved his hand at the jet skis.

"I'd like you to put those back in the truck that you brought them in and go home to Pattaya, you're not welcome here." Uncle Tong's voice, as I heard it in my earphones, was polite, almost apologetic. The leader of the thugs, all balls and no brain, mistook the politeness for weakness.

"Who the fuck are you?"

Nat stepped forward, but Uncle Tong put a hand on his arm, stopping him.

"You need to get back to Pattaya and fix those jet skis."

"Beer, shoot the yellow one," I said into my mike.

"What the fuck are you talking about, old man – fucking crazy old man."

"Like that yellow one there."

I heard the loud bang that came from the jet ski, and it jumped a meter sideways, bursting into flame. Beer had hit the gas tank – nice shot, very effective.

I watched carefully through the glasses. If anything was going to go off, it would happen now.

Tough guy didn't look so certain of his position. He turned around to check if his gang was still there. Safety in numbers can be a false notion.

"Beer, take out the red one nearest him."

"And that red one doesn't look so good," Tong, listening in on the multi-channel, said to Beach Boy standing frozen in a half crouch since the yellow jet ski had exploded into flame. The red jet ski spun when the fifty-caliber bullet hit the front cowling. It hadn't stopped spinning when he held up his hands.

"Okay, okay, sorry, boss, we're leaving."

"Uh-uh, tough guy, life ain't that easy – before you leave, I have a question, and I want you to answer honestly, or our guy with the gun is going to shoot you. Do you understand? I said, do you understand?" Uncle Tong's voice had taken on a hard, tempered edge.

Beach Boy was nodding his head, and from the way he was standing, it looked like he was about to get on his knees and start begging – that was the smartest thing I'd seen him do since I'd laid eyes on him.

"What I'd like to know is what made you think you could come down here to our market and get away with this shit? Are you just stupid or what? Well, answer me, you fucking dog, before I order my man to blow you in half."

Beach Boy fell to his knees, survival taking precedence over face, and from the sound of Uncle Tong's voice, it was another smart move. I was surprised.

"We were operating out by Don Muang, and this guy told us to come here. Paid us ten thousand."

"What did this guy look like?"

"He was a little younger than you, Uncle, and he had a deep scar on his chin."

"Ask him if the scar ran horizontal just below the upper lip," I said to Uncle Tong and watched while he repeated the question to Beach Boy.

Beach Boy's head nodded in the binoculars. Somboon had turned. That probably meant the 'hot' Ferrari and Speedy's dead body were also probably in play – fuck.

"Uncle Tong, thanks for your help, and get them the fuck out of here." I watched him raise his hand in a salute to me. I got out of his Vigo and walked back to the Defender. Standing by the vehicle, I looked back and watched as they crossed the water and got down on their knees. A loud cheer erupted from the crowd that had gathered in the market. Job done, time to head home.

At the traffic lights, a boy was selling newspapers. I remembered what Mother said and waved him over. Got the *Thai Rath* morning edition, gave him a hundred – keep the change – spread the wealth.

Sankit was front-page news. According to the story, Sankit had phoned in the burglary and reported the theft of the dowry of ten million baht to the police. The police had arrested someone called Chatree, apparently the son of Sankit's personal secretary at the Ministry. A woman he'd fired two months ago. What made the article front page was that Chatree admitted he'd stolen the money, except he said his share was twenty million and "there was too much money in the room for us to carry away". Backing up Chatree's version of events was the twenty million in cash he was caught with. Sankit was now being invited by the NACC (National Anti-Corruption Commission) to make a statement and had been temporarily transferred to an inactive post at the Prime Minister's office. In Thai political speak – that's the dog house. Sankit's whereabouts were reported as 'unknown'.

A car horn blared out behind me. That's unusual in Thailand. Normally people are more polite and just wait. On any given day, except when there're floods, riots and Chinese New Year, there are over ten million cars driving around Bangkok. You'll hardly ever hear a car horn. I looked around. It's funny the little things that save your life. In this case, the car horn. The passenger-side window exploded. Sound of shots close by. Slow motion kicking in, driven by adrenalin coursing through the blood, two little holes in the driver's side window registered, and then survival mode kicked in.

I scrambled out from behind the wheel and dived through the passenger-side window, hitting the ground hard. Shots coming hard and fast. Crouching behind the Defender, I looked underneath. Could see a motorbike's wheels and two left feet wearing a construction boot and a cowboy boot. Good, they were still on the bike. If they got off, I was a dead man. My Glock was in the glove compartment of the Defender. I scooted around to the back of the Defender, staying below window height. The driver who'd honked the horn was sitting upright, her mouth hanging wide open. I waved her to get down. Glass from the windows of the Defender rained down on me and the sidewalk.

The shooting stopped. I waited. I heard shouts of, "Go, go, go," then the sound of the bike taking off. I ran back to the passenger door and ripped at the handle. It was locked. Reached in, got the glove compartment open and the Glock out. Racked one in the chamber and came around the front of the Defender. They were gone. I could hear the bike, but the sound was a quickly fading howl. By the time I got back in the Defender, they'd be long gone.

Safety back on, I slipped the Glock inside my belt at my back and walked around to the driver's side. The engine of the Defender was still running. I got in and, ignoring the red light, drove away. I watched in the rear-view mirror as the woman who'd honked at me lifted a mobile phone to her mouth. I wasn't concerned, this was our patch, and I was only five minutes from home. I noticed as I drove through a pedestrian crossing that I was driving on autopilot. I glanced at the bullet holes in the window to my right. They were exactly head height.

The soi just before our house is wide enough for cars to park on either side. Trees provide shade in summer and protection from getting too wet in the rainy season. I pulled over. Stopped the engine. That had been close. Really close. My knuckles white where I gripped the steering wheel. I released the wheel, fumbling in my jacket pocket for a smoke. I finally found the packet. I got out of the Defender and lit one up.

Mother's Benz turned into the soi, pulling to a stop in front of me. The passenger window came down. It was Tum.

"I thought you were dead?" I said, throwing the butt away and walking forward to lean into the car and look in the backseat. Chai was driving, Joom and Por in the back. I had to smile. It hurt.

"I think I was dead for a while," Tum said.

"Did you get any lottery numbers while you were over there?"

"If I did, I can't remember them."

"It's good to see you, Tum."

"What happened to the Jeep, Chance?" Mother said, nodding at the bullet holes. Most of them were through the driver's side window, but there was another group through the door and a line that extended down the length of the Jeep. Either the shooter had used an extended magazine or two of them had been shooting.

"Someone tried to kill me just outside of the market downtown."

Mother nodded, expression steady, eyes hooded. She bit her upper lip. I reached in with my hand. She reached up and grasped it, squeezing hard. A tear escaped from her eye. I thought of Suchada.

"Let's get back home. We can talk there," Mother said with a tight little smile on her lips.

I leaned back out of the window, and Chai pulled away.

I puffed my cheeks and let out a long breath. The day had finally taken a turn for the better. I opened the door to the Defender. On the passenger's seat, Pim's blue phone, light blinking fast. Missed Call or SMS. I grabbed it. An SMS. I opened up the Message List.

Unknown Number: Goong didn't rape the Sullivan kid – a friend.

I might have been a bit optimistic about the day's progress.

naam raawn bplaa bpen naam yen bplaa dtaai — Warm water fish live, cold water fish die

DO IT OR DIE

Pak Nam, Sunday, 30 October 2011, 4:30PM

Showered, I had needed to get the cold sweat of fear off me, I taped myself up and sprayed my ribs from one of the cans of anesthetic that Chai had left in my room; he'd picked them up from the Police Hospital. Which is where Mere Joom, Por and Beckham had been taken after being caught on the island. I had a hundred questions, the first being why Por had shot Here Leng, and how they had gained their freedom but first, at Mother's order, we had to eat. Questions would have to wait.

We sat around the outside dining table next to the pool, with the door to the kitchen open. Mother and Ba Nui cooking while Por, Chai, Tum, and I drank Chivas and soda, talking. Beckham was in the house out back with Dr. Tom and a couple of nurses attending to him, lying in the same bed Por had recovered from his coma in after the bombing. Fully equipped with state-of-the-art medical equipment to Dr. Tom's specifications, Beckham couldn't be in a better place than where he was right now.

We'd called everyone in. Every person we could count on was on high alert, putting people on notice that we considered ourselves under attack. Approach with caution, we're going to shoot first and to hell with questions. Come to us with empty hands and honesty on your lips. It's our way of surviving.

To my knowledge, the only people who knew Pim was missing were the hotel manager, Por, Mother, Chai, me, and of course, whoever had taken her. The whole district knew that Virote's sons had made a move on Big Tiger's territory – which was tantamount to a slap in our face. The only way they could have thought they could make such a move was if they thought they had the leverage to pull it off. The hit on me didn't fit unless they were taking a 'belt 'n braces' approach – which was possible, I suppose… but it didn't fit, so I had no fast ideas about that.

"Khun Por?"

"Yes, Chance."

"What happened at Here Leng's house?"

"It was the girl. And again, your mother saved my life." A grin of pride and a long look at Mere Joom cooking in the kitchen.

"Once you and Chai left, Leng took a call, and after he finished, he told the girl to go upstairs and get more ice. All this time he was talking to Mother, telling her how he was the last of his line, he was all washed up, not interested in life anymore, that kind of thing. The girl came back down. I noticed she was shaking, and then I saw that our ice bucket was still full. She saw I noticed the ice, and she grabbed for the basket. Came out with a gun. Your mother was so quick. She threw her glass, and it hit the girl in the face. Then shooting started out front of the house. The girl brought the gun up, but Mother was faster. Here Leng dived for the gun in the girl's hand, and Mother put one in him. Then you joined us." He took a long drink of his whiskey. Chai was grinning, looking at Mother whisking eggs in a bowl.

Three plates of rice and half a bottle of whiskey later, Por sat on Mother's comfortable deep sofa and I was in the matching chair opposite him. Mother sat to his left. Chai had left us alone, saying he was going to look in on Beckham. Tum had made himself scarce. Ba Nui had served coffee and retreated to her quarters on the other side of the house at the back of the kitchen. Now it was just the three of us.

"We had to make a deal, Chance." Por leaned forward and picked up a large snifter of cognac. He dropped his nose in and inhaled deeply, hooded eyes watching me above the rim of the glass.

"I thought as much – what's the deal?"

"Well, we were being held by that son of a bitch of a police colonel over in Phra Pradaeng until he got a call from someone up high. And I mean really high. We were taken to the Police Hospital, where they fixed Beckham up, and that's when they approached us. We were taken up to an office, and they laid it on the line. They want a billion, and then the evidence disappears. I told them who the hell has a billion baht lying around, and that's when they told us about Chatree, the twenty million baht he was caught with, and Sankit's missing billion."

"So they really think I took it?"

"They do, yes. I half convinced them you didn't, but either way, they've given us, you actually, the job of getting it back and giving it to them. Greedy bastards."

"And this was the deputy…"

"Both deputies and the Interior."

"Shit."

"Yep – that's about right." Por reached over the low coffee table, awkward for him to do having to shift his plastic leg out of the way, and tapped me lightly on the leg.

"I had to promise I would leave town – they made me swear – bastards – I thought I'd go to New York. I'll go alone. I can get the leg sorted, and I'll get back as fast as I can. I promised them I wouldn't fly back to Bangkok for a couple of weeks. I didn't promise that I wouldn't drive, sail or walk back within that time. I was careful with my words, and none of them picked up on it. Dumb but cunning those bastards."

"When do you have to leave?"

"Before midnight tonight." He shook his head. "Bad time to be leaving – bastards."

"You shouldn't have mentioned his sons. You know it's a sore point with him," Mother said.

"I was explaining what happened with Here Leng."

"Here Leng just came to the end of his rope. He wanted to die, just didn't have the courage to do it himself. Wanted us to do it for him." Her glass put back on the table with a slight bang. Still keyed up. Killing another human, no matter how times you've done it, is not a question of breaking eggs to make an omelet. Killing someone you liked and considered a friend cuts deep. I know. I've been there. Por leaned over and kissed her cheek.

"Thanks for saving the life of this foolish old man, my dearest." A look passed between them. I've seen it countless times. A look that when we lived in the old house, with the teak wood floors, when I was a kid, would have meant falling asleep to soft laughter, moans, grunts, creaking floorboards and wondering what all that noise was about.

"That SMS you got. The one saying Goong didn't rape the farang kid. That might explain a lot. We need to dig a little deeper on that. Feels like someone might be playing us."

"I'm thinking Virote's sons."

"Maybe," Por nodded and stroked his chin, "but we don't know yet. Don't want to judge too quickly. How's your judgment of Goong working out?"

Ouch. Por had never spared me when it came to lessons. Not malicious in intent, his way of educating was to show the error of one's thinking. Correct the thought process and everything else should work out. He did this sometimes subtly, but at times, it was like getting hit in the face with a motorbike helmet.

"I judged him, it's true, but his death was an accident, and I'm not sorry he's dead. What I might've missed is he was just a patsy. He was perfect for someone to lay the crime on. He'd done it before a couple of times. Why would we doubt he'd done it again?"

"Right, and what did they hope to achieve?" Por took

another sip from the snifter and sat back, looking at me over the rim of the glass.

"They wanted us there. Whatever happened, we would have visited Here Leng. Goong dying was a bonus for them."

"Maybe. So who was there the last time Goong did this? We still don't know who was shooting at us at Here Leng's place. Think about that. From what I'm hearing, his boys have all moved on. So who would know we would be there and want to kill us? Who knew enough about what happened back then to plan that we would visit Here Leng if it happened again."

"Virote's boys moving on our territory and Somboon taking off with the car and body at the same time? Too much coinciedence, Por."

"Right, but what if someone is using them as a distraction? The attempted hit on you can't be discounted either."

I nodded, swirled the cognac in my glass, looking into it, thinking… more questions than answers.

"Well, I better go pack. Tum and your mother will take me to the airport. You get on with finding Pim. Use whatever and everything you need. If you have to give everything away, don't think twice. You get my daughter back, and I'll get back here to help you sort the rest out."

I slipped off my chair, kneeling by his side, and gave him a deep wai.

He stood, Mother standing at the same time. "I'll help you with the packing."

Por smiled at her. They headed for the stairs, Joom with a sway in her hips, Por with a bounce in his step.

I downed the rest of the cognac, its heat coursing down my throat, settling in my belly, joining the fire already there. Por was right. Someone was playing us. Pim, the Ferrari covered in DNA, and Speedy's dead body, all leverage against me. Leverage against something I didn't have – the money. Or was it something else, something as simple as revenge?

Face value and 'Face' are two entirely different things. Face is a delicate game in Thailand. I had the feeling I might have put too much faith in one and not enough in the other, but which, I couldn't tell you.

I went outside, slipping on a pair of Crocs, our favorite brand of house shoes, by the French doors leading to the pool and guest house. Chai sat on one of the two rattan comfy chairs on the deck. I sat down in the other. A steady drizzle, hidden in the dark, hit the water of the swimming pool, causing the pool lights to shimmer and dance in the water. I glanced at the time on my cell. Nearly 7pm.

"Any word on Pichit?" I asked Chai.

"Nothing. He's either with them, or he's dead. He wouldn't hide. If he were in danger, he'd come here."

"Somboon was a bad mistake. We let him get too close."

"People change. All kinds of reasons, pressures. We can't know how each individual around us is going to act over time – can happen to anybody."

"Not you."

"I'm not 'people'."

I looked sideways. It was dark on the deck, but the glow from the lights inside the house showed enough of Chai's features for me to see that he was being entirely serious. I took out a cigarette, tapped it down on the packet, and fished the lighter out of my jeans pocket.

"Those things will kill you."

"I know." Out of the corner of my eye I saw his nod, and I lit up. Death from cancer was the least of my concerns. A cold breeze punched its way across the porch, strong enough to sway the branches of the trees on the far side of the pool. Another front coming in, bringing more rain, more flooding. Mother had said she'd take care of the issues at the farm and run back-up. Her spy network had been put on alert. No 'feelers' out about Pim yet, but feelers on Suchada and Sankit were out in full force. More effective than a UN Red Notice, Mother's word on the street seldom fails to yield results.

"Anything on Lek yet?"

Chai shook his head.

"What about the guard. The senior guy?"

"He's in the trunk of the Benz."

"What?"

"He's in the trunk of the Benz. Probably still sedated."

"Probably?"

"Yes, I stuck him with enough juice to keep him down for eight hours, and it's been a little over that now."

"Well, we better question him, then."

"That's what I was thinking – Pit 51?"

"Yeah, that's what I was thinking too."

naam thuaam bpaak – Water floods the mouth

PIT #51

Pak Nam, Sunday, 30 October 2011, 8:25PM

The mere sight of Pit #51 is enough to get anyone to talk. There's a look of dawning horror when the hood is taken off, and there, in front of them, the myth, dark urban legend, stuff of tales mothers use to scare their kids is proven real. The #51 painted large in black on the concrete walls of the twelve-foot-deep pit.

The guard, whose name was Chakan, at least that's what was written on his ID card, pissed his pants. Crocs' eyes showed red in the beam of light coming from Chai's flashlight as he played it over the dark pit. We hauled Chakan over to the pit's edge, leaving his hands and feet tied, and sat him down, the rancid smell of his piss coming off his faux military guard pants. His shoulders heaving, chin on his chest, he looked dammed miserable and very scared. This part of the job I like the least, that's to say, I hate it, and I confess Pit 51 even gives me the creeps.

The worst of our crocs are here. Almost uniformly 'salty' and female. A few Siamese crocs too, small, but they can grow to a couple of meters and can be extremely aggressive, especially the females when protecting a brood. All of the crocs in here had killed humans; most I think enjoyed doing it. The last one in, the female that had taken down Ken the Yak last year in his swimming pool.

Chai cut through the gaffer tape he'd wound around Chakan's head and mouth and then ripped it off, shining the flashlight in Chakan's eyes.

"Stop crying and listen carefully. Nod your head if you understand me."

Chakan nodded, not looking up.

"You have one chance to get this right and only one chance. If I think you're lying, then the guy shining the light on you is going to kick you into the pit. Then we're going to cover you in chicken blood because we're in a hurry. Nod if you understand what I've said."

Chakan nodded again, still didn't look up, but sobbed louder.

"Good. Now tell me what you did at the hotel."

"I turned off the CCTV."

"Who told you to do this?"

"Lek, he was a temp hire bellhop."

"What happened to the regular guy?"

"He was hurt in a motorbike accident. Please don't kill me."

"Keep talking – when did Lek ask you to do this?"

"Just after he came on shift, about 6pm. We work a

twelve-hour shift."

"And what did he ask you exactly?"

"Sometime during the shift I was to kill the cameras for the floor of the Presidential Suite and the lift lobby. He told me it was because someone important wanted to meet with the people in the suite and couldn't be seen."

"And you chose to believe that? From a bellhop? How much did you get?"

"Ten thousand."

"How were you paid?"

"Five before and five after."

"And what happened?"

"I watched you leave with this guy here, and then Lek came to see me and told me to turn the cameras off for the lift lobby on three as well because they were leaving now by the back entrance."

"And you turned the cameras off?"

"Yes, and reset the time on the server so that the ten minutes wouldn't show up. I'm sorry."

"What time was this?"

"3:30am exactly. Lek told me to keep it turned off for ten minutes, and that's what I did."

"And then?"

"Lek called me later that day and said he'd made a big mistake and he was getting out of Bangkok for a while, maybe the country if he could. I was angry with him because he'd lied to me and involved me in what looked like a kidnapping. He said he had been lied to as well. I asked him why he was running, I was scared too, and he said some very heavy people were after him, had been to his apartment, so he was running. I figured with him gone, I was in the clear."

"And then?"

"That was it. I didn't hear anything more. I swear, take me to any temple, and I'll swear before the Buddha, I just went back to work like everything was normal. That's what I wanted. I plan to donate the ten thousand to a temple, nothing but bad luck on that money. I went back to work. Please don't kill me... I've got two kids."

He'd given what he had and, with nothing left to bargain with, begging seemed like a good choice. In a way, this idiot was directly responsible for Pim being missing. His duty was to take care of the guests in the hotel, and he had failed in that duty. Something didn't fit.

"Why did you believe Lek? You said he was a temp. How long had he been there?" I tried to remember who had taken our bags to the suite. We hadn't gone directly to the suite. We'd gone straight to the ballroom. I'd told the concierge our bags were in the trunk and left him the keys to the car.

Chakan kept sobbing. Chai stepped forward and rapped him on the collarbone with the flashlight.

"Answer." Chai's voice was soft, hard to hear above the noise of the rain.

Chakan sniffed deep. "It was his first day, first job, that was the strange thing. His first job was the Presidential Suite. He came down and told me that a guy in the Presidential Suite had told him some VIPs were coming that night and asked a favor of him."

"And you didn't think it was strange that a guy would ask a bellhop this?"

"No. Farang make strange requests and do strange

things all the time."

Okay, I could concede and see that one, but I still smelled a rat. "You were the one to get Lek his temp job. Lek is a friend of yours. You left that out. You want to tell me more while I make up my mind about kicking you into the pit?"

Chai let out a very audible sigh. "I'll go get the chicken blood," he said and handed me the flashlight.

I got down on my haunches directly in front of Chakan. Turned the flashlight off. He stopped sobbing and looked at me, eyes blinking.

"Talk now, tell me everything, and you can live. But leave out a single detail, and you will go into the pit covered in chicken blood. If you love your children, tell me the truth."

**

The digital clock on the dashboard showed 23:55. I'd seen Por off at the airport. Exchanged a few words, mostly polite, with the cops that had come to make sure he got on the plane. A promise is a promise, and Por got on the plane to Los Angeles. He'd connect there with another flight to New York. Mother was back at the farm. The situation at the dyke had remained stable, but more water was on the way. A lot more judging from what I was looking at in the beam of the headlights.

We were in something closely resembling a monster truck on the outskirts of Nonthaburi, approaching the Pathum Thani area, driving up AH2. Water was everywhere in front of us, above the wheels of our jacked-up pickup truck. In the cab behind me, Chakan, Nat and Beer. Chai was driving, and I was studying our progress on GPS. In the back of the pickup was a black rubber boat with a 35HP Mercury engine and a couple of spare twenty-liter fuel tanks.

Chakan had told me that Lek was likely staying at his uncle's house in Phak Hai. Normally that would be an hour's drive. Floods aren't normal. The entire area was under at least two meters of water at sea level and in low-lying areas as much as fifteen meters. As soon as the road ran out, we'd have to use the boat. It wouldn't be long.

Usually, even at night there'd be lights all over the countryside. Especially along the road. Not just street lamps but the lights of bars, restaurants, vendors' stalls and factories working overtime. Outside, it was completely dark. No electricity here, apart from what you might get out of a portable generator. Completely cut off from road access, the only way to get to Phak Hai was by boat or helicopter. Mother had tried to get us a helicopter, but they were all in use.

Chai pulled off the highway. Ahead of us, a dip in the road and water covered the roof of what had been a roadside stall. Only a quarter of the streetlight poles showed, a line of dead lights showing the path of the road underneath. A flooded road led to a gate to a rice mill, abandoned now; the gate was locked. Chai parked next to the gate and slipped a pair of bolt cutters under the water. Minutes later we crawled slowly up the loading bay ramp until we reached dry ground.

While the others unloaded and stocked the inflatable, I sprayed myself with more local anesthetic. Chai knocked on the window. I lowered it.

"You can stay, drive back home. I'll find him if he's

there."

"No, it's better to be doing something, you know?"

Chai nodded, understanding. I got out and walked over to the boat tied up to the loading ramp. Chai handed me a pair of night vision NVE-7 goggles. US military spec ordered via the internet and shipped overnight to an address in South Carolina and on to us as a video game, they'd earned their USD5,000 cost back many times over. For a moment the rain stopped, and the clouds above parted to show the moon. I felt like I hadn't seen it for a long time, couldn't remember when the last time was, but it felt like a long time. The gap in the clouds closed, and the darkness closed in around us. I put the goggles on.

I took up a position opposite Nat. Chakan was up in the bow. Beer had taken the truck home and would be waiting for our call. Chai stuck the Mercury in forward gear, and we slipped away from the loading bay. Through the gate and up the soi we had just come down, we crossed the main highway, and Chai opened up the throttle. It was forty-one point seven eight kilometers to Lek's uncle's house. At best, we could do about twenty knots. The trip would take a little under two hours. With the boat up on plane, I wedged myself as tight as possible into the seat in the middle of the boat, trying to ignore the little jabs of pain finding their way through the anesthetic.

The government had evacuated nearly all of the land around these parts, but many people had refused to leave. Knowing that thieves and looters were operating at full strength was a strong deterrent to leaving their homes. Ten minutes after leaving the truck, all I could see in every direction was water. Kevin Costner's movie came to mind, only difference being this was fresh water. I took out my cell phone. No reception here, all the transmitting towers had either been turned off or were shut down for lack of power. A dog barked at us in the night, eyes glowing green in the goggles. Chai shouted something.

"What?" I turned and cupped a hand to my ear.

"We'll pick him up on the way back. I marked the spot on the GPS," Chai shouted above the sound of the Mercury and gave me a thumbs up. Chai likes dogs, dogs like Chai.

There's not a hell of a lot to do when you're heading out on a mission like this except think. You're too keyed up to sleep, and you've already checked your gear ten times. The landscape, not that there was much land to be seen, was depressingly bleak, dotted here and there with the roofs of sunken houses and the occasional telephone pole. We were cutting a direct line to Phak Hai, a line made possible by the flood.

It was obvious that someone had planned the snatching of Pim very carefully. The element that didn't fit was me. How did they know that I would leave? I couldn't figure that out because I hadn't known I was going to leave. It seemed a tenuous hook upon which to base a plan to kidnap someone. Usually you'd want a bit more certainty than 'he may or may not leave the room'.

I hoped to get access to Chatree, Sankit's ex-secretary's son, tomorrow. Mother was working on it, but they had him locked up deep inside Nong Khaem Police Station under twenty-four-hour guard. Not an easy place for me to visit without a calling card in my hand. Between him and Lek, I hoped to establish that I had nothing to do with the theft of the money and hopefully get Pim back. The big assumption in that equation was that the reason Pim had been snatched was the money. I dreaded to think it was related to Virote's boys, the Brothers Grim: one of the reasons we had to keep Pim's disappearance out of the news. If they learned she was missing, they'd start looking and put out their own offers. Leverage I couldn't afford to give them.

We passed an ancient pagoda with just its top poking out of the water. Judging by the height of the pagoda, the water was at least four meters deep. A green Ayutthaya slid out of view behind us to our right; in front of us, a flat plain of water where rice would usually grow. On a bank to my left, by a clump of trees, a crocodile walked slowly into the water. I remembered standing with Por looking down at Pit 51 just after he'd had it built. He said to me, pointing his chin at the crocs, "Remember, we're not like them. We do what we do, but we do it with honor. We don't kill for pleasure or profit or because we're hungry. We protect our own, mind our business, and take revenge when needed, sometimes that means killing, but we do it because it is needed not because we want to." I was ten or maybe eleven at the time.

A thousand thoughts later, each more depressing than the last, Chai cut the engine. According to the GPS plot, we were about half a kilometer away from Lek's uncle's house. Paddling hurt, the pain putting fire into each stroke, but against the strong current, all of us had to pull our weight.

The house belonging to Lek's uncle had been pointed out on Google Earth back at the farm by Chakan. We brought him along to talk to Lek and guide us to the house once we reached it. He wasn't needed. We could smell what I guessed would be Lek twenty meters away from the house. The second floor still above water, the wooden railing made a convenient place to tie up. We kept silent, just in case, but there was no need. We wouldn't be waking anyone up.

The pencil-thin beams of our flashlights made the rats run for the cover of darkness. Lek and his uncle were both dead, lying next to each other. They had been dead for some time by the look of their bloated bodies and the rats dining. Shot in the head and chest. Three bullets each. Whoever had done it had been close. I turned Lek over and found a wallet in his jeans pocket. Counted fifteen thousand baht. On the wall, black-and-white photos in simple wooden frames, pictures of Lek's uncle when he was young, with his wife outside a department store in his army uniform, and surrounded by his children; everyone smiling and looking awkward and self-conscious. He looked more awkward, but less self-conscious now. I felt sorry for him; none of this was his doing, just caught up in the current. It was a bad way to start the week.

Ya wang naam bor na – Don't hope for water at the next well

AUNT DAO'S DREAMS

Aunt Dao, Star, lived with her maid in a single-storey house in the compound Por and Mother had built for his minor wives. The first of his minor wives, Aunt Dao was also the only one who, in her own words, "Was no beauty queen." Aunt Dao was the only daughter of a mafia godfather who had ruled Bang Phli with an iron fist. In the violent gang warfare of the mid to late sixties, he and Dao's mother were cut down while having dinner at a Chinese restaurant. Dao had been saved by a visit to the ladies' room. She was twenty-seven years old. Aunt Dao, twenty-seven years old, weighed over a hundred kilos and had lost everyone and everything. She was alone.

Whether Mother acted out of kindness or politics, she's never let on, and no one's brave nor stupid enough to ask. Mother told Por to take Dao in as his minor wife. They had no children, but Aunt Dao was loved and respected by all of us. It's what's on the inside that counts.

We lived in a wooden house on stilts then. The floorboards, teak planks hundreds of years old, were worn smooth by the feet of five generations. Like many Thai families, we all slept in one big room on the second floor of the house. No glass in the windows, just wooden shutters. Chai and I shared a space underneath the shutter that opened to a view of the river behind us. Once we'd eaten and showered, electricity hadn't reached our neck of the woods yet, Mere Joom would light an oil lamp and would either read or tell us a story. We liked her stories best, and one of our favorite stories, one that was first told to us the day after we'd received a spanking from her that I can still remember, was the story of how Aunt Dao saved Por's life.

We'd received a spanking because we were teasing Aunt Dao. Mother had heard about it, asked us if it was true, and when we admitted it was, sent us to go and find a bamboo cane with which she was going to spank us. We were sent to bed early and ordered not to cry, we'd brought it on ourselves. The next day Mother asked us if we were sorry we'd teased Aunt Dao, and of course, we said yes. I think I was about nine then and Chai eight. Old enough to know better. Mother asked us if we were sorry because what we'd said was disrespectful to Aunt Dao or because we got whacked (her term). The one thing that Mother never tolerates in anyone is a lie. Of course, we again admitted the truth, thinking the worst – we were going to get sent for bamboo again. Instead, Mother squatted down in front of us and told us to sit down.

We sat down on the hard-packed earth underneath the house.

"Por was going to attend the wedding of a friend." Mother had a certain 'story voice', and when we heard it, I remember Chai and I sharing a look of relief and a little grin of anticipation for the story we knew was coming.

"It was a big wedding, and everyone knew about it. Por was going to speak for the 'Chao Bao', the groom. He had a new suit made, and everyone knew he was going. The day of the wedding went smoothly, and in the evening Por returned to get his new suit. He came upstairs and opened the closet, and his suit was gone. He asked me if I knew where his suit was, and I didn't. He looked around the house and down by the laundry but didn't find his suit. Por was running late by now, so he decided he would just have to wear one of his old suits and went back upstairs.

"When he got back upstairs, he happened to look out the window, the one that you boys sleep under. He saw that down near the water's edge Aunt Dao was holding his new suit. Por was wearing a pakama, a red and white chequered one. I always told him it made him look like a table in an Italian restaurant. Por ran down the stairs and shouted to Aunt Dao to give him his suit because he was late. Aunt Dao turned and ran to the river, where a boat was tied to the pier.

"Por ran down to the pier and jumped into the boat. Then Aunt Dao pushed the boat away from the pier. The current there is strong and because of the curve of the river takes you out to the middle quickly. I don't want you boys swimming off that pier, remember that. Anyway, the boat, that one over there," she pointed out a traditional shallow wooden canoe, "drifted out into the middle of the river, and Aunt Dao threw the paddles over the side. Por floated halfway to Hua Hin with Aunt Dao." Mother had laughed out loud at the memory and then got her serious, 'here's the moral of the story' voice going – we paid attention.

"She knew Por would be furious with her, and she put up with a lot of shouting until Por got back and heard the news. That evening at the wedding reception a bomb had gone off. It killed five people, all sitting at the guest of honor table. Everyone thought Por had planted the bomb because the only empty seat was the seat with his name on the table in front of it.

"Aunt Dao knew that if she told Por she'd had a dream about a bomb killing him at the wedding he would still go. So she'd made a plan to steal his suit and get him on that boat so she could push it out to float in the Gulf and Por would miss the wedding." Mother leaned in close, her voice a whisper. "That woman you were teasing yesterday cannot swim and is terrified of the river."

Gutted by the sorrows of shame, I don't think either of us slept a wink that night.

I pressed Aunt Dao's doorbell. She opened the door. "Oh god, you look terrible still. Come sit down. I'm relieved you're here. I've been so worried about you. Would you like some coffee?"

I gave her a kiss on the cheek. "Yes, thanks, Aunt Dao. Why have you been worried about me?"

"Sit. Sit first, and I'll get you some coffee, then we can talk."

Aunt Dao's house was decorated in the style of an overstocked antique shop with overtones of gypsy fortune-teller. I sat down on an overstuffed, flowery sofa.

"I've asked Nok to get us some coffee," Aunt Dao said and lit up a Siphon 'Falling Rain' cigarette. I dug out the packet of Marlboro.

"What are you doing?"

"I was going to join you in having a cigarette."

"You're supposed to be baby-making with Pim; you can't smoke. Don't say another word, and put those away." I complied as she waved away the wafts of smoke in front of her.

"I was afraid something bad was going to happen. I saw it, but I didn't understand what I saw, and I didn't want to cast a cloud over your wedding day. I'm sorry, I should have said something."

"What did you see?"

"For three nights I dreamt about you. Each dream was different, but they all involved you. At first, I thought it might be because I was thinking of you getting married, but when the second dream happened the next night, I knew it wasn't an ordinary dream. Not that any dream is ordinary, they all mean something, but well, you know what I mean." Aunt Dao stopped talking while Nok put a pot of coffee and two cups on the table. Aunt Dao waited, puffing on her cigarette, until Nok had left the room.

"Where was I?"

"Wasn't an ordinary dream…?"

"Yes, so, I knew it wasn't an ordinary dream when it recurred. That only happens with my special dreams."

"What was in the dreams?"

"In the first dream you were surrounded by well-wishers and then later you were in an empty house, opening doors, one after another, calling Pim's name." That was a close description to what had happened when I discovered Pim missing.

"In the second dream you were in a jungle, near a waterfall, you were hunting for Pim but couldn't find her." She stopped talking and put her hand on my leg. Her lower lip was trembling.

"It's okay, Aunt Dao. You can tell me…"

"In the third dream, Pim was waiting for you, and you'd been shot. Chai was kneeling over you, trying to bring you back, but you were dead." A tear rolled down her cheek. I've had better starts to the day.

"Aunt Dao, let's look on the bright side. Your dream means Pim's safe, and your dream has warned me. I'll be on my guard. And your dreams don't always come true, right? You remember when you dreamt about Por and the bomb, you saved him, right?"

She looked doubtful. "I dreamt I saved Por," she said in a soft voice, another tear rolling down her cheek. I gave her a hug, not sure who needed it more, me or her. Being the subject of one of Aunt Dao's death dreams is the equivalent of being told you've got cancer.

"You're right, Nong Oh. Now you know, be on your guard." She still looked doubtful.

Mother called.

"Yes, Mother?"

"I got you clearance to talk to Chatree. You have five minutes with him before lunch. You'd best leave early; the area is going to get more flood water. Have you talked

121

with Aunt Dao?"

"Thanks, and yes."

"Don't think too much about that right now, stay focused on Pim."

"Yes, Mother."

"Por called to say he's fine, and he'll be back in a few days at most." She hung up.

"Aunt Dao, I have to get going, some business I need to take care of." I gave her a wai and left her standing by her door, cigarette in hand, feeling her eyes on my back all the way to the gate.

Chai had got us another monster truck, standard black with eighty-percent-dark film on the windows, your basic 'I'm a gangster' kind of vehicle. An appropriate choice for what we had to do.

"Where to?"

"Nong Khaem Police Station. Mother's organized for us to talk with Chatree."

"How is Aunt Dao?"

I looked at him. "Am I the only person who didn't know what Aunt Dao dreamt?"

"I think so, yes." Chai shrugged, nodded, and handed me the *Thai Rath* newspaper.

Sankit, Chatree, the missing billion, and the flood shared top billing. Rumors, more than a few with my name attached, flew like a flock of swallows on Wireless Road at dusk. Chatree had talked a lot but not said much. Just that the amount of money he saw was huge, he only took twenty million, and he and the other two guys he'd done the robbery with were drinking buddies whose names he didn't know. If something looks like bullshit, smells like bullshit, and feels like bullshit, there's a good chance it is bullshit – one of Uncle Mike's favorite sayings.

There were a lot of things that smelled like bullshit: Suchada moving her maid out and hiring a temp just before the wedding. A temp bellhop just before the wedding. Her and Sankit's disappearance, which I could understand in the light of the news, but not in the light of their only daughter being missing. Mother and I had sent both of them messages saying what had happened – silence the only response. About the only thing I knew was that Lek's murder was to cut the link between me and whoever had taken Pim.

The law in Thailand is that the investigation of a crime stays in the district where it happened. Puttamonton Sai 3, Soi 39, where Sankit and Suchada lived, was in Amphur Nong Khaem. The whole area was about to get hit with the water we'd been floating on up near Ayutthaya and would be under a meter of it by evening, according to Twitter. The FROC was telling everyone the worst was past. People in Nong Khaem were heading for the high ground. Smarter to believe in the street than the government.

Chai parked at the rear of the police station, a foot of water already in the parking lot. I'd been wearing boots ever since the morning in the jungle. That seemed like days ago, when it was just a day ago. The black phone rang. Chai answered it, grunted a couple of times, then covered the phone, putting it against his thigh.

"It's Virote's boys. They want to meet, talk, said they have a car to sell you."

I shook my head.

"He has enough cars," Chai said. Listened, put the

phone on his thigh again. "Car's still wrapped in plastic with the passenger in the back."

I nodded.

"All right, we'll meet. We'll send you a message later when we're ready." Chai hung up. Unlike Mother, he doesn't do that with those he loves.

"We have to find that car."

"Yes, we do."

"Let's go see what Khun Chatree has to say for himself."

ying gra soon nat diaao dai nohk saawng dtuaa —Shoot one bullet, get two birds

A Real Bastard

Nong Khaem, Monday, 31 October 2011, 11:55AM

One glance at me, as he slouched his way into the room, was all it took. Chatree tried to bolt for the door. So he knew who I was. I was sure I'd never met him before. The cops calmed him with a couple of slaps in the face and sat him down opposite me.

"Khun Oh, the sergeant said ten minutes, no more. The colonel will be back by two, and it wouldn't be good…" He shrugged, raising his eyebrows and his hands palms upwards at the same time. I smiled and nodded as he backed out of the room. He shared an 'it's all on you now' glance with his pot-bellied brother in brown who'd taken up sentry position by the door and closed it behind him.

I turned my attention to Chatree. He had a petulant

little pout on his lips and a shiny bruise on his cheekbone. One of the cops must have been a bit too enthusiastic in their questioning. He was lucky they hadn't used cattle prods – it's been known to happen.

Chatree studied a doodle someone had drawn on the table, intently not looking at me.

I slapped the table hard. Having given myself another good spraying in the car park, I could do that. Chatree jumped and looked at me with a sullen glare and a strange look of smugness in his eyes. The look was tinged with fear now, but it had been there.

He looked at me, then slowly turned his head and looked at the cop by the door, then back again to Chai and then again to me. It was time to deal with his smugness.

"Khun Chatree, you're probably thinking that all you have to do is keep your mouth shut, do your five years, and you'll come out a rich man. Well, I've got some bad news. You won't be coming out. You won't make it. You see, you've pissed off some very powerful people. And painting that nine on the wall, well, that pisses me off no end. You probably won't even make it to sentencing." I leaned forward, put my hand on his, and he flinched. "Your mother won't be able to help you with this."

Now he looked worried.

"I didn't paint the nine on the wall." That was as good a place as any to start.

"Who did?"

"No one. I mean no one I know of. We didn't do it. We robbed the place, sure, but we were in and out – no time to paint anything on any wall." Beads of sweat on the bald patch of his head.

"When did you hear about the money at Sankit's house?"

Chatree twisted his head and looked at 'pot-belly' by the door. Pot-belly studied the ceiling. Chai took out his Ka-Bar and looked at me. I gave a little shake, 'no', and muttered, "Not yet." Chai put on his hungry Doberman face. Chatree turned the color of the Formica tabletop.

"About two weeks ago. I overheard my mother on the phone with Sankit."

"Sankit fired your mother two months ago. Why was he talking to her again?"

"They were, you know…" He shrugged his shoulders, wobbled his head, and rolled his eyes around. I took that to mean his mother and Sankit were lovers. He smiled at Chai, eager to prove he was helping. Chai's upper lip twitched – very well done, I thought.

"Sankit asked your mother to rob his house? Is that what you're trying to tell me?"

"No. Like I told the other officer, Sankit just told her that he'd buy her another house and that all the trouble was over."

"What trouble?"

"Suchada trouble. Sankit moved my mother with him to the new Ministry. Suchada caught them in a delicate situation one day when she barged into his office at the Ministry and demanded that Sankit fire her."

I didn't want to know the details. Just the thought of Sankit in a 'delicate situation' was enough to make anyone hurl.

"How did you find out about the money?"

"I asked my mother why she was happy. She told me

Sankit was going to buy her another house and when he retired he was leaving Suchada to live with her. She was happy."

"I asked her where Sankit got his money, and she just laughed, said he had lots of it. She knew for a fact that the night you were getting married he would have ten million in cash in the house."

"I told a couple of my drinking buddies, and we decided to rob the place. We checked it out. Just a drunk old guard and the maid, so we robbed the house. Then we got caught." He blinked twice and wrinkled his nose, looking from me to Chai. Chatree sunk his head into his bony shoulders tortoise-like, spread his hands in the classic 'believe me' posture. Chai continued to twitch his lip; he leaned forward a bit more. The twitch became a silent snarl.

"You're lying."

Chai swapped hands with the knife.

"Oh, give me a break, come on…" Chatree was jerking his thumb at pot-belly and rolling his eyes.

Okay, I'll play, I thought. "Officer, could you step outside for a moment? My client here wants to tell me something in confidence, and he can't do that with you in the room."

"I'm sorry, sir, but I was ordered to stay in this room no matter what."

"What kind of car do you drive?"

"I'm sorry, sir. I don't understand."

"What kind of car do you drive? It's a simple question."

"I don't, sir. I share a motorbike with my wife's brother, sir."

"I asked a simple question. What kind of car do you drive?"

Understanding broke over his face like a new dawn over a field of wheat. "A Honda Accord, sir."

"Black?" I ventured, thought there might be a trend.

"I prefer light blue, sir, like the sky." So much for trends.

"Two…" I looked at Chatree, held five fingers up, "five minutes, officer. Please keep watch outside the door for us." Give the cop his due. He looked at Chatree, who nodded his assent, and with a smile eased his belly out of the room.

Chatree looked terrified. As if he'd suddenly realized he was alone in a room with two violent killers. If he had realized that, it made him smarter than I was giving him credit for being.

"Talk. You have five minutes to convince me you're telling me the truth." I sat back in my chair, giving him the hooded eye look. With the way my face looked, I knew it was intimidating, scared the hell out of me when I'd looked at it in the mirror.

Chatree leaned forward, his chin almost on the table. A drop of sweat rolled off his bald head and hit near the doodle. I noticed it was a doodle of a dick – appropriate. I flicked my eyes back on his.

"It was my mother's idea."

Man – this guy was more than just a bastard on paper. Who'd shop his own mother? What a charmer. I was tempted to sic Chai on him; his 'unleash me now' act wasn't all act.

"Go on." I kept the disgust out of my voice. I needed

him to talk.

"Sankit told her he was going to give her ten million, but he needed her to keep quiet. Someone was asking questions about money he had, and he wanted to know if they'd called her. Also he didn't want to give her the ten million; he wanted her to steal it. He'd set it up, but she had to find someone to do it. He'd handle the cops and get the blame placed on someone else."

"Who?"

"Who what?"

Chai moved fast, coming across the table, a hand on the back of Chatree's head pushing down hard once. The sound was still echoing off the walls and Chai was back in his seat, snarl back on his lip.

"Fuck, fuck, sorry, shit, I think you broke a tooth. Fuck. Can't you control him? Shit."

I shook my head. No look of smugness now. Just a cold reality that there was no way out. It looked like he was going to cry. I really hoped he wouldn't. I flashed on Goong. I shouldn't be judgmental.

"Who?"

"You, for fuck's sake, he was going to blame it on you."

I looked deep into the fear in his eyes. He was telling the truth.

"Tell me about the robbery. What time, and who are your drinking buddies? I don't care about the cash you stole. I just want to verify your story."

"There weren't any drinking buddies. I made that up to delay sentencing. I was hoping the original plan was still going to work. That's why I couldn't take more. I couldn't believe it. There was so much of it."

"Tell me exactly what you did."

***

Standing on the top step in front of the police station, I lit up. It had stopped raining for the moment. Muddy brown flood water swirled over the two bottom steps. Chai was bringing the pickup around to the front.

Chatree had been set up by Sankit. I could see that. And I could see Sankit's plan. It had all of his hallmarks. Chatree had said his mother told him the money was kept in a room on the third floor, two doors down on the right. But when he got there, the door was locked, and the one at the end of the corridor was open, with the light on. There was a room there, and we had to go back and take a look at it, but I was reasonably sure we'd find that there wasn't one robbery that night at Sankit's, there were two. One Sankit had planned and one that he hadn't. They were connected, but the only connection I could see was that whoever had pulled off the unknown robbery wanted Chatree to see the billion.

It occurred to me that standing on the top step I made an easy target. Just when I was thinking of retreating back into the station, Chai swung out of the parking lot and, with a nice bow wave, parked in front of me. I waited for the waters to calm down and walked around the shoulder-high front grill of the pickup, treading carefully as I couldn't see the ground under my feet.

"I'll drive. You take shotgun and stay hands free."

Chai nodded and slid over.

It was a short drive to Sankit's house, couple of kilometers, maybe less. At the front of his soi, a guy was cooking satay on a barbeque. The barbeque rested on overturned plastic crates to keep it out of water that was up to his knees. I slowed right down, didn't want the wave to hit him. He saw it and smiled, waving his bbq tongs in thanks at me. I hadn't eaten since leaving the house and pulled over opposite him. Chai opened his window.

"Ten sticks, please."

"Coming up, boss."

"You not worried about the flood?"

"Nothing I can do about it. Why worry?"

"This your spot? You sell here all the time?"

"Oh, sometimes here, sometimes up near the bridge, but that's flooded worse than here."

On the far side of the road, behind the guy selling satay, some guys were breaking a wall down using a jackhammer and picks. I got an idea.

"Back in a minute," I said to Chai and got out.

I sloshed my way over to them. The guy with the jackhammer stopped it as I approached.

"Hey, could you guys give us a hand? We've got a wall needs breaking to ease the flood. Just down the road here, shouldn't take longer than thirty minutes or so. I'll pay you."

"How much?" This from a lanky guy, older than the rest, leaning on his pick. I doubted the guy with the jackhammer had heard a word I'd said.

"A thousand each."

"Sure. Show us the wall."

I walked back to the truck with them in tow. They climbed into the back. The rain had started again. I stood on a little piece of slippery high ground next to the satay vendor.

"Hey, last Saturday night you see anything strange happening down the soi?"

His face went from Smiley to Politburo in a millisecond. Bland as dough.

"Nah, I usually pack up early evening and head home." Hear no evil…

"Sure, no problem, thanks for the satay." I handed him the black phone general number and a thousand baht. "If you do see anything strange, give us a call, okay? Keep the change." A hardy spirit and a cheerful outlook are qualities I admire.

The guys in the back were already soaked to the bone, but at least they'd have some cash in their pockets. I got in the cab. The smell of the satay peanut sauce made my mouth water, but first we needed to get the guys to work.

Sankit's gate was locked, and the guys in the back of the truck looked a bit worried when Chai deployed a pair of bolt cutters on the problem.

"It's okay," I said. "The owner told us it'd be locked; that's why we have the bolt cutters." That satisfied them.

Gate open, I drove over what I knew to be Sankit's carefully manicured putting green, avoided the pond I knew to be there, and went around the side of the house. Executed a nice turn with an accurately gauged reverse maneuver, putting the back of the pickup right in front of the 'Berlin Wall' art.

We disembarked onto dry land. Sankit's house, like many, was built on raised earth.

"Can you guys break through the wall a meter on that side and a meter on this, without breaking the wall in the middle? Then load the bit you cut out into the back of the truck? That'll help the water outside the wall flow better through the area."

They nodded. I don't think they'd believed a word of what had been said since the bolt cutter moment, but a thousand baht on a rainy day is worth the risk.

"How long?"

"About thirty minutes, maybe a bit longer."

"Go to it, then, we'll be back in thirty."

I grabbed the satay, Chai the bolt cutters, and we headed for the back door to the kitchen. Chai tapped the glass in, and in we went. The door to the living room was open. Chai took a quick peek and shook his head. No one home.

"I have to eat. I'm starving. You hungry?"

Chai shook his head.

I remembered where the plates were from my last visit. As I pulled one from the cupboard, a cup at the front fell and smashed on the counter. White shards of china everywhere. I got a towel off the sink and swept them to the edge of the counter. Grabbed the small plastic bin and pressed the pedal with my hand. I was about to sweep the remains of the cup into the bin, but I stopped. In the bottom of the bin were five empty bottles of red nail varnish. The maid hadn't used nail varnish. I remembered clearly her fingers clutching the nearly empty glass of rum. Khun Suchada's nails had also been plain. The red of the number nine written in Thai underneath the upraised finger came to mind.

naam maa bplaa gin moht naam loht moht gin bplaa – When the tide is high fish eat ants, when the tide low, ants eat fish

TRICK OR TREAT

Pak Nam, Monday, 31 October 2011, 6:45PM

We had agreed to meet the Brothers Grim at 7:30pm. I was reasonably sure they'd set up the hit on me after the jet ski incident, and that wasn't something we as a family could tolerate or allow to go unaddressed. They'd called us, so by the unwritten rules of the mafia code we got to set the time and place. We agreed we'd talk, but we planned to kill them. It was as simple as that. And as complicated as that.

Killing anybody is a difficult thing, unless you're a raving psychopath, but sometimes what needs doing, needs getting done. Since their father had died, his sons had shown no respect, tried to kill me, and encroached directly on our territory. All because they'd turned one of our guys, had a Ferrari covered in our DNA and with a dead body in the trunk – vacuum packed no less. We hadn't found the Ferrari or Pichit yet, but we were looking. We were sure Pichit was dead, couldn't see him turning, and he'd have shown his face by now. He was dead or locked up. We looked hard; he was one of ours. We'd pulled up all of the land title deed information connected to the entire Virote brood, identifying likely locations, marking them on detailed street maps. When the time was right, we planned to move. The time would be right at 7:30pm; it was Halloween.

While Chai and Tum were briefing the boys on this evening's activities, I inspected my newly acquired 'Berlin Wall' piece in the garage. Dry now, three and a half meters tall and as many wide, it dominated the rear of the triple garage. I was also loading up. It's like folding a parachute, just something you have to do yourself. For tonight's event I was going with a Desert Eagle, Glock 23s, two of them, an AA-12, and an M-4 combat assault rifle. Mars Model 12 covert body armor on the bench next to the weapons. I might be coming to the party a little overdressed, but every weapon had a purpose, and we'd already gone through the sequence.

Like all good plans, it was simple. We'd drive up, pop the trunk using the modification that had been done at Mother's shop, Tum would sit up in the trunk and fire an RPG at the brothers' vehicle. Depending on the result of the RPG, we'd either speed off or attack; deed done, we'd quickly change vehicles, dump all of our weapons, and go somewhere public.

The first and most important element of our plan was that the two brothers were together and it was really them in whatever vehicle they chose to show up in. We assumed that they'd be coming in an armored vehicle, hence the RPG and, in my case, the Desert Eagle. Loaded with custom armor-piercing incendiary rounds, if they stayed in their vehicle, I could do some damage. The grenade launcher slung underneath the M-4 was back-up in the event the Desert Eagle didn't get the job done. If the job hadn't been done by then, they would have either sped off or engaged us on the ground. That's where the Glock 23s, but first the AA-12 came in. When it gets up close and personal, it's hard to beat the AA-12 for the amount of flying metal over a wide area it generates in a short period of time.

Like all plans, it would probably be the first casualty of the engagement.

The middle finger and the fist to which it was attached had been spray-painted on with a high level of detail. Knuckles were detailed, and wrinkles had been added to the raised finger. The nine wasn't a nine. At least, not originally. A circle had been added to the bull's horns to turn it into a nine, but the red color of the varnish was clearly different.

This was no ordinary piece of art. This was a personal 'fuck you' message. Whoever had robbed Sankit of his billion had painted this and taken their time doing it. Looked at in the cold light of a hot dry lamp, the amateurish attempt to turn the horns into a nine was laughable – but it still fooled you for a few days, I thought. The thought led me to what else I might have missed, and that took me everywhere. One problem at a time.

I turned away from the 'art' and faced the wall above

the bench where I had laid out my gear. A3 sized color prints of the entire area taken from Google maps and updated by one of our computer guys with the latest flood info had been pinned to the corkboard lining the wall.

The meet would be at a piece of vacant land in between where two expressways crossed, just inside the district of Bang Phli, our territory. The toll booths were empty, expressways being free because parts of them were flooded, and on this particular stretch, there wasn't any parking. It was too far out for the motorcycle taxis to offer a service. Anyone waiting on the expressway would stand out on the approach, and it would be too much of a long shot to get anyone in place between when we drove past and arrived at the meeting point. Little chance of getting sniped from the expressway meant only worrying about the surrounding area, and due to the way the vacant land was in a slight dip, still dry because the roads around it were high, the dip took it out of the line of fire from the surrounding houses. All in all, it was a safe place to meet and had good escape routes.

The side door to the garage opened, and Mother walked in. She walked around the wall art. Glancing at it, she turned to me with a raised eyebrow.

"It was painted on Sankit's the night of the robbery."

"The nine is wrong, not the same kind of paint."

"Yes, I think it was done by Suchada or Sankit. Does the 'Red Horns' signature mean anything to you?"

"No, but they're like buffalo horns."

"And red. I think the color is significant. Otherwise why not just paint on in black, it would be quicker."

"Yes, but then it wouldn't stand out as much. Could it

be something as simple as running out of black?"

"No, I don't think so. The person who planned this was meticulous. I doubt they'd forget to bring enough paint to get their message across."

"Whoever painted it hates Sankit or Suchada, maybe both. Do you think they have Pim?"

"I can't see who else, except, of course, for Sankit and Suchada. Right now my money's on them as getting Pim out of the hotel without a fuss – I can't see anyone else pulling it off. She's too savvy. If it was someone dressed as a hotel employee, she'd demand to speak to the manager to get a confirmation. It had to be someone she knew and trusted for her to walk out of there."

Mother picked up the body armor. I ducked my head, and she slipped it over, patting it down on my shoulders. I adjusted the straps. An awkward silence.

She reached out and turned my chin to look at her. "Are you thinking about what Aunt Dao said?"

"No." I shook my head and smiled at her. "Just one moment, one day, one thing at a time, like you taught us. I've been thinking about how we're going to kill Virote's boys."

"Good. Stay focused and behind cover." Mother turned for the door. I think she didn't trust herself to keep it together in front of me. Stressful times. "I'm just going to check on the car again." She stopped at the edge of the door, looked at me. I smiled at her as she slipped through it never taking her eyes off me.

***

My heart thumped like an overly enthusiastic drum player for a marching band, as Chai turned off the Bang Phli

Suk Sawat Expressway and into the vacant lot. I spoke to Tum on the comms.

"You ready back there? We're coming up to the place now. Thirty seconds."

"Ready, boss, say the word." The word was 'Shoot'. The heavy Benz's solid rubber tires crunched gravel that looked like cat litter, and there, in the center of the vacant lot, a black Cherokee Jeep with tinted windows. Chai slowed us down a fraction.

"Tum, twenty seconds, it's a Black Cherokee Jeep. Aim for the middle of the rear door."

"Got it, boss."

Chai slowly swung us in a wide circle to bring us on a parallel track with the Jeep. Tum was facing the driver's side of the Benz, so that had to face the Jeep. We pulled up about twenty meters apart and parallel. No one stepped out of the Jeep. Chai kept the engine running. I waited, watching over Chai's shoulder, Desert Eagle in my hands between my knees.

"Wait, hold it, not yet, can't see anyone yet."

Tum had his own release handle inside the trunk. I didn't want him going off early. I felt sweat drip slowly down my armpit.

A rear window, passenger side, started opening on the Jeep. Interior looked dark, hard to make out who was inside. I had to be sure.

"Shit!" The twin brother of the weapon Tum was balancing between his feet in the trunk of the Benz had appeared in the window of the Jeep. That's the trouble with weapons and plans, everyone has them.

"Drive," I shouted, but Chai already had the Benz

in reverse, wheels spinning on the cat-litter gravel, white dust flying by as I watched the RPG fire toward us. It missed us with a roar, hitting a shed on the far side of the lot with an explosion that rocked the Benz sideways. Chai threw us into first, looked at me, and nodded.

"Now, shoot, now," I shouted into the mike and popped the trunk. I looked over my shoulder. Nothing happened; the trunk was stuck.

"Tum, go manual, the switch has failed."

"I'm pulling it, boss, but it won't open." Tum's voice a hoarse, hollow rasp. Bad place to be, locked in the trunk of a car during a gunfight.

Chai had the Benz in second, heading straight for a chain-link fence at sixty. He swung us over hard, a long sliding curve of a turn later we were headed straight for the Jeep. Its tinted windows coming down. I braced myself as Chai floored the Benz for the final twenty meters. We T-boned them hard and fast, pushed them a few meters, and the Jeep flipped over on its side, wheels spinning uselessly and steam pouring from the grill.

Chai got us in reverse, I looked back and saw the trunk in the rear window. It had decided to open. Murphy's Law.

"Hold your fire. I think it's all over," I said to the wind in my earphones.

Chai drove us slowly past the Jeep, nothing moved. He stopped once we'd got around and had a clear run at the exit. We got out. I kept the AA-12 leveled at the Jeep, just in case. Chai, Glock pointed at the Jeep, walked sideways till he reached the popped-out front window. He leaned in and then pulled back out, shaking his head at me and showing me three fingers. Three men, Brothers

Grim not there. He jogged back to the Benz, opened the back door, and got out a five-liter tank of gasoline.

Thirty seconds later, Tum looking a lot happier in the backseat of the Benz than he'd sounded in the trunk, we exited the lot and rejoined the expressway on-ramp. A whoomph sounded behind us as the gas tank of the Jeep caught, and we were already doing one hundred and forty heading back towards Pak Nam.

The Brothers Grim had ended the phony war with a bang. Now we'd find out who was with us and who was against us. Aroon the Shopkeeper over in Phra Samut Chedi and Chainarong over in Bang Sao Thong to our east, the only surviving district bosses. I was reasonably sure of Aroon, he and Por went way back. Chainarong, the other district 'boss', wasn't exactly a newcomer, but he'd always been one to hang back, hold the last vote, be the last to pass a judgment. In other words, an expert fence sitter.

Chai pulled up next to our first escape vehicle. A BMTA commuter van, or at least disguised to look like one. I got out, post-action adrenalin fall-off hitting me like a sledgehammer. That and it had been forty minutes since I'd last got a spray across my ribs, and with Chai's stunt, I thought I might have broken the rest of them. Once again, though, he'd got us through without a scratch. I looked over the roof of the Benz at him. All business, clearing and packing weapons, the model of efficiency.

The side door of the Urvan opened.

"Shit."

Virote's boys, weapons leveled at us, grinning.

"It's okay, boss, I got this," Tum said in the earphone

still in my ear. I realized he was behind the Benz by the open trunk. Mother's words, "Stay behind cover," came to me. The door to the Benz still open, I dropped to my knees behind it and scrambled for the interior.

"Shoot, shoot, shoot," I shouted, the sound of gunfire outside barely muted by the still-cool interior of the Benz, playing the beat of the dull, flat – plunk – sound of the bullets as they hit the Benz's armor. I saw Chai in the backseat, swiveled around, and pulled the door shut. The ugly snout nose of the RPG appeared in the corner of the rear window.

Tum fired, and I watched as the rocket went right between the two brothers and out the far window. It deflected beyond the van and smashed into the smiling teeth of a woman advertising Colgate on a huge billboard. The explosion ripped the billboard off its foundation and, ripping down power lines on the way, wrapped itself around the Urvan.

I could see Somboon's face, twisted as the metal the van was wrapped in, consumed with pure hatred as he looked at me. Firing a machine gun from chest height, he stood in the doorway of the van. While Somboon and the brothers were shooting, their driver was trying to get them out of the tangled mess of the collapsed billboard. Chai handed me the M-4. I waited, saw the elder brother, Khemkaeng, start to change magazines, and I got the door of the Benz open. Saw him look up, got the barrel of the M-4 in between the door and the frame, and started shooting. By some miracle, their van pulled free of the billboard, turning away from us. As it turned away, Khemkaeng gave me the finger. I got out of the Benz and emptied my magazine at the back of the van. A torn piece of metal from the van's roof waved at me as it sped away.

Ears ringing from the gunfight, I looked around, trying to listen for sirens. Nothing yet. Chai got out of the Benz. Khemkaeng giving me the finger, making me think about the 'Berlin Wall' art, but some things are coincidence.

"You hit?" he asked.

I shook my head and looked behind him for Tum. I walked past Chai, speeding up, a sickening feeling hitting my gut. On the ground, lying on his side, Tum had paid the ultimate price. Chai was beside me.

"He was a good soldier." That was about as high a compliment as you'd ever get out of Chai for anyone.

"Yes, he was." I flashed on Tum and Somboon sitting together, drinking whiskey in the sala at last New Year's party. I swore to myself I'd get them together again before this year was out.

ngaai meuuan bpaawk gluay khao bpaak — Easy like peeling a banana and putting it in your mouth

CONTROL DAMAGE

Pak Nam, Monday, 31 October 2011, 8:15PM

I was on the phone to Mere Joom, Chai driving the shot-up, battered Benz back to the farm. We skipped the remaining escape vehicles for obvious reasons. Tum was in the back seat – the trunk still would not close and we had tinted windows. I turned around and looked at him. That was a mistake. Eyes and mouth open, I reached over and pulled his eyelids down. The only way to deal with it is to turn grief into anger and, as fast as you can, get it up to a quiet rage. You kill one of mine, I kill ten of yours. That's the math.

"Bang Bo's on fire," Mother said, referring to the district Virote's boys ran. "We got at least eighty of their buildings. The rest we had to pull back, or the fires were put out quickly. We got their massage parlor and the

145

gambling dens."

"Good, let's keep them closed. Perhaps an anonymous email to Khun Chuvit?"

"Yes, good idea."

Brothels, what we call massage parlors, earn big, fast cash; same with the gambling dens – what would hurt the most would be the lost equipment. Gambling is illegal in Thailand – you can't just order another roulette wheel from the store down the road; the equipment has to be smuggled in from abroad. Not a big deal, but it would cause a week or so delay in operations.

"Everyone safe?" Another guilty look into the backseat.

"All safe and out of harm's way. I've told everyone to be extra vigilant, and I've got the police and media covered. Now we wait and see."

"Any sign of where the brothers and Somboon went?"

"We got the CCTV of them coming off the expressway in a damaged van, heading into Bang Bo, and then we lost them. But it looked like they're heading back to Khemkaeng's house."

I'd been to his place a few years back. Birth of his first son. I flashed on his baby boy, dressed in blue, very red face; I remembered thinking he looked like he'd been pickled – in a way he had been, we all had been. His boy would be four or five by now; a walking, talking, thinking, human being and certainly old enough to hate the man who had tried to kill his father.

"Chance, are you there?"

"Sorry, Mother, just thinking about Khemkaeng's place."

"Don't do it. Not worth it. Going in hot, without

thinking, is a good way to get yourself and Chai killed. I know you're upset about Tum, but now's not the time. Come back here."

"We're almost at the farm, just got off the expressway. I'll see you in ten." She hung up. Five minutes later, we reached the farm and dropped the Benz off for 'cleaning'.

Mother was looking down on what she had dubbed her CNC center on the fifth floor of the Crocodile Farm's main administration building. I was sitting in one of the 'observer' seats slightly behind her. Beckham had called it a 'War Room', and Mother had swiftly corrected him.

"No, Moo, it is not about war. It's about command and control." She called him 'Moo', a play on Beckham, or more exactly the 'ham' in Beckham, ham being pig, pig being moo, said the same way as you farang imitate a cow. She'd then showed him a picture of NORAD's war room. Mother's war room wasn't quite at the level of NORAD's; it was, however, more sophisticated than the Thai police's traffic control room, mainly because it contained much of the same information, but her equipment was more up to date and more numerous.

Large-screen Samsung monitors displaying CCTV bought and paid for from the Highways Department technicians was simply enterprising use of government assets. This coupled with monitors linked to Google maps, an integrated contact management system for the one-time phone system, and a PABX interface allowed Mere Joom to stay on top of things and coordinate operations as complex as the selective burning of Bang Bo. Specifically, the properties inherited and owned by the three sons, their wives, and anyone associated with them in business.

Beckham had coordinated the event with Mother. The plan had been to start the fires at the same time we had killed the two brothers – the third brother, Supot, we hadn't decided upon yet. It looked like he was in hiding or dead. Either way, it didn't matter, we hadn't succeeded.

Mother and Beckham had succeeded and over eighty properties in Bang Bo and its neighboring districts were on fire. All of those who had set the fires were out of harm's way – for the moment.

There were two reasons for this plan of attack. One was to 'sight unseen' burn the Ferrari and our DNA with it; two was to hurt them, publicly and financially. Take away the cash, they lose support fast. Embarrass them publicly, they lose support and, maybe due to the loss of face, their cool.

I watched as Mother picked up a phone, and then I looked down at the floor below. A young woman, perhaps thirty, answered her call.

"Send a tweet to @FROC: Bang Bo. Strong surge of flood. Klong Suan many fires from cooking gas," Mother said, and she pushed another button on the phone. Another woman, older, picked up a phone. I watched her nod as she received Mother's instructions. "Call Narongchai at *Thai Rath*. Tell him you heard a rumor that Virote's sons are fighting over the district."

Mother turned towards me in her chair. She looked immaculate as usual: back straight, hair like she had just stepped out of the salon, a small smile upon her lips, only the furrows in her forehead gave away the pressure she was under.

"You should head back to the house. Get some food

and sleep; it's going to be a long night. Por will call you later tonight, around ten New York time. Before then he's being fitted with a new leg. He sounded good. I asked him about the red horns and Sankit; he didn't make any connection but said he'd think about it."

I hauled myself out of the chair, my ribs on fire, desire for revenge running hot through my veins. She offered me her cheek, which I kissed on my way out.

I kept seeing the back of Tum's head. Caved in by a few rounds, blood matting the hair around the holes, "I got this, boss," playing over and over in my head. Time to cool down.

Back at the house, I headed straight upstairs to my room and stripped off. Got the bandages, gauze, tape, and various Band-Aids peeled off. On the bridge of my nose a cut about two millimeters deep ran horizontally from the top halfway to my cheek. Underneath each eye, a rainbow of dark purple, green and mustard yellow covered an inch or so. A split upper lip with three stitches in rounded out the look. My torso had similar coloring to the bruising under my eyes, the green slightly darker on the twin bruises left by Lek's motorbike; the diagonal red strip running from my left shoulder to my right hip was new, courtesy of the seatbelt. My kneecaps had new scrapes on top of the old. I thought I might be looking at bone in one of them, but I wasn't sure. On the counter in front of the mirror I was looking at – a couple of painkillers and a glass of warm water. Chai, ever practical and always thinking.

I stepped into the shower, ignoring the painkillers on the counter. I wanted the pain. It balanced the devastating pain of losing Pim. A pain I couldn't get rid of with anesthetic spray or pills. A pain founded on guilt and all-consuming in fear. I was scared I'd never see her again. Scared this was payback for all the people I'd disappeared. Scared because you can't make a deal with someone who hasn't called or left a ransom note. Scared because I couldn't make promises to Buddha that I wouldn't be able to keep. My hands pressed against the walls, pushing out as hard as I could, the cold water splashed hard on my neck. Use everything you have to bring to bear on a situation, spare nothing; consider it all, make your choices, and move in a predetermined way. Por's words in my mind, as clear as the day he'd said them during one of my 'lessons'. Take the pain, take the fear, acknowledge it, and park it. It gets in the way of getting the job done. Every scenario I had for Pim's kidnapping led back to Sankit and Suchada operating together or singly. Find them, you find Pim.

Dried off and in my boxers, I sat in the French window seat, smoking a joint, looking at the river at the bottom of the garden. I called Uncle Mike. I hadn't spoken with him since the night of the wedding.

"Chance, how you, buddy? I heard the news. Joom called me – what do you need?"

"I need about twenty-five mill."

"Thai or US?"

"U.S. Sorry."

"Don't mention it. Take me a couple of days, okay? I've got to free some stuff up."

"Thanks, Uncle Mike. And hey, listen carefully. We've got a lot of activity up here. Keep a close eye out and the guys Mother sent you closer, okay?"

"As soon as I've squared this cash away for you, I'll

be going sailing for a while – you can reach me on the batphone." I smiled, the first time he'd called his sat-phone a 'batphone', Mother thought he was talking about the battery in the phone. It ended with Uncle Mike taking her to see a Batman movie.

"Take care, Uncle Mike, I'll send the account details through."

"You take care, Chance. It sounds heavy up there. You know that stuff Aunt Dao came up with, man, don't pay any attention, man, you know – it'll be cool, dude, it'll work out."

I rang off. There was a knock on the door.

"Come in, it's open."

Chai walked in. "Por called while you were in the shower. Gave me the name of a guy in Surat might know about the red horns."

"Did you call him?"

"Can't. He doesn't have a phone. We have to go see him."

"Don't we have anyone we can send?"

"Por said we should go. The guy's an old man. Blind. Por said he was stubborn as a mule. We have to go."

"Okay, five minutes." I swung my legs off the window seat.

"You didn't take the painkillers?"

"No."

"Take them. We've got at least a five-hour drive ahead of us. No point being in pain." He had a point. Surat Thani is six hundred and sixty kilometers from Bangkok. I checked the time on my phone. 9:45pm and a new SMS. Unknown Number, again.

'You want to know who ordered the boy raped – follow the money. Your friend.'

If this person was such a friend, why didn't they just give me a call instead of sending cryptic bullshit messages? I planned on delivering that message when I found out who was sending them. I couldn't do anything about Goong – death cannot be undone – plus I had other priorities. Whoever and whatever had happened would have to wait. Of course, whoever was sending these SMS's was playing their own game. Another job for another day.

***

The dirt road we were driving up apparently led to the home of Khun Thanit. Former bandit, sheriff and currently retired due to his being blind. He was also, according to Por, a walking Who's Who of the Thai criminal world. We came to a fork in the road. We'd taken the wrong road four times already. We were somewhere just off Route 401 near Khao Wong in Surat Thani. GPS didn't cover the dirt roads that crisscrossed the hills and mountains here. We'd arrived in Surat at 4:30am in the morning. A brief nap and some food at the local 'big hotel'. Chai had asked me after tasting the congee if I wanted him to kill the chef. I told him we weren't doing freebies right now.

"Left or right?" Chai asked.

"Let's take a look," I said, climbing out of the Fortuna. The Fortuna wasn't fancy, but it was armored. The side panels had scratches where twigs and branches crowding in on the road had made their mark. Not many people had come up this road recently. I trudged up the path a ways.

"I think a truck..." I was talking to empty air. Chai

had disappeared. I walked up the rutted, red earth road, trees lining the side so thick you couldn't see more than a couple of meters in, most places less than that. The sun hadn't got high enough to touch the path. The only sounds were the buzz of insects, occasional whoops from some happy birds and the gravel that crunched beneath my feet. The road bent right around a large gnarly old tree, branches covering the road that would scrape the roof of a saloon car. Clever.

As I got abreast of the tree, an old man stepped out. A double-barreled shotgun pointed at my stomach in his hands.

"Khun Thanit?"

"Who wants to know?"

"I am Chance, son of Jor Por Paknam and Mere Joom."

He grunted and raised the shotgun a little, aiming at my chest. Chai came out of the jungle about five meters behind the old man. He didn't notice. Chai's Uzi was pointed at the old man's head. I shook my head.

"What do you want?"

"I need information. Por told me that you knew everyone in these parts. I want to know what you know about a police colonel called Sankit and anything about a red horn signature."

"What's Sankit to you?"

"I'm the son-in-law he tried to kill last year."

He lowered the shotgun muzzle, pointing it at the ground by his feet. "I heard about you, Dek Farang. Come up to the house, we can talk more comfortably there. Have you eaten yet?" He turned to walk up the path and turned back.

"Might as well tell your man up there with his gun pointed at my head to join us." His eyes as white as mountain snow, the wrinkles around them crinkled as he smiled.

"His gun's not pointed at your head anymore."

He barked a laugh and chuckled his way to the door of a one-storey house about a hundred meters further up the path.

He put the shotgun on a rack over an ancient TV set. We followed him through to a large kitchen built on the side of the house just off the living room, cool and dim in the early morning light. Steam rose from a rice pot, and the smell of fresh coffee dominated the room.

"Sit over there."

We sat down on the stools he had pointed out.

"I never give out my true address. The people you talked to earlier always give me a call. Told me a Thai-speaking farang was looking for me, with a bodyguard who moves like a Thai boxer only silently. I figured it might be you." While he was saying this, he laid out the table. Fresh steamed rice, two different curries, and a plain soup. My stomach growled.

"Hungry, eh, well, eat first, go ahead, don't wait for me." He put a couple of plates, forks and spoons on the table, walked over to the bench, unplugged the rice cooker, and put it on the table. We tucked in. He sat down opposite us, a fresh cup of coffee in his hand. I ate and waited for him to talk.

sen phohm bang phuu khao – A strand of hair blocks the hill

THE BLIND LEADING THE BLIND

Surat Thani, Tuesday, 1 November 2011, 6:15AM

"When Sankit first came to Surat, as deputy head of the city police, I was still a bandit, still had my sight. These dammed cataracts hadn't yet taken over." He waved a hand in front of his eyes and slurped at his coffee. The food was delicious. Chai eats like a soldier, 'Fast and Furious', but even he was taking his time. *Thaan*, pronounced 'Tun', is a title given as respect. It can be used for anyone you respect. A blind man who'd got the drop on me and then served a delicious breakfast had my respect.

"Thaan Thanit, when was this, what year?"

The skin around his eyes crinkled, and he chuckled again. "Thaan, is it? Your parents raised you well. Please give my regards to Por and, of course, to your beautiful mother. What year is it now?" His old man act didn't fool me one bit, he was sharper than a samurai's sword and twice as tough.

"I will, Thaan, thank you. It is the year two thousand five hundred and fifty-four." In case you were wondering, farang, Thailand's calendar is five hundred and forty-three years ahead of yours, and you call us backward.

"Umm, two, oh, five, four, eh." He let out a long sigh, blowing the steam from his coffee cup before he took another slurp, his Adam's apple rising and falling between two deep leathery ridges. "Ah, how time flies. Sankit came up here just after Songkran, twenty-five years ago, two-oh-two-nine." Nineteen eighty-seven on the Western calendar, farang. He put his coffee down on the table in front of him, wrapped his hands around the mug, and his low gravelly voice reminding me of Por, he continued.

"He was a tough, mean, cold bastard, Sankit. Got stuck in right away, didn't mess about. Put the word out that nothing happened without his okay. One of the local mafia robbed a bank. Week later the press gets an anonymous phone call about a bunch of dead guys in a house in a rice field. All handcuffed and shot through the back of the head. The handcuffs Sankit's way of telling everyone he'd done it. No one robbed a bank for a while. Not unless they'd cleared it with him, anyway. Then, well, no one has proof, but rumor has it Sankit wired the chief's car up with a little C4 and blew him up. Couldn't wait for the old guy to retire, and he was due to in just a couple of years." Thanit tapped out a Krong Thip, and I held a light up. He moved the tip of the cigarette to the lighter and sucked deep. He smiled as he blew out a long stream of smoke.

"The wise man sees with his mind. Fools use their eyes," Chai said, then continued the constant flow of rice and curry to his mouth. The old man's smile grew wider.

"Your friend is young but wise and built like a tractor. A good friend to have, and a good friend is worth more than all the gold in the world."

I was wondering if they'd start quoting Buddha next, or maybe the King, but they were both right. I had nothing wise to add to their statements, so I did what any self-respecting Thai would do, shoveled another spoon of Thaan Thanit's delicious curry into my mouth and kept listening.

"After Sankit had taken out the chief, he used the bombing and attack on the police as the reason to wipe out the remaining gangs who hadn't bowed to his rule. He put up a wall of cops between the north and the south. Meanwhile he kept all the right people fed. Mainly it was Suchada, his wife, and she's as cold as he is, if not colder, who took care of the money side of things. Surat's a big province, covers the whole of the Thai area east-west, everything going north or south passes through here, and he took a clip off everything he could. Smuggled oil, drugs, guns, gambling, women, illegal workers, cars, you name the crime, and Sankit was on it – like flies on buffalo shit. He bought a boatyard and a fishing boat. He didn't go fishing, though; all he ever did was feed 'em. There're a lot of bodies off the coast of Surat just below the low-tide line, to this day the fishermen say it's a good place to catch lobster."

"Thaan Thanit, what about the red horn signature? Does that mean anything to you?"

"Sure. He was the reason they sent us the bastard Sankit in the first place."

"He was a cop?"

"No, at the time, he was one of the biggest bandits in the south, and for sure the biggest in Nakhon. He gave everyone the runaround. Ran circles around all of them. Left a pair of red horns painted wherever he'd struck. Of course, there were a lot of copycats, but still he made the cops look like fools. There were rumors he was a communist operating out of the mountains and jungle west of the city. But nothing was proven. There were rumors he'd robbed Sankit's own house. There was a picture of the red bull signature on the wall outside the house. It was in the papers. Sankit finally caught him, but it took him a couple of years. It was how he got his promotion."

"So this happened just before Sankit was sent up here?"

"Yes, six months before. The trial took a while, but in the end they gave him death."

"He was executed?"

"No, he was lucky they suspended the use of the death penalty that year, so he escaped death, but he got life. The papers were full of it at the time. Many thought he should have been shot, he killed an on-duty cop when they went to arrest him, but he got lucky, if you can call being locked away forever lucky. Personally I'd prefer to go down fighting."

"Do you know if he is still in prison?" I sat back and placed the fork and spoon in the middle of the plate. Thanit picked my empty plate up and, turning around on his chair, placed it on the counter by the sink.

"He never made it to Bang Kwang. He tried to escape and made it into the jungle near the sea. The cops tracked him down, surrounded the house he was in, and when they started shooting, it went up in flames, and he was killed." Thanit passed me the coffee pot and a mug.

"I'd bet he wasn't killed, and I'm not a gambling man," I said, pouring myself a cup of coffee.

"It's a bet you'd lose. That doctor, the one with the funny hair, she came down from Bangkok and did the forensics on his dental records. It was in the papers."

"I'd still make that bet. Khunying Pornthip would have based her findings on dental records. And I am sure that the dental records matched those of Red Bull. I'm also sure that the dental records would have been switched with whoever did die in that house."

"I'll take that bet. How much?" He rubbed his forefinger and thumb in the universal sign for cash.

"I tell you what, Thaan Thanit, if I'm right you agree to go to Bangkok and have my doctor look at your cataracts. If I'm wrong, Chai here will deliver the car we're driving and you can keep it."

"Car stolen?"

"Nope, it's legal."

He held out his hand, and we shook on it. I was reasonably sure the car was safe, but the only way to prove it was to find Red Bull – Krating Daeng – same as the energy drink, but not from the same family.

"Why was he called 'Red Bull'?"

"Because he drank it all the time, said it kept him healthy, swore by it. Had a bottle with him always; that

159

little fact was also in the papers along with the forensic report. What kind of car am I winning?" He had a big grin on his face.

I laughed out loud.

"Thaan, please prepare yourself for a trip to Bangkok, and please don't shoot the guy I send to pick you up, unless of course I've asked you to shoot him."

He cracked up laughing and slapped the table so hard my coffee mug bounced on it.

Thaan Thanit gave us his number and a map of the way to reach his house from the rear, over the top of the mountain behind it. As we walked down the path, I looked back. As I looked, shotgun in the crook of his arm, he raised his other to wave, the blind man who could see.

"Where to?"

"Good question. I've got to call Mere Joom and find out the state of things. Otherwise, we need to find the prison guards who were transporting Red Bull from Nakhon Si Thammarat prison to Bang Kwang. One or more of them was on the take, must have been. We need to find out everything we can about this Red Bull. Why, after twenty-six years on the lam, does he come out of hiding and rip off Sankit?"

I called Mother. Chai opened up the car and put the air-conditioning on. The late morning sun beat down on our heads through the gaps in the jungle around us.

"Mother, how are you?"

"Chance, I'm fine, no problems. Everything is under control. I've brought in some extra help, the flood waters are dropping, and the rats are staying in their holes. How are you?"

"Good, I've found out a bit more about the red horns, they mean Red Bull, but no relation to the current family. It was the call sign of a bandit down here in the South, Nakhon Si Thammarat mainly, but he might have had some national coverage. He had several run-ins with Sankit and was supposed to have been killed in a police shootout about twenty-five years ago in 1987-88. Apparently Khunying Pornthip handled the forensics."

"Wouldn't be the first time she got something wrong," Mother said. "I'll find out what I can and send it to you. Follow your instinct, it will lead you to Pim. I spoke with Uncle Mike. He mentioned your request. Do you think that will work?"

"I don't know. Cash has a way of drawing people out. What we can't see, we can't fight."

"Yes, all right, but allow me some time to sort out the phu yai, otherwise they'll just grab it. By the way, the funeral rites for Tum have been cancelled. I'll send you a file later." Mother cut the connection.

So Tum had betrayed us. I looked up at the sky. Clear aquamarine blue with not a cloud in it. I thought about the blind old man up the road who could see and felt like I was the one who was blind.

yohn hin thaam thaang – Throw a stone, follow the path

CHASING DOWN A WHO DO THERE

Nakhon Si Thammarat, Tuesday, 1 November 2011, 1:15PM

Nakhon Si Thammarat has more hit men than any other province in the country. Included with the information Mother had sent me, a cautionary note: The Brothers Grim had put a price of one million baht, about thirty-three thousand US dollars, on my head. I wasn't sure that news of the bounty would have reached here yet, but I didn't want to find out the hard way. We stuck to the back roads.

Mother's information pack on Red Bull included old newspaper clippings, his autopsy report and interestingly that he had no identification card or number. His alleged name was, Preecha Arooncharoenboonmee, and now you know why we make up nicknames and use first names for everyone, hence, 'Red Bull' or in Thai, Krating Daeng.

One of the articles had a picture of him, supposedly taken in Bangkok in 1976. I was surprised. It showed a young, slim, pale, academic-looking man, leaning against the rear of a car, of average height, wearing glasses and smoking a pipe. He looked more like a teacher than a master bandit and bank robber. Something troubled me about the image. It was grainy, as a copied, old, black-and-white photo from a newspaper will be. There was something about it, but I couldn't put my finger on what. Perhaps it was just the difference in my expectations. I'd been expecting a mountain man, outdoors guy like man vs. wild, and got someone who looked like an accountant.

He'd been tried and found guilty at the provincial court. A photo of a much younger, slimmer Sankit with a crueler, thinner face than the one which he had acquired since coming to Bangkok – the similarity between him and Chatree was obvious. I felt the tiniest twinge of pity for him, Chatree that is, as for Sankit, my disgust for him had grown exponentially over the past twenty-four hours. Mother hadn't found the names of the guards who'd transported Red Bull, but the location of his demise was clearly detailed in the autopsy report.

Chai crossed Route 401 heading east, and within a kilometer, we turned right, running on a small dirt road next to the ocean, not far from Tha Sala. Coconut trees, shrimp farms and small, mainly Muslim populated fishing villages lined the road. I opened the window of the car, baseball cap and sunglasses on. The sharp smell of the sea combined with the pungent aroma from the racks of squid drying in the early afternoon sun. We passed a temple, and then it was all scrub and coconut trees until the road ended in a small track and a wall of bamboo.

"This is it," Chai said and put the Fortuna in park. He pulled his Uzi out from under the seat and starting checking it over.

Foliage had reclaimed the abandoned track, the path just wide enough for Chai and me walking side by side. It broadened into a clearing containing a broken shell of what had been a house, the walls blackened and cracked by fire and time, vines creeping towards a roof that wasn't there. I walked around the side. Chai went the other way. At the back, where the scrub reached the base of the blackened wall, I forced my way through and entered what must have been the back door.

Remains of a fire in the corner, used condoms, broken glass and empty glue pots provided a trashy history of current use. The house was small, one room with a separate toilet and shower in one corner of the room. The toilet bowl had seen recent use, fat indolent blue flies eating shit off the torn newspaper it had been smeared on. I turned back to the main room. From here to the main road was over a kilometer. For a man in shackles to run for a kilometer didn't seem likely. The story went that the officers transporting him stopped at the gas station on the main road to use the toilet. While they were in the toilet, the prisoner unlocked the back of the van, which was padlocked from the outside, and then made his escape. Tracker dogs followed his trail to this house, and a shootout ensued when they had surrounded the house. Oil barrels, reported to have been smuggled oil, went up in flames, and the prisoner died in the fire.

It sounded like something we would fabricate and

then pay everyone to believe. My phone vibrated. Another email from Mother. There were three guards transporting the prisoner. Two were still alive, and both were in Nakhon. One lived outside Nakhon on the other side of the city; the other lived right in the city center next to the Big C shopping mall.

The drive through Nakhon was about forty kilometers from where we were. I sighed, looking around at the debris and the mess. Thinking – what the fuck am I doing here? This was a complete waste of time – a red herring thrown here by whoever had ripped off Sankit. They could easily have gotten the same information that Mother had sent me.

I checked the images she'd sent me and read through the text again. None had shown or described the red horns, but there was mention of it being painted on the wall of a gold shop Red Bull had robbed in the early eighties. The gold shop wasn't far from the address of the second guard. It would probably be long gone, and it was a risk, but it was all I had to go on. I didn't have time to waste; it had been over four days since I'd lost Pim. I let out another long breath, walked out of what had been the front door, and looked around for Chai.

I couldn't see him, felt a little flash of annoyance, knew it for it was, and took a deep breath. More than most, judging by those I've met, I am a product of my environment. I was trained from when I was five to be not just a soldier for the family, but the boss. Mother had put a gun in my hands when I was nine, and it wasn't a toy. More important, Mother had put knowledge of behavior in my head.

Chai emerged from the brush at the side of the house. He came over and stood near me. I had my emotions back under control. The façade of cool a national trait admired by many, mastered by few.

"The woman who owns this land lives in Nakhon. Land's been in her family for as long as anyone can remember. No one from the village comes here. They all know the story of the bandit being killed, called him by name, Preecha or Red Bull, and they reckon the place is haunted."

"Were any of them here when it happened?"

"Some of the older ones must have been, but they all denied it."

"Did any of them know where this woman lives?"

"She's a niece of the late governor; the governor who commissioned the Jatukam."

"Shit, that's all we need. All right. Let's head into town. There's a gold shop I want to look at, and we can talk to the guard and woman." As we walked up the path, I looked back at the ruin and heard Aunt Dao's words, "I dreamt I saved Por…"

***

The gold shop was easy to find. In a row of five-storey shop-houses, of the type that are common in cities and towns across Southeast Asia, the gold shop we were looking for was the only one which had a pair of red bull's horns painted on its wall. It even had a plaque under it. I couldn't read what it said from where we were parked across the street. It looked exactly like the horns painted on Sankit's wall, only smaller. If you're robbing a gold shop in broad daylight, you don't have much time to spend on art.

"Let's go and have a chat with the owners." Gold shops are typically Thai-Chinese family businesses and rarely sold. There was a good chance that whoever had owned this shop when it was robbed was still there. We crossed the busy street. The plaque, written in Thai, read, 'This shop was robbed by the infamous bandit, Red Bull, 21 March 1983'; the date was, of course, from the Thai calendar.

Twin glass-topped counters ran the length of the shop, at the end another counter in front of a curtained door in the rear of the shop. Behind the counters, five shop assistants tended to customers. It was busy, mainly single women and elderly couples, all focused on the gold resting on cushions of red velvet. CCTV cameras in all corners covered the entire shop. I walked to the far end counter and what looked like the oldest shop assistant. He sat on a stool, bent over the counter, studying a gold and ruby ring with a loupe at his eye.

He glanced up at me, taking in Chai at my side in the same sweep of his eye. He opened his other and the loupe fell, to be caught in a move that had been made a million times.

"Good afternoon, is there anything I can help you with?"

Chinese-Thai gold shop owners don't like to waste time chatting when they could be making money. I pointed at one of the gold chains, about a five-baht chain. We measure our gold in baht weight. A baht being equal to 15.244 grams or a little less than half a troy ounce, if sold as weight, if sold as jewelry 15.16. He smiled; a five-baht chain is about four grand in USD. His hand parting the red curtain in the back of the counter and snaking in, he brought the chain out, handing it to me.

"I noticed that plaque on the wall outside..." I said and hefted the chain in my hand. I'm not big on jewelry of any kind, and gold chains mean nothing to me, but I feigned interest.

"Yes, my father put that up. He was famous, you know."

"Your father?"

"No," he smiled, "the bandit, 'Red Bull', he was famous. After he was caught, father put up the plaque. A lot of people came to look at it and talk with him. Some of them bought gold. It died out after a little while, but we just left it there."

"I'd like to buy it."

He looked confused.

"The painting and the plaque. I'll pay you two hundred thousand, and I'll repair and paint the hole in the wall, but it has to be the original, and I need to confirm it."

He laughed.

"I'm serious. I'm collecting Red Bull art. I already have one of his pieces. I'm looking for more. Do you know of any other places that have the signature?"

His eyes turned crafty. Money has that effect on people. "No, no, I don't. This is the only one I know of."

I handed the gold chain back to him. "Were you here when he robbed the store?"

"No, but as I said, my father was."

"Is your father in the shop?"

"No, he passed away seven years ago now, but my

mother was, and she's here. Let me talk to her, and I'll come back."

"Okay, thank you."

I turned back to face the entrance, leaning against the counter. One of the customers near me, a bored expression on his face, glanced our way, raising his eyebrows, and then back at the gold chain in his companion's hands. She was poring over about fifteen different chains, trying to make her mind up, asking the shop assistant about each chain. I heard her boyfriend sigh from where I was standing.

"Okay, enough. Just choose a chain. I'm hungry." That won him a glare and a frosty pout. Buying gold is serious business, not to be rushed. The act of shopping, just as much, perhaps more so than the goods, for many women is an act to be lingered over and enjoyed.

"Come on, come on, I'm going to faint if I don't eat something soon." This guy was a real charmer. The girl slammed the chain she was looking at down onto the counter with a bang that turned heads. Back straight, chest out, head high, she stomped her five-inch cork platform shoes to the door. Charmer shrugged at the assistant and the other customers, pointed at one of the chains, and took his wallet out.

Nearer the door, another couple walked out. As they went through the door, the guy looked back and tried really hard not to look at me. Too hard. Chai was already moving. Walking swiftly through the shop, he took position by the door, keeping an eye on the street. He raised his hand, thumb and little finger to his ear, and left the shop.

"Mother would be happy to talk to you about that

day."

I turned around and smiled.

"Please, follow me. By the way, what's your name? My name's Vichien."

"My name is 'Oh'. Pleased to meet you, Khun Vichien."

"Come this way, Khun Oh."

I followed him through the curtain at the rear of the shop. Behind the curtain, the shop's guard sat on a stool, shotgun in his hands. He smiled at me. You don't get many farang gold shop robbers.

Wooden stairs led up to the second floor of the gold shop. We removed our shoes and went up. At the top of the stairs, an iron grille gate was open. Vichien went through the gate, and we came into a living room. His mother sat at a table on the street side of the room. I noticed how quiet it was and how still. A shaft of afternoon sunlight filtering through a gap in the curtains split the dark room in two.

"Would you like some tea or coffee?"

"Coffee, thanks." I walked over to his mother and gave her a wai, which she returned and with her hand indicated the seat opposite her at the table. The table was large enough to seat four, heavy teak, varnished to a mirror-like gloss. Dust specks swirled in the light behind her.

"My son tells me you want to buy the Red Bull signature?"

"Yes, that is correct, krub." We say 'krub' on the end of everything, ka if you're a woman, well, mostly everything, and only when we're being polite.

"For two hundred thousand baht?" She had a little

smile on her lips as she took off her glasses and laid them on the newspaper on the table. I looked down at the street below. Our car was still there but no sign of Chai.

"Yes, two hundred thousand plus the cost of taking it out and repairing the wall, but only if it is the original."

"Oh, it's the original. I watched him paint it."

"What happened?"

saawn jaaw ra khaeh waai naam — Teach a crocodile how to swim

HIT MAN ALLEY

Nakhon Si Thammarat, Tuesday, 1 November 2011, 4:30PM

"It was the first of the month. We always stocked up for when people got paid, so we had a lot of gold. It was a Wednesday, just before lunch. He was very polite and calm, his whole team were. No one threatened anyone."

"How did he come in?"

"He came in through the back. We found out later they'd rented the shop behind us and broke into our backyard. The guard sits at the back looking into the shop, so he didn't see them come up behind him. Now we have a camera, of course, but back then we thought the three-meter-high walls topped with barbed wire were enough to stop anyone coming in through the back."

"Wouldn't breaking through the wall have made a lot of noise?"

"Before he came into the shop, a truck with road workers appeared across the road, and they started digging up the road. My husband went out to complain to them, and they said they had their orders, nothing they could do. The equipment they used was very loud. We could hardly hear ourselves talk inside the shop."

"The road workers were a part of his gang?"

She smiled. "He was very clever and funny. Although we were nearly bankrupted by the robbery, no insurance, we were able to laugh about it later. What can you do? It happened, and some of the things he said were funny, but yes, he was super clever. The day he robbed us, the police got calls from three different banks saying they were being robbed. So when my husband pressed the alarm, no one came."

"What do you mean by funny – funny strange or funny like a joke?"

"Like a joke. They made us laugh years later. When he walked in carrying a ladder over his shoulder, we were confused and asked him what he was doing. He replied that he was from the department of wealth redistribution, and my husband laughed. Then he took out a very short, ugly looking shotgun and pointed it at the ceiling. My husband stopped laughing; he realized we were being robbed when Red Bull said, 'Allow me to introduce myself, my name is Red Bull, and I am the new owner of your gold.'"

"You said he didn't threaten anyone, but he had the shotgun?"

"Later we found out that he had never killed anyone, except for that poor policeman when they finally caught him."

"You mean when he was killed?"

"No. The first time, when he was caught at his moobahn near Krung Ching."

"He killed a policeman?" I knew this, of course, but I wanted to test the waters. We have a saying: throw a stone, follow its path.

"Really? You're buying up Red Bull's 'art', and you don't know his story? Spending hundreds of thousands of baht – how much did you pay for the last one?"

"I paid about five thousand?"

"Dollars?"

"Baht."

She sat back in the chair, grabbing her glasses from the newspaper and putting them on, and leaned forward. Getting up close, she searched my face – her eyes loomed large. She leaned back, took the glasses off, and put them back on the newspaper.

I didn't say anything. Times like this, it is wiser to wait. I didn't have to wait long.

"You don't look crazy. You do look like you've been in some trouble, though, those cuts and bruises on your face. I also know that you don't read magazines, do you?"

I wondered where this was going now that I'd thrown the damn stone. "No, not much, only if I'm at the dentist or getting a haircut."

She reached down and lifted the newspaper. Underneath it was one of the society rags, celebrity gossip, that sort of thing. Pim and I were on the cover. Lesson #1: Never underestimate anyone.

"I do. I read a lot. Books, magazines, the newspaper.

I read about your wedding to Sankit's daughter, and just four days later, you show up in my shop asking about the Red Bull signature painted on the wall outside. Now do you want to tell me what this is really about instead of knocking down the wall of my shop?"

I gave her a wai. It's a cultural thing.

"I'm sorry for the deception, Aunty. Someone stole the dowry money from Colonel Sankit's house the night of the wedding. I really do own a piece of the art, and my offer stands, and I really did buy it for five thousand baht. That's what I paid the guys who cut it out of Sankit's wall. Whoever did the robbery left a slightly larger version of the red horns on his wall." I left out the part about the 'finger', it was too vulgar to discuss with this lady.

"Did the painting include a finger raised like this?" She gave me the finger.

I burst out laughing and sucked in hard when my ribs protested.

"Are you all right?" she asked, dropping the finger with a tight smile.

Arms crossed, folded over, I nodded and held up a hand; the pain had left me short of breath.

She continued, "I ask about the finger because that's what was painted on the wall of Sankit's house the last time Red Bull robbed him."

I got the pain down to a level where talking would hurt but was possible, and she had my attention.

"Is Sankit's house still here? Did he sell it? The house I mean, not the finger art."

"Yes, it is still here, or at least it was a year ago when I last passed it, and I'm not aware that he's sold it. If he has, no one has moved in, not in over twenty years. Of course, the painting's not there anymore if that is what you're interested in. Sankit had the wall repainted immediately, but it didn't do any good. Red Bull had taken a photograph of it and published a pamphlet which was spread all over the city."

"What was in the pamphlet?"

"Oh, it was all about how Sankit was a murderer, a thief, corrupt policeman and exactly how much had been stolen from the house. Which was a lot, back then a fortune, in cash and gold. There were photos of that as well. The gold and the cash, I mean. It looked like about thirty million, the gold was at least ten million, and there was a big pile of thousand-baht notes."

"And what do you think, if I may ask? Was Sankit all of those things that Red Bull said he was?"

"Oh yes, your father-in-law might wear the uniform of a policeman and he might be a minister in parliament, but we all know he's a crook. Nothing to be done, though, they have the money to buy whatever they want; except respect, that they can't buy."

"Did you know his wife, Suchada?" My phone vibrated against my thigh. I sneaked a peek. An SMS from Chai.

'Don't use front entrance to leave shop. Gunmen waiting.'

"No, I never had the pleasure of meeting her, a shame I'm sure. As far as I know, Sankit was still single then. I think he married Khun Suchada shortly after Red Bull was caught." The smile playing around the corners of her pursed lips betrayed the true intent of her words, sarcasm dripping like molasses from a ladle.

"Aunty, thank you for your time and information. Please think about my offer. I really would like to have the artwork."

"Oh, don't worry, you can have it. I feel that two hundred thousand is too much, though. Just take it and pay for the costs of repair and painting the front of the shop; that will be enough."

"Thank you, Aunty, please don't get up, I can see myself out." I waied and left.

Back in the shop, Vichien was again sitting on his stool.

"Khun Vichien, do you have another way out of here apart from the entrance?"

He looked at me, a frown closing in on his face. "Should I ask why?"

"No, but there are some men who have been paid to kill me waiting outside your front door to try and do that very thing right now."

"Oh. Yes, you're right. I don't want to know. Will they come in here?"

"I doubt it." That wasn't as conclusive as he might have wanted, but it was the truth as I saw it.

"There's one way, but it's a little dangerous."

"A little dangerous is better than the lot waiting out there. Let's go."

He nodded, and we headed back up the stairs. This time we didn't take our shoes off. Five flights and a triple-locked solid metal door later, we emerged onto the flat roof.

"This way, this way," Vichien whispered.

"I don't think they can hear us up here, Khun Vichien."

"Oh, right. Well, anyway, follow me, please."

I hoped I hadn't offended him. He and his mother seemed like good people. Wobbly steps made from ex-packing-crate wood, the stencil markings faint with age and sun, enabled us to cross over the walls that separated the different shop-houses on the roof. Like most upcountry cities, Nakhon has only a few multi-storey buildings, most are no higher than the one we were on. Passing rows of laundry and under the watchful eyes of an army of stray cats, we crossed to the corner of the block. Another row of shop-houses, set at a right angle to the building we were on, was about five meters away. Vichien pulled out a long, thin plank that was stashed behind a water tank. I figured out what he meant by a little dangerous.

I helped him get it into place over the alley below. I looked down; the winner for softest thing down there was a toss-up between the concrete paving slabs or the metal dumpster. Also rans: the air-conditioning compressor units. I took off my shoes and socks and rolled my trousers up a little. Vichien got the plank in place. I took a look. It didn't look good. A few hit men were beginning to look like the less dangerous of the options. I called Chai.

"I'm on the roof, far right side. Going to cross over to the next building, can you pick me up?"

"Give me ten minutes to get transport. I'll be there. There're six guys out front that I can see. Three in a silver Civic, and three in a low-slung purple pickup. They're parked too far apart for me to get at them, and it looks like they're using two-way radios."

"No way to get at the car?"

"None, and I watched one of them put something

underneath it – judging by the way he ran back to their car, I'd say it was an IED." We don't call them bombs anymore. We get the same movies and media you do.

"Okay, ten minutes." I hung up and checked the time. 5:17pm. I looked at the plank and then at Vichien. He smiled at me.

"It bends a little in the middle, but don't worry, it won't slip off. I used it a few times when I was grounded."

"When was the last time that happened?"

"About thirty-five years ago."

"Right, thanks for the tip and the help, I do appreciate it. Here's my card. Please go ahead and get the artwork out of the wall and send me your bank account details. I'll wire the money."

"You go. I'll hold the plank while you climb on. Good luck." He grabbed the plank where it crossed over the wall, and putting my hands either side of his, I heaved my body up, getting my knees onto the plank. I looked down the length of it. Narrow and thin and what looked like a long way to fall. I remembered reading somewhere five storeys is what it takes to guarantee a suicide by jumping off a building. Not a good time to have that thought. I considered crawling across, but I didn't think both knees could fit together on the plank. I took a deep breath and slowly stood up. Vichien reached down and handed me my shoes.

"Thanks for all your help, Khun Vichien. I can take it from here."

He nodded, smiled, and with a wave, he walked away.

Luckily there was no wind. It was hot, but that wasn't why I was sweating. I don't like heights. When I look

down from a great height, my mind always does a quick
– wow, what would it feel like if you fell – thing. I don't
know why it does that, but the resulting flip-flop in your
stomach is not pleasant.

I figured a shuffle would do it. A step at a time and
don't look down. My phone vibrated again. Not now.
A shoe in each hand, I spread my arms out and tried a
shuffle forward. Not too bad. I took another shuffle. I
speeded up. Shuffle, feet warm on the plank. Luckily
it was smooth. Slide foot, stop. Slide other foot, stop.
Shuffle. Eyes focused on the end where the plank crossed
to the other building. Getting closer to the middle, the
plank sagged, but it was gradual. The plank was teak, solid
and strong. I could trust it.

Sound of car wheels skidding below.

"Hey." Shit. Halfway, nearly there. A chunk of wood
flew off in front of my foot. Shots echoed loudly in the
alley. I ran, got the bounce in the plank wrong, slipped,
dived for the edge of the wall, and knew I'd miss. Time
slows when the adrenalin is pumping. Something happens
to the processors in our brain, speeding them up to hyper
speed, making everything go into frame-by-frame slow
motion. I hit the wall and dropped, landing hard on an
aircon compressor unit. Still three floors up and nowhere
to hide. I was wedged in tight between the compressor
and the wall. I couldn't see the guy shooting at me, but I
could feel them as they hit the aircon in front of me. I got
an elbow over the top of the compressor and pulled myself
up to take a look.

Two guys, silver Civic. Not more than twelve meters
away from me. Sitting ducks have more chance. The Glock

was in my shoulder holster under my left armpit, where I couldn't get at it. I was trying to think of something relevant before I died. The guys below smiled, taking aim, careful now I'd stopped moving. I couldn't come up with a clever thought. I was going to die with that as my final thought.

As I watched the guy nearest me start to tighten his finger, he jerked forward against the car door he was leaning on, his gun falling to the ground. His partner turned and was cut down. The driver's expression was panicked as a hole cut into the front windscreen of the Civic and his brains splattered around it. Being on the wrong end of a silenced Uzi on full automatic is a bad way to end a day. Chai rode up on a motorbike, a helmet draped off one handlebar, and parked next to the Civic. He looked up at me. I was still three floors up, at least twelve meters – and that's a long way to jump or fall.

Chai got off the motorbike, pulled the dead driver out of the Civic, climbed in, and parked it under me. He got out the passenger side, aimed his Uzi at the sky. A silenced Uzi makes a clattering sound, like one of those old ticker tape devices they used to have before digital. The plank came crashing down. Chai picked it up and climbed onto the roof of the Civic. He braced the bottom with his foot and leaned the plank against the wall below me.

"Slide down," he said, with a grin on his face.

I slid. I think it was Winston Churchill who said, "If you're going through hell, keep going." I knocked Chai's feet out from under him, which probably saved his life as the other three guys from the purple pickup showed up. I reached over, grabbed the windshield wipers, and pulled myself down over the hood of the car. Got a close-up of the inside of the driver's head as I went – bad image to have. I got the Glock out. Chai had rolled into the gap between the car and the wall.

I poked my head out to take a look. One of the guys ran out, a bottle with a flame, a Molotov cocktail, in his hand. I fired, missed. He heaved it. Chai stitched a line of bullets from his stomach to his chest. We ran for the back of the alley. I heard the Molotov go off with an air-sucking whoomph. At the end of the alley, a metal dumpster offered cover, and we ducked behind it, bullets hammering into it and the wall behind us. Cement chips and ricochet bullets flew around us. I heard sirens. People down south know the difference between gunfire and fireworks.

A squeal of tires. I looked out. The pickup had taken off. Four dead bodies, a burning car, a motorbike, and a plank on fire. I felt sorry about the plank. Nowhere to run, but somewhere to hide. I nodded at the dumpster. Chai made a cradle with his hands, and I climbed in. Scrambling over old rice, rotten vegetables, broken glass and all the usual crap that people generate and dispose of, the blind man's breakfast joined it.

Chai behind me, we shoveled the crap to one side and lay down in the trench. I heard Chai puking, and that set me off. Heard the sirens loud, echoing down the alley. I wriggled deeper down into the muck, pulling the crap back over me. Made a little tent for my head with a broken toaster and a plastic stool. I breathed out long and slow and breathed in as slowly as possible, trying to calm myself and filter the stench.

Loud shouting from pitched southern Thai accents

mingled with the siren. I couldn't make out what was being shouted. Staring at broken eggshell stuck to the inside of a plastic bag an inch away, I could hear my heart thumping in my ears. My ear pressed up to the metal wall of the dumpster, I felt more than heard the boots coming down the alley. Sounded like two men running. Could make out the shouting; they sounded nervous.

"Check, check there, behind the dumpster."

"Nothing."

I resisted the urge to pee and then thought, what the hell, it wouldn't make much difference, let it go.

"Check the dumpster." Voices still loud, excited.

Bang! I was startled but didn't move. One of them had hit the dumpster with something hard, probably his truncheon. I felt something run over my bare foot. Rats or mice. I hoped the only place I was bleeding was my face. The garbage shifted to the left of my head. Something hit the toaster up against my right ear. Hit it again harder. Hurt my ear. The metallic sound seemed to satisfy.

"Nothing here, all clear." The shout less loud now.

"Put a couple of rounds into the garbage, make sure." Oh, shit.

"I've checked it to the bottom. There's no one there, just stinking garbage and rats."

"Don't fucking argue with me. I am your superior. If I tell you to shoot the garbage, then all you do is ask me how many times, Sergeant. Do you understand?"

"Yes, Sergeant, how many times, Sergeant?"

"Twice."

After the first shot, I couldn't hear anything with the ringing in my ears, but I felt the second shot as it cut a groove in my right thigh. The boots went back up the alley. Only the siren cut through the noise in my head. I wondered if Chai was alive. I nudged him with my ankle, wouldn't use my foot, of course. He made a thumbs up on my foot. Okay, good. As the adrenalin drained away, every pain that it had smothered let itself be known afresh. I shut my eyes and groaned softly into the mush, pulling myself into my mind, minimal breathing long and slow. After a while, I fell asleep.

graloh baang dtaai chaa graloh naa dtaai gaawn – Thin skull die slow, thick skull will die before

AN EMPTY FISHBOWL

Nakhon Si Thammarat, Tuesday, 1 November 2011, 11:30PM

I woke up with Chai shaking my shoulder, reached down, and touched something furry and alive, which bit me on the web of skin between my thumb and forefinger. I've woken up in better circumstances but also in worse.

The alley was empty, except for the scorch marks on the floor and walls. My cell had fifteen missed calls, most from Mother. I called her.

"Where are you?"

"Nakhon, we had a bit of trouble and had to hide for a while. We're both okay, no problems. We need a car to pick us up, some fresh clothes, and I need a pair of shoes."

"What have you two been up to? Don't answer that, you can tell me when you see me. Where?"

"There's a row of gold shops off Tewarat Road. We're

in the alley behind them. Ask the driver to flash his lights twice. How is business? Anything new?"

"Business is quiet. I've talked with the phu yai (big shots), and they think you've already found the money and plan to keep it."

"I wish we had that problem."

"The yakuza rumors are remembered. I need more time to work on them, so don't make the call yet. Is that okay."

"Yes, I can hold off. It's a shot in the dark anyway."

"A stone thrown into the forest?"

I laughed softly, Mother had taught us all of the idioms, and flashed on Vichien's mother giving me the finger. At least they hadn't gotten involved with the bloodshed.

"I'll sort out a car for you. Stay where you are." She hung up. I hated being the cause of the fear in her voice when she'd answered the phone.

We stayed out of sight behind the dumpster. It's a glamorous life, the one I lead. I lit up a cigarette.

***

An hour later, I was having another cigarette, lying in a bathtub, the water milky with Dettol, drinking scotch on the rocks, my second, feeling a whole lot better about life. We'd holed up in a friend's massage parlor. It was the only place we could think of to get a bath. A shower wouldn't cut it. The customers and girls had left, and the place wouldn't be occupied until about eleven in the morning. Until then we had the place to ourselves except for the guards we'd hired.

There was a knock on the door.

"Yes?"

"It's me," Chai said.

"Come in, it's open."

He walked over to the table next to the bed and mixed himself a Chivas with soda. Raised his glass to me, and I lifted mine in response.

"That was close," he said.

I knew he had something on his mind, but with Chai you have to wait, be patient. It may never be shared or be a year before he referred to it again, or sometimes he'd just get it off his chest. Chai doesn't talk much. Some people make the mistake of thinking that means he doesn't think much – big mistake.

"Pim's going to be mad with you for smoking."

"Well, she's not going to find out, is she?" I liked that he was talking about her in the future tense. It shored up a thousand hopes.

"You'd lie to her?"

"Of course I would. Do I look suicidal?"

He smiled, which is a rare thing. Chai doesn't relax much; he's 'on' twenty-four seven, always alert. I often wondered how he'd adapt to old age. Never thought of asking him – I knew the answer. Live every moment, moment by moment. Like a mantra, only he imbued it with a rigor of discipline to which few mortals could ever hope to aspire. Certainly not me. My best guess was that he would enter the monkhood, and Chai would make a good monk. So I waited and sipped my scotch.

"Mother told me about Tum."

I didn't say anything, rested my head on the edge of the tub, shut my eyes, took a drag of the smoke, and listened.

"Three million in his bank. All coming in over the last week, the first deposit the day after Goong died. The day before the attack at Here Leng's place. From his phone we know he had been talking with Somboon, so they were working together. But when Somboon was shooting at us from the van, I'm certain he was aiming at Tum, and he looked mad, like he wanted him dead."

I heard the clink of the ice in his drink as he took a swallow, thinking about what he'd said, about Somboon's face above the sights of the AK-47 blasting away.

"Another thing, the guys at the hospital, the group that chased us, we haven't seen them again. I thought they were from Here Leng's gang, but I didn't recognize any of them when we were in the jungle, and I would've. They must be part of another gang."

I heard the clink again, but silence followed.

"Don't fall asleep in the bath. I'd have a hell of a time explaining to Pim how you drowned in a massage parlor."

I smiled and heard him shut the door. I brought the scotch to my lips and took a deep swallow, ice cubes melted now. I opened my eyes to squint at the ashtray on the edge of the tub. Flicked the ash off the cigarette and took another long drag.

Chai was right. Tum and Somboon were working together. Somboon had the car; he was the one who drove it from the farm. Killed Pichit and then... and then what? He'd obviously tried to sell the car to the Brothers Grim, but so far it hadn't surfaced. That could mean it was destroyed, they didn't have it, they had it but hadn't used it yet. Was Tum also working with the Brothers Grim, or was he working for someone else, maybe himself? Too many questions.

I stubbed out the smoke and hauled myself out of the tub. I dried off and put on the pair of boxing shorts that the driver had bought. I felt like a boxer, one who'd just done fifteen rounds with Mike Tyson. Laid out on the bed, I looked up at the full-length mirror on the ceiling. I looked like a Picasso, wild diagonal stripes of blue, purple and black-tinged reds.

The day replayed itself in my head, images, emotions and pain. I got up, crossed the slippery tiles to the tub, collected the ashtray and my empty glass. I sat back down on the bed, poured myself another drink, didn't bother with the ice, and rolled a joint. Sparking it up, I laid down again, blowing smoke at the Picasso.

I thought about my conversation with Por before he left for New York. He'd said Here Leng had taken a call just before the girl went back upstairs for ice. When she came down, she had a gun in the basket. I wondered who had called Here Leng and what they'd said. Chances were it was Tum who had sold us out to whoever had tried to kill us at Here Leng's place. I needed Here Leng's phone.

I couldn't discount either Aroon or Chang Noi. Either was capable of manipulating Virote's sons, neither were capable of taking us on their own. The vacuum caused by Big Tiger's disappearance last year sucking in greed, ambition, and power, the forces needed to fill it.

I knocked back the rest of the scotch, stubbed the joint out. A glance at the cell, 2am in the morning. I shut my eyes and sent out a thought, Pim, if you can hear me, I'm trying my best, I'm looking, stay safe.

I was dreaming about Big Tiger, he was about to

whisper in my ear who was playing us when I felt a hand on my shoulder. Chai with a finger to his lips. He leaned in close.

"The guards have gone."

I came awake quick, looked at the time, shit, only an hour's sleep.

Chai's phone lit up. He answered, keeping his voice low. I pulled on a pair of jeans and quietly racked the Glock, putting one in the chamber. Chai hung up.

"Just heard from Tommy. Someone's told the guards to leave or die, and two pickups are headed this way out of Nakhon. They left ten minutes ago."

Tommy was the guy who owned the massage parlor. One of Uncle Mike's loaders from the old days, he'd bought a massage joint with his profit.

"How'd they find us?"

"One of the guards told his sister, she told her boyfriend, and he overheard some guys talking about us today and decided to cash in."

"Shit. All right, let's get out of here." I grabbed my stuff, put the cheap trainers on that the guy who'd delivered the car had bought for me, and followed Chai out into the third-floor corridor. Chai flicked his little mini Maglite to find the exit to the stairs. Every step hurt, I was soaked in sweat by the time we reached the ground floor. As we were walking past the empty fishbowl, the place where the girls sit with numbers pinned to their chests waiting to be bought out, headlamps swung light across the room.

We crossed to the doors and looked out. It was Tommy. He jumped out of his Benz and ran over to the doors. They were locked from the outside with a padlocked chain around the door handles. He got the chain off and the doors unlocked. We'd been betrayed too much for me to put the Glock away, but I didn't point it at him. Trust is hard to win but easy to lose.

"You guys have to get out of here now. Go. I don't want these assholes shooting up my place." Tommy looked nervous, like we were going to argue with him or something.

"We're out of here. Thanks for the help, Tommy."

"Don't mention it, Oh, say hi to Uncle Mike when you see him next."

"Will do," I shouted over my shoulder, running for our car.

The Camry that Mother had bought for us was old, one of their earlier models, and lacked power, but it was a hell of a lot better than being on foot. One thing it had going for it was its color, black. I drove, leaving Chai free to fill his hands with the Uzi. The massage parlor was on Route 4102. Exiting the parking lot, I turned left instead of right. Right would take us out of the province, which was probably the smarter move, but I had unfinished business here, and I figured that whoever was coming for us wouldn't think we'd head back into the city. Three kilometers down the road, we passed two pickups loaded with men headed in the opposite direction. They didn't turn around; we were in the clear.

I turned left onto Route 4016 and eased up on the speed. I'd decided to head up to Red Bull's old hideout, which according to Vichien's mother had been a moobahn, a village to you farang, up near Krung Ching waterfall. Thai communist insurgents had built a large base in Krung

Ching. It was captured sometime in the late seventies, but according to Vichien's mother, sympathizers had supported Red Bull long after the camp was taken. About a sixty-kilometer drive from where we were, I swapped places with Chai, the booze and pills were taking their toll, and I was afraid of falling asleep at the wheel.

I woke up with a crick in my neck, one pain of many and the least of them. We were parked by a small stream outside the National Park Office for Krung Ching waterfall. I couldn't see Chai anywhere, but knew he was around somewhere. It was pitch black outside, and it felt cool even without the air-conditioning being on. For the thousandth time I felt despair creeping in; five days now and I was no closer to finding Pim. Despair is a wedge that can split you open given the tiniest of cracks. I got out of the car; keep moving and trust your instincts.

I checked my cell, no reception. The park's office looked empty, which wasn't surprising. It had just turned five in the morning, it would probably be at least three or four hours before someone showed up. Further up I saw a stream by the light of a small campfire, had to be Chai. I joined him, the warmth of the fire held the cool of the morning at bay. Sometime later, light showed in the sky, the sun behind the high mountain peaks that surrounded us. Chai went down to the stream, Uzi in his hand, and ten minutes later, we were eating river trout.

I caught another nap and woke up feeling worse. Chai pointed at a pickup with the Park Ranger logo on the door. I walked over as a man dressed in khaki got out of the pickup.

"Hello," I called up the hill.

The man jumped and spun around to face me. "You startled me!" He looked to be in his early sixties, but age is hard to tell when your life in a tough environment is taken into account.

"I'm sorry, didn't mean to."

"Ah, that's all right, you speak very good Thai for a farang."

"Thank you, I work at one of the newspapers in Bangkok. Up here doing a story about the old communists."

"Hah. Haven't had anyone up here talking about them for a long time. Hardly any here now, most died or got money and left."

"I was looking for a moobahn. I was told many people in the village supported them."

"Ah yes, Seri Din Daeng is the moobahn you're looking for. About ten kilometers that way." He pointed his arm out towards the northeast.

"Would you know a road that we can get there on?"

He laughed. "No roads. This parking lot is where the road ends. From here there is a trail, well-worn, to the Krung Ching waterfall. Many tourists use it. Follow that path, takes about four kilometers, and then there's a smaller trail. Follow that, then you'll come to a huge boulder in the path. Take the right trail if it's still there. Haven't been that way for a while, and after the rainy season, the trail sometimes disappears. Gets swallowed by the jungle. You're going in there dressed like that, are you?"

"Er, yes, didn't think I'd have to do any jungle trekking, but the story has to be with my boss before tomorrow morning."

"Have you got mosquito repellent?"

"Um, no, haven't got anything." If you excluded the Glock and Uzi plus what Chai had on him, that was true.

"Well, hang on a moment, then, I think we've got some up at the hut. I'll get some for you." He walked away, muttering about dumb, crazy farangs. He had a point. He unlocked the hut, went in, and emerged a couple of minutes later, an old camouflage army jacket in one hand and a can of mosquito repellent in the other.

"Here, take this, it's old, but it'll help against the thorns and brush. And this, use it often, your sweat will cause it to come off, and the mosquitos in here still carry malaria. Bad thing to have malaria, had it myself a couple of times. Wished I was dead most of the time I had it, and I sure as hell hope I am before I catch it again."

"Thanks, I'll return them when we get back. Are there many people in the moobahn?"

"Just two old men and their wives remain. One of them is blind and the other a cripple, but they're both still sharp and enjoy a drink." That I did have; I would take the Chivas with us.

"Well, thanks again, see you later."

"I hope so. If your car is still here tomorrow morning, I'll send someone to look for you."

He gave me a smile that didn't inspire much confidence in the trip ahead.

nee seuua bpa jaawrakhaeh — Run from a tiger to a crocodile

A WALK IN THE PARK

Nakhon Si Thammarat, Wednesday, 2 November 2011, 8:30AM

Chai set a fast pace but stayed with me while I tried to keep up. Even in good health that would have been difficult; in the shape I was in, it was practically impossible. The trail to the waterfall had been easy. As the park ranger had said, it was well worn, but after the waterfall, about two kilometers further, the trail disappeared into jungle. Then the going got really tough.

In front of me, hacking away at a thorny bush in our path, Chai looked like he had just started. I was exhausted. Mentally and physically.

"Chai. Hold up, man. This is a waste of fucking time. I don't know why I brought us here, chasing the ghost of some bandit who died twenty years ago. This is dumb. Let's head back."

He just kept hacking at the jungle in front of him.

"Chai, did you hear me? I said let's go back. This isn't working."

He stopped hacking and turned to face me. "We should go on. There is something here, your instinct is right. I don't know if Pim is here or not, but we should go on. If there's nothing here, then we have one less place to look. Remember Aunt Dao's dream – the second one?"

Arguing with Chai was a waste of time. Once he'd made his mind up about something – then that was the truth. I could order him to leave with me and he would, but he was right. And if I collapsed from exhaustion, as I was reasonably sure I was going to at some not-too-distant point in the near future, then it would be his job to carry me out of here. With that thought to cheer me up, I joined him in bending back the brush so we could squeeze onto the small trail behind it. No helicopter could land here. Looking up at the top cover, I doubted they could drop a hoist in. No cell reception had made it into this valley, the air only alive with mosquitoes.

An hour later, we made it to the large boulder the ranger had mentioned. The trail eased up and headed down a gentle slope. A breeze that somehow managed to keep itself intact amongst the trees gave some respite to the constant lawnmower buzz of the mosquitoes. I dared not remove my trainers and didn't want to think about my feet. I had blisters on both heels and at least one elsewhere on each foot. The spot where the rat had bitten me was sore, puffy, and looked infected. The scratches on my face burned with sweat that didn't cool, just dripped away. In other words, to use an English term, I was completely fucking knackered.

Reaching the bottom of the slope, the trail crossed the stream.

"Chai. Stop for a break. I need to tend to my feet."

He nodded. I sat down on a large rock and started to take the trainers off. Chai knelt down beside me and one by one eased them off. The white socks were covered in pink and yellow, transparent where they had stuck to the skin. Not a pretty sight.

"Do you see the waterfall?" Chai said, flicking his eyes upriver.

"Hands in the air, please."

Fuck. The voice came from across the stream. Chai looked at the Uzi lying on the ground next to him. A bullet pinged off the rock I was on.

"Don't even think about it. Now put your hands in the air, or I'll shoot one of you."

We put our hands in the air. Seemed like the smart choice.

"You, on the rock. Throw that gun of yours onto the sand there by the stream. Use your left hand."

Actually, I can shoot well with my left, spent a fair few hours on it, but you have to be able to see what you're shooting at, and all I could see was jungle. I eased the Glock out and tossed it onto the sand, thinking Chai still had his Ka-Bar.

"You, standing. Throw that knife of yours next to the gun. Nice and easy, you look like the dangerous sort."

Now that pissed me off. I don't look dangerous?

"Now both of you take five steps back from where you are. Big steps now, go on."

This guy was really beginning to piss me off. I could hear the laughter in his voice.

I got off the rock and slowly backed up five paces. Chai was standing in front of me, back straight, arms up like he was guiding a jet onto an aircraft carrier. I heard a gun cocking behind me and slowly turned my head around, to look directly into the twin barrels of a shotgun about a foot from my head. Behind the shotgun, looking older, still wearing spectacles, was the man from the newspaper clipping.

"Red Bull."

"Hello, Chance." He pointed the shotgun into the air, bringing it to a rest on his shoulder, as if he'd made a point, which he had. "Pick up your weapons and follow me." He walked past me and turned. "And don't bother with those shoes, they're not worth wearing."

I thought I saw Chai grin, but it's always hard to tell; it might just have been a twitch. I left the shoes and followed. The stream's cool water was better than a spa, the blisters stung, but that was a small price to pay.

When we crossed the stream, the park ranger who had been so kind earlier in the morning walked out of the jungle with a rifle over his shoulder. He looked cheerful. I thought about shooting him. In the kneecap. We walked through a clearing, up a grass bank and into a car park where the park ranger's pickup truck was parked.

I sucked it up. It's all you can do sometimes. But it will never be mentioned again, on pain of Pit 51. That's a promise. Chai, openly grinning, put a hand on the side of the pickup and vaulted into the back, settling himself against the back of the cab. I waited while Red Bull moved the front passenger seat forward and then climbed into the back of the cab. I propped myself up behind the passenger seat, legs stretched out.

The park ranger drove, with a smile on his face. The road was brand new and very smooth. After about fifteen minutes driven at an easy speed, we arrived back at the park ranger station we'd left in the morning. Red Bull and the park ranger burst out laughing. I looked out of the rear cab window. I couldn't see Chai's face, but I could see his arm shaking. If you can't beat 'em, join 'em – laughing hurt my ribs. The park ranger, I was beginning to call him the Lone Ranger in my head, stopped next to the Camry.

Chai jumped down.

"Follow us, we have a place about forty-five minutes from here," Red Bull said.

Chai looked at me, I nodded, and Red Bull raised the window as we turned around. With Chai following, we went further into the mountains away from the coast and after a while turned onto gravel, then dirt roads, climbing higher all the way. With the pickup in first gear and struggling, we crested onto a small plateau. An area of about thirty rai, fifteen acres or so, nestled in a dip between two peaks, a thousand-foot drop off the road to our left.

We pulled to a stop in front of a house that wouldn't have been out of place in the French countryside. A large, rectangular, two-storey house with a deck running around the sides and back on both levels. The garden around the house was well manicured with roses and green lawn surrounding the gravel driveway.

Red Bull and the Lone Ranger stepped down, and I

followed. The cramped space of the truck hadn't done me any good, and it hurt to straighten up. The door opened, and a woman came out. She had a shy smile on her face. I'd seen her before somewhere. It took me a moment. Khun Suchada's temporary maid, Ba Noi. She waied me, and I returned it. No hard feelings, nicely played.

I hobbled towards the entrance.

Red Bull turned to me. "Call me Preecha, I prefer it. I have a room for both of you, upstairs. You are welcome as guests in my house. You are free to leave anytime you wish, and no harm will be done to you by me or others here. I suggest, though, that you take a shower and rest for a while, and then we'll eat and have a talk."

We followed him into the cool interior of the house. I looked at my cell, 10:45am, and noticed once again there was no cell reception here, or he was using a jammer. He led up wide wooden stairs to the second floor and showed us to our rooms. Chai's room first, next to mine, which was at the end of the corridor on one end of the house. The view from the room was a breathtaking vista of the surrounding mountains and lush green forest below.

At the door, he turned to face me.

"Noot will bring you some fresh clothes. Rest now, we'll talk later. We have a lot to talk about. I'll turn off the jammer so you can use your phone, but I would appreciate it if you didn't tell anyone where you are."

I nodded, and he left, closing the heavy dark wooden door behind him. I waited for the click of a lock, but there wasn't one. I went to the door and tried it, opening it a crack. I poked my head out of the doorway and saw him watching me with a smile on his face. I ducked back in and softly closed the door.

I showered, wrapped myself in a towel, and lay down on the bed. I called Mother.

"Chance, are you all right?"

"Yes, Mother, we're fine. Any news?"

"Still quiet, but it appears the phu yai are hardening their negotiating stance. They've had the police issue an arrest warrant for Por for the murder of Here Leng."

"Have you heard anything from Aroon or Chang Noi?"

"No, nothing, should we have?"

"No, but I suspect that one of them, maybe both are playing games."

"When will you be back? Where are you?"

"I should be back tomorrow morning early. I'm still in Nakhon, but in the country. Could you ask Aroon and Chang Noi to lunch tomorrow? I want to get a look at them."

"I'll try."

"Any news of Virote's boys?"

"Last report was they're staying at the elder one's house."

"And no news of the Ferrari?"

"Nothing."

"We might have got it, then?"

"Maybe, but we're still looking for it. I've been doing some work on that."

"Is there any way that we can find out who deposited the cash in Tum's bank account?"

"Difficult. I've been trying, but we don't have anyone on the inside at Krungthai Bank, and I haven't found anyone to help us yet. Any news on Pim?"

"Maybe, I'm with the artist now, we're meeting this evening, and after that, we'll drive back."

"Take care, Chance, the bounty on you has been raised. It's five million now. I've put out a counter message that anyone who takes the contract will never get to spend the money, but five million is a lot of reasons to be stupid." She hung up.

There was a knock on the door.

"Come in." It was Noot, the maid I'd known as Noi.

"Some clothes, they should fit, but if not, let me know, and we'll get some new ones for you." Her accent had no trace of Issan and wasn't southern, sounded more Bangkok than anything.

"Thanks. Have you been with Khun Preecha long?"

"Dinner will be at six, and we usually have a drink before, at about five." Ignoring my question, she gave me a small tight smile and left without saying anything further.

Rest and get your head together. The mistakes I'd made yesterday and today had done my ego no good but had served a purpose. I wasn't dead, and I knew I'd screwed up – bad judgment and going off half-cocked will get you killed, fast, in our business. I was angry with myself, but it was in the past; get over it, learn, and move on. Guilt has no value unless it's spelled without a 'U' – one of Uncle Mike's favorite sayings.

I set the alarm for four thirty and shut my eyes.

bplaa yai gin bplaa lek – Big fish eat little fish

RED BULL'S TALE

Nakhon Si Thammarat, Wednesday, 2 November 2011, 4:55PM

I heard laughter as I reached the bottom of the stairs. I was still stiff, sore, and my ribs hurt like hell, laughing was something I'd try to avoid.

"Ah, Khun Oh, or do you prefer the farang version, Chance?" Khun Preecha, AKA Red Bull, stood, poured a red into a huge wine glass, and handed it to me. Chai, looking relaxed, had a glass in front of him, as did Khun Noot. Khun Noot looked a lot younger and slimmer than she had in Suchada's house and, wearing a long cream-colored skirt with a blue sweater, distinctly unlike a maid. Her height hadn't changed, but that's a difficult thing to disguise.

"Either is fine," I said, taking the glass from him.

He indicated the seat next to him, and I sat down.

"Cheers," he said and raised his glass. We touched glasses, and I waited. It was his show. Took a sip of the wine, it was outstanding. Glanced at the bottle, a Petrus, Khun Preecha had expensive tastes.

"How's the wine taste?"

"It's excellent, but I'd expect that from a Petrus."

"Knowing they're stolen from the governor's cellar makes them taste even better." He had a grin on his face that was hard to resist, as if he had a very funny joke that he wanted to share with you and could hardly contain the anticipation.

"You've kept a low profile since your death."

"I wasn't in Thailand most of the time, but yes, when I've been here visiting Noot – she's my daughter, I have two – I've kept a low profile."

"Where did you go?"

"I travelled. China, Europe, the Americas, Cuba for a while and, after, back here."

"Do you have my wife?"

"No. Suchada and Sankit have her, as far as I'm aware. I assume they're waiting for you to find me and then return to them their ill-gotten gains."

"How do you know this?"

"Noot saw them leave with your wife. Sankit's driver picked her up and delivered her back to the house about ten minutes after you left. She heard Suchada talking with someone, asking if the house had been cleaned and saying they'd be there before lunch." He continued, anticipating my next question, "This was about 4:55 in the morning. And the other reason I know they've taken her is because this isn't the first time they've done it."

"And no other indication of where they might have gone?"

"No, although I'd dearly love to know, it was too much of a risk for Noot to follow, and we were well on our way back here by then."

"Where's the money?"

"It's in the cellar."

"What did you mean by it's not the first time they've done it? You mean kidnapped someone for money?"

"No, I mean, specifically, it's not the first time that they've taken my daughter."

I was confused, wondering if he'd maybe shaken a marble loose at some point, but he seemed perfectly serious and normal.

"They took Khun Noot before?"

"No, they took your wife before. Chance, your wife is my daughter. I want her back safe and sound as much as you do."

It's funny how the obvious becomes when it is made so. The feeling I'd had looking at the old grainy photograph had reminded me of Pim. She made the same pose when she was distracted by something. And their eyes were the same. I also understood a lot more about why he'd robbed Sankit.

"You went for the dowry?"

"Yes, when I heard she was getting married and the papers reported the dowry, I decided to steal it. After we put Noot in place, she got a look in Sankit's secret room, and then we decided on a different plan, but the original idea was to steal the dowry, yes."

"The business with Chatree?"

"I set it up. I fed the idea to Sankit's mistress through another contact; steal the money and blame it on the son-in-law. Sankit planned to take it one step further and blow you up. Sankit's driver planted a bomb on your car while it was parked in the hotel. Their plan was to accuse you of stealing the dowry money, and then when you drove out to see them, they were planning to blow you up. I locked the second door, but left the door to the room with the money open and the light on. When they found out all the money had been stolen, they thought Chatree might have done it, then they saw the sign I left, and they knew. Sankit wanted to come after me after killing you. I guess you could say you owe Suchada your life because she talked him into using you to track me down. And you did. At the time I didn't know you were against Sankit. I learned your mother basically got him the position of Minister, and I assumed you were allied with him. Thanit, whom you met, is an old friend. He told me he didn't think Por would ally with a cop like Sankit, but circumstances make strange bedfellows, and I assumed that was the case in this instance."

"Did Sankit know you were alive?"

"No. He honestly thought he'd got me in Tha Sala. Sankit was never smart enough to catch me, but I underestimated Suchada. I shouldn't have. I knew she was evil, but I didn't think she'd stoop so low as to kill her sister just to spite me."

"Suchada killed Pim's mother?"

"Yes, not directly, she didn't pull the trigger, but she caused it." He paused to stuff a pipe with tobacco. I hungered for a Marlboro. Chai leaned across and laid a packet on the table in front of me. After lighting his pipe, he handed me the matches. I lit up. The windows of the living room were open to the view and the soft breeze that had a cool salty edge to it. The sweet somewhat cloying smell of his pipe tobacco drifted across the room. He sat back in the chair and continued.

"I was born in Bangkok. My father and mother were civil servants. We were well off, my father as corrupt as any, probably more than most. I went to Thammasat University; it was 1976. I was seventeen, a gifted student, so they said, and also a leftist. I was on the campus the day the Red Gaur and the police attacked, but I was lucky, I hid under a pier in the river. I wasn't a communist before that morning, but by evening I was, and helped by other comrades, I came south. We had a big camp in Krung Ching then, and I was joined by many who fled Bangkok. I saw some of them last year. Thida and Weng, they were both in Krung Ching as communists then. Now they're leaders of the Reds, don't know if they're still communists or not, but what they have now is a sham compared to then. Now it is about money and power. For us, it was about the common man." He chuckled to himself. "Our time in the camp was short. Early in '77, Thai Marines came in, with air and artillery support. We fought hard, but three months later the camps were taken and we were on the run. My parents, despite being corrupt, had leftist sympathies. They were arrested and thrown out of the Civil Service; they committed suicide. With nothing to return to, I stayed. Plus, I like the jungle. There's a brutal honesty to it." He poured more wine and relit his pipe, which had gone out.

"Communism wasn't defeated by the army. Communism was defeated by human nature, particularly greed. Look at China now, more millionaires there than Thailand, same with Russia. Well, we were scattered but not yet defeated. My first job was propaganda; that's where the Red Gaur, you called them Red Horns, came from. It was a propaganda tool initially to blame the robberies on the Red Gaur. I hated them; they were thugs of the worst sort, brutal. When we ran short of funds, I started robbing banks and found out I was good at it. I robbed trains, gold shops, banks, department stores and factories. Anyone who had a lot of money. In the beginning I gave it all away, but as the movement fragmented and faded away, there were less and less comrades to give it to. Finally, in the early eighties, we were keeping what we stole. We still gave away a lot, to those who supported us and there were many, but we kept most of it.

"I'd just robbed the train to Hat Yai, and we were hiding in a moobahn not far from here. The man whose house we were staying in, an old sympathizer, had two daughters: one, a very beautiful woman, smart, and kind, her name was Gulab, Rose; the other a mean-spirited, jealous woman called Suchada. Suchada wanted me for the sacks of money and gold that we had with us; Rose because I loved her and, for some inexplicable reason, she felt the same about me. Rose and I got married, which is to say, she told her father she was leaving with me. Her father was a good man and had no concerns other than for her safety. I let him down on that score. He died not long after she did. I was still in prison. I was told he died of a broken heart." His voice had faded as his memories drifted back, a tear formed at the corner of his eye. He wiped it away, cleared his throat, took a sip of his wine, and smiled at us, his eyes full of regret.

"Sankit, just a young police lieutenant then, was given the task of capturing or killing me. He couldn't do either. He's about as smart as this table and less useful." He tapped the table with the stem of his pipe.

"After I robbed Sankit, I decided to quit the bandit life and retire. We were staying at a moobahn not far from here, close to Rose's father's home. Rose was pregnant, and she wanted her father to see his granddaughter. After the baby was born, Rose went to stay with her father for a while. I stayed at an old hideout in the jungle, visiting when I could. Suchada even then kept trying to sleep with me. I never told Rose, didn't want to upset her, I should have. Suchada told Sankit where I was in exchange for half the money and marriage. He came out to where I was hiding. Held the baby up and put a gun to its head. There was another cop there, a sergeant; he started to argue with Sankit about the baby. Sankit shot him and killed him. Sankit was raving mad. I was sure he'd kill her, so I surrendered. Later, when he'd caught me, he described in detail how he'd killed Rose. He told me that he was keeping the baby, and if I said anything at any time, he would kill her. I believed him, still do." He spread his hands. The pipe had gone out again.

"That's my story."

"The man who died in the house on the beach?"

"He'd died three days earlier in another fire. We got him from the morgue, created dental records for him, swapped my name onto them, and bribed an officer to slip it into my file. He was in the house two days earlier. We rigged the house with a mix of napalm, diesel and gasoline. I never went near it. I climbed into a car at the gas station while the cops were in the toilet. The guard I bribed dropped anti-constipation pills into their noodles. Before they left the prison, the transport guards would always eat because they'd be on the road for a while. We gave them each a triple dose. By the time they reached Tha Sala, they were shitting themselves." He smiled more broadly this time, but he still looked sad. His sadness and the story had me in a wild swirl of rage and sorrow, I could hardly breathe, and it had nothing to do with my ribs. Some pain will never heal nor go away.

A gong sounded somewhere out on the deck. Khun Preecha stood up. "Shall we eat?"

I got up and turned to go out to the deck. He grasped my elbow.

"I'm sorry for the trouble you had yesterday. I wasn't expecting you to be quite so unpopular in Nakhon. We were keeping an eye on you, but things happened quite quickly after you reached the gold shop."

"Khun Thanit?"

"Yes, I've invited him for dinner. I hope you don't mind. I think of him as family."

"No, not at all, may I ask you something?"

"Please, feel free."

"Would you be offended if I called you Khun Por?"

"Only if you drop the Khun, no need to stand on formality."

I got down on my knees, not an easy thing to do in my shape, and waied, bending over deep to his feet. It was something I hadn't done for Sankit the day Pim and I were married. He took me by the arms, lifting me up.

He looked me in the eye; a tear rolled down his cheek. "She made a good choice."

I swallowed hard. "I'm going to get her back, and then I'm going to kill them both," I said.

"I know, I know," he said, and I could see the fear in his eyes as he remembered a similar promise.

phuu cha na kheuu phuu gam noht gaehm – The victor is the one who chooses the game

FISH OR CUT BAIT

Bangkok, Thursday, 3 November 2011 7:55AM

Dao Kanong bridge was heavy with traffic. Bangkok had not flooded, and now its inhabitants were flocking home. The government had survived. Stories of corruption abounded, accompanied by just as much finger-pointing, and while Bangkok, for the most part, was dry, everything around was flooded. Floods, riots, coup d'état, business and life in Bangkok goes on.

My phone rang, Mother, the latest in a series of calls that had been going on since four in the morning.

"Yes, Mother?"

"It's set up. Are you coming back here?"

"No, I'm going to Prachachuen. I'll go from there. I need to see Thomas. Is he still treating Beckham?"

"I'll send Thomas. Are you all right?"

"Yes, I'm fine, a little banged up, but nothing that won't heal. I just need another forty-eight to seventy-two hours, and then everything should be sorted. These proxies, they understand they'll have to decide then and there? No waiting, we're moving today." Truth was I pissed blood when we'd stopped at the last gas station. The anesthetic spray wouldn't help; it only works on the outside.

"They'll have their bosses on-line. We still have a problem with the chief. He's heard about our deal, and he wants a cut, or he's proceeding against Por and me."

"How much?"

"Two fifty." About eight million dollars.

"Greedy."

"Very but he's got the evidence. There are also rumors, but not from the same source, an arrest warrant is going to be issued on you. The car was mentioned."

"Is the paperwork on the car sorted?"

"Done."

"Thanks, Mother."

"Be careful, Chance." She hung up.

I had a plan. It wasn't fully fleshed out, and it had holes you could comfortably fly a 747 through, but it was a plan. I looked in the rear-view mirror. Khun Preecha and Noot were in a pickup behind us, towing a horse-trailer with a 'wild' buffalo and a billion baht in it. The buffalo wasn't really wild, but that's what the sign on the rear of the trailer said.

I called Moo, the corrupt cop from Phra Pradaeng who'd driven us off the island. We'd been using Moo to keep an eye on the Phra Pradaeng chief and had him reporting to Beckham. Mother called them Moo Moo boys. Beckham was offended.

"Hello, is that Lance Corporal Moo?"

"Yes, speaking, who's this?"

"How's the Camry going?"

"Oh, yes, great…"

"How do you feel about doing another little job for me? Nothing dangerous and well paid."

"What's the job?"

"I need you to get a phone for me."

"What kind of phone?"

"A second-hand one."

"Okay, any kind of special features?"

"No, but I want a particular second-hand phone, not just any second-hand phone."

"Oh. Which particular second-hand phone do you want?"

"Here Leng's phone."

"Oh."

"Can you get it?"

"Yeah, I think so. We can work something out, but I'll have to involve the sergeant taking care of the room. I'll negotiate something with him."

"Keep it reasonable, and let me know. And Moo?"

"Yes, boss."

"Thanks."

***

I watched the phu yai's front-men enter the Fuji Restaurant in Siam Square. We'd booked a private room, and after a few minutes they entered it and sat down. I was watching on a notebook's screen in a van in the parking lot outside. You can buy all of this surveillance gear in Panthip. The screen was divided into three segments. The top third of the screen split into two images of the corridor outside the room, the bottom two-thirds an overhead image of the room. I could select another camera and change the image, but the one I was looking at showed the men's faces clearly. None of them said a word. The time in the top right corner of the screen read 11:11AM 3/11/2554. All the one's added up to six, a bad omen. I changed the regional settings on the notebook, and then the time read: 11:11 AM 3/11/2011 and added up to eight – a good omen. We're flexible like that.

"Okay, looks clean. Good to go," Chai said over the comms. He was monitoring the same images I was in the private room next to them. Nat was with him, and they were both loaded for bear. Steve had lent a couple of his yakuza boys to add atmosphere to the golf bags they'd used to smuggle the weapons into the restaurant. We didn't think anything would happen, but we were still fighting a war.

I got out of the van and walked across to the restaurant.

"I believe you have a room booked for me, 'Khun Oh'…"

The waitress checked the tablet in her hands. "Yes, sir, please follow me." The restaurant had a sizeable crowd; it almost always does.

She slid the door open and stepped aside as I entered the room. The three men, representatives of some of the most powerful men in Thailand, sat in a row facing me, green tea thermos flasks by their cups.

"Good afternoon, gentlemen, please don't get up." I eased down onto the bench seat opposite them, swinging my legs into the well below the table, thankful we weren't sitting cross-legged on a tatami mat. Thomas's drugs were good, but I doubted they'd be good enough to handle that and still keep me upright.

They didn't say anything, and they wouldn't. I'd called the meeting, and it was my show.

"I have the money, and you can have it, but I have conditions. When these conditions are met, I will turn the money over to you."

The one on the left, a well-known lawyer, after looking at his companions and getting the nod, answered me. "How do we know you have the money?"

This was a fairly predictable question. I took out an iPhone and handed it to him. A photo of me sitting on the money reading today's *Thai Rath* on the screen. He nodded, passed the phone to the senior cop sitting next to him, who passed it to the prosecutor sitting to my right. Although proxies, each of these men had a face seen on television screens nationwide many times, and they were powerful men in their own right.

"Like I said, I have the money. Do you have the authority to make a deal?"

"We do." Same looks down the row, same nods. Consensus is a wonderful thing, especially when you're on ten percent of the deal.

"Number one: I want the charges against my father dropped."

The prosecutor sat back in his chair. The cop spread his hands, the prosecutor sucked in his cheeks, and the lawyer said, "I'm afraid that's nothing to do with us. It's a personal matter between your father and the station chief.

If the complaint is removed, we can make it disappear, but the complainant is the station chief, and we cannot influence him. According to our understanding, he is quite upset with your father for killing off a major source of his income."

"All right, you say this is personal and you're hands-off. I take it you won't mind me dealing with it personally, then?"

The lawyer got the consensual flicks of the eyebrows and the shrug from him was an answer in the affirmative. The Phra Padaeng station chief had just been thrown to the wolves, well, actually, me. No one said a word; they knew we'd have the room wired for sound, and no one wants to be a viral hit on Youtube, but everyone in the room understood exactly what had been said.

"Number two: You will stage a press conference at 5:30pm today, where you will reveal that you have caught one of the gang with over a hundred million baht – that money comes out of your cut, by the way. At the press conference you will announce that you are looking into certain matters in Minister Sankit's past that may be related to the robbery. You will not ask this man any questions nor restrain him in any way. After the press conference you will release the man and you will also release Khun Chatree. This is non-negotiable. If any of you disagree with this, then a deal of any kind is of no value to me and I will get up and walk out of here."

"Let us make a call," the lawyer said. Three phones on speed dial. A brief synopsis, each man with his hand over his mouth, phone pressed hard on his ear. Lots of, "Krub Pomme's," 'yessirs' to you farang.

The phones slipped back into pockets, nods up and down the row. "We can do that," the lawyer said.

"Number three: It's possible that some evidence is going to come up in the next few days that may implicate me in a murder. The evidence will be a car. You will impound the car, not find any evidence related to me; however, you will find a dead body in the car and want to question the car's owner."

"Who is the car owner?" This came from the prosecutor in whose hands the 'peuk ron' hot potato would land.

"I don't want to accuse anyone unjustly; let's wait for the evidence," I said.

"It will depend on who brings the evidence to the attention of the prosecutor…"

"Where it may be dealt with according to the decision of the prosecutor…"

"True, however, as you know, it still depends on who is behind the evidence. If it is someone with influence, then we cannot guarantee a solution."

"… and if it is someone without influence?"

"Then we will take care of the matter according to your wishes."

"Each one of these clauses is worth three-hundred and thirty-three million baht. That's my deal."

"We've already told you we can't do number one." The cop looked angry, red flushing up his neck. The lawyer next to him looked embarrassed; emotional outbursts and lack of insight are not admirable traits.

"And I've conceded that. My counter proposal was that I have free hand to deal with the problem myself, which I understand you have agreed to?"

The lawyer laid a hand on the cop's arm. Cooling him down. His boss was bigger; the cop cooled down.

"Yes, we're agreed. We have a deal. Where do you want the press conference to take place?"

"It should be at Nong Khaem police station, right?" I said and looked at the cop. He had the 'dead look'. Being calmed down in front of me had made him lose face. I'd made a fresh enemy, he was telling me with his eyes. The lawyer clenched his jaw. It's with these little signals that most of our negotiating is done, usually with a smile.

The cop cleared his throat. "Yes, it would be proper procedure to hold the press conference at the station."

I stood up abruptly. The prosecutor spilled his green tea, hand headed for the gun under his armpit. I gave him a little grin and kept my hands on the table.

"Gentlemen, I think our business is done. Thank you for your time." I didn't wai them, nor they me.

As I slid the door to the room open, I turned back to them. "There is one other thing, and it's a deal-breaker. If any word of our talk here gets out to anyone apart from us and the people you talked to on the phone, then the deal is off. Is that understood?"

They looked at each other; then three heads nodded slowly. The heat behind the cop's eyes had increased. Job done, I slid the door shut behind me.

Five hours later, wearing a huge pair of Aviator Ray-Bans, a NY Yankees baseball cap, a fake moustache and my hair dyed black, I was standing at the rear of the conference room in Nong Khaem police station. In front of me journalists jostled for position Thai style – cutting in front of each other and then apologizing with a meek grin and a low wai. Khun Preecha sat at a long table, a hundred million baht on it and about thirty journalists in front of him. The deputy police chief stood behind him, waiting for the flashes and questions to stop. It didn't take long; no one wants to piss off the deputy chief of police.

"I will make a short statement about the status of the case of the robbery at the home of Minister Sankit's, which occurred on the night of the twenty-eighth of October two thousand five hundred and fifty-four at approximately ten p.m."

The deputy chief looked up from the piece of paper he was reading and scanned the room. The fraction of a pause as his scan hit on me was missed by all except a couple of the journalists, who glanced at the back of the room and did their own scan. He was just letting me know he wasn't happy with the orders he'd been given. Tough shit; orders are orders when they're backed by leverage. That's reality. The levers and fulcrums of Thai society are a blend of family, money, position, ruthlessness – take your pick, farang, we're an old society with a deeply woven fabric – a Gordian knot of relationships and power.

The chief looked down at the paper shaking in his hand. I knew what he was going to say; I wrote it.

"Acting on information from an anonymous tip-off, we raided an apartment in Bang Bua Tong. In the apartment we found two pistols," he waved his hand at the guns on the table, "and one hundred million baht in cash. We found a mobile phone on the person who was sleeping at the house. In the mobile phone were photos of Minister Sankit's house and a room with boxes filled with cash. We arrested Preecha Arooncharoenboonmee on suspicion of the robbery of Minister Sankit's house. The photos are being printed now and will be given to you when you leave. Khun Preecha has not confessed to the crime. He alleges that he was drugged and put in that room by a well-known influential figure, whose first name begins with the initial 'O'. Furthermore he claims that the influential figure stole the billion baht, and he was merely at the house to present a claim against Minister Sankit for alleged offenses that occurred when Minister Sankit was a police officer serving in Nakhon Si Thammarat. That is all we can tell you for now as the investigation is ongoing. The office of the National Anti-Corruption Commission (NACC) has requested that Minister Sankit appear before them at 3pm on 8 November. Thank you."

The chief gave me another hard stare and stalked out of the room. His abrupt departure surprised the journalists, the questions and shouting starting as the door closed behind him. The noise died as the door reopened and a sergeant walked in with a pile of A4 sized envelopes. Copies of the photos we'd made during the day inside; the top photo the finger, this time without the nine, just the wild buffalo horns. As the journalists dived for the envelopes, the sergeant helped Khun Preecha out of his chair and I slipped out the door. The final part of the first act of our three-act play would be another statement to the press, in a couple of hours, saying that Preecha had been released on bail paid by Mother.

I left the station by the rear entrance. Chai was waiting for me in a Mercedes-Benz Vito. Mother had cut a deal with a second-hand car dealer on Ratchapisek to buy up a fleet of Vitos. During the day, we had all of them fitted with the same license plate, just a simple, 'O 9'. Twenty of them were driving around Paknam and Bangkok. Bait, you have to cut it to catch the big fish.

Chatree also left the station by the rear entrance. His mother parked her Benz, hazards blinking, in the road blocking the exit. A cop standing next to the door saluted her. Chatree came out, furtively looking left and right as if he had somewhere to hide. A lesser version of Sankit, that's really making a statement about someone. Then again, between a guy who'd rat on his own mother and a guy who'd shoot a baby in the head, the guy with the gun wins as the lowest of the low. I'd known Sankit was bad. I had no idea he was that bad, or I'd have killed him long ago. And regrets are about as useful as tits on a bull.

We had fifteen people in taxis, in cars and on motorbikes following Chatree, and his mother's Benz had a tracker in the right rear wheel arch. Chatree's phone, handed back to him at the station, had a new chip in it. This one would call the notebook on the seat in front of me and start a recording of every conversation that took place and every SMS that was sent or website surfed – in short, the notebook was a duplicate of Chatree's phone. This cannot be bought at Panthip.

The crew we'd hired to follow Chatree were from a private detective agency. Run by former members of DSI and staffed, mostly, by serving DSI, I was reasonably sure they would not lose him. He was worth a lot of money to them.

phlik wi grit hai bpen ohgaat – Turn a problem into an opportunity

A Grim Deal

Bangkok, Thursday, 3 November 2011, 7:35PM

The easiest way to get the 'invisible hand' to show itself was to make a deal with the Brothers Grim. Most times the obvious isn't so until it is.

"We need to talk – just you, me, your brother and Chai. No funny stuff, meet like men and we can work out a deal. Leave Somboon out of it, and come and talk with me."

"Where?"

I wasn't surprised by his answer, the war we were having was costing us both, but our pockets are deeper. "Parking lot two, Suvarnabhumi (pronounced Soo wanna poom), fifth floor, as fast as you can get there."

"We can be there in about fifteen."

"See you then." I cut the connection. The airport's

car park is a good place to meet – more cameras than Hollywood. The chance of something 'going off' there was slim. I was sure now that the 'hand' was either Aroon the shopkeeper, Chainarong, or both; my money was on the latter, and I'm not a gambling man.

Going into the car park, security ran the mirror under the car. In the trunk were a couple of M4s, smoke canisters, three hand grenades, two Remington pump-action shotguns, and enough ammunition to take on a small nation. We popped the trunk. The red suitcases the weapons and ammo were in didn't get a second glance.

The brothers had parked next to the far corner on the left side away from the airport's entrance. Leaning against the wall next to a Porsche, they turned and walked forward, hands showing, as we parked opposite and got out.

No smiles. No wais.

"Thanks for coming," I said, talking to both of them, but starting with Khemkaeng.

"We're here. What have you got to say?" Khemkaeng said. His tone was even, eyes on the level. It wasn't a jai ron, 'hot-hearted', look, but neither was it compromising. I returned it in kind.

"The only thing that will come out of this war between us is pain and loss. We can stop it right now, today. Us standing here…" I looked at each of the men in turn, Chai, Khemkaeng, and his brother, Damrong. They were listening, so I went on.

"You can hurt us, you already have, but we can hurt you, and we've proven that too. I remember the day we named your son," I said to Khemkaeng. His eyes and jaw softened. "Yeah, I do. And your wedding, Khun Damrong, to your beautiful first wife. Can I make her a widow? Sure I can, as you can do to mine. Por will be retiring this year. When he does, he's going to ask me to take over. I don't want the job, but it's my duty to do it. I want him to feel good about retiring, not that the districts are at war and we're killing each other." I had them nodding now.

The brothers looked at each other, unspoken words passed.

"How do we stop, stand it down?" Damrong said. Each word getting a nod from Khemkaeng as it was said.

I smiled, moved in a bit closer, lowering my voice till they leaned in. I paused till everyone was within whisper range.

"We don't, we expand it." I waited for their reaction. I hadn't done much work with these two brothers, and that was to my remiss. If we were going to survive together, we had to know each other.

Khemkaeng smiled first, it reached his eyes, and he held out his hand. I shook it. Same with his brother.

"Let's talk business," I said, and Khemkaeng pulled out a packet of Marlboro reds. He offered me one, and I took it, cupping my hands around the flame of the lighter he held up with the practiced ease of a long-time smoker. A guilty thought, Pim's words about smoking in my head. I pushed it away; there was business to talk about.

"I am very sorry for your father's passing. He was a great man, and all of my family had the utmost respect for him. I think someone poisoned your thinking towards us in your time of grief. I understand this and am not angry, as I hope you can tell. I would like to know who did the poisoning."

Khemkaeng held up his hand. "Khun Oh, I was told you'd put a contract on me by Aroon. This was about three weeks ago. I waited to see what moved. After the death of Goong, I thought you were taking out the next generation." Damrong nodded. I looked at him straight; hard pill to be delivered.

"I was told by Por, who was told by the gunman who was given the contract, it was your second wife, Som, who bought the contract on your brother." His cigarette stalled halfway to his lips.

"When did Por get his information?" It was polite and smart of him not to question the truth of the information nor the source.

"A day or a couple of days before the accident with Goong. She also planned to kill your first wife," I said, watching his eyes. Genuine shock there; this was all news to him, or shock that I knew?

"I'll ask her when I get home and let you know," he said. The cigarette trembled in his hand, but there was no expression on his face.

"One other thing," Damrong said, "remember the wedding of the sheriff in Chorakhe Yai?"

"Yes." They'd invited Por. I went in his stead. I hadn't stayed long. Just long enough to slip the petty, fat, corrupt sheriff an equally fat envelope and deliver up a few hundred wais.

"Chainarong's sister left with Tum."

Chang Noi's sister left with Tum, I thought, wondering why he'd say that.

"Interesting. Well, we don't have time to spend

unraveling the past. Here's what I propose moving forward. I've got a family in mind to take over running Here Leng's district. The family I'm thinking of will work out for all of us, but it's early days yet – I haven't spoken with them. When I have, I'll introduce you. Big Tiger's old territory is mine…" Khemkaeng's mouth had opened as if to ask a question and then shut again. I stopped, raised my eyebrows.

"What if Big Tiger comes back?" he said.

"He won't. I shot him in the back of the head over a year ago." The fact that they didn't know was a testament to the quality of the secret. Khemkaeng nodded. I'd handed him a little piece of trust, and he'd picked up on that.

"The other thing," I paused and looked at each of them hard, "you guys have to stop fighting each other – this is not the time for personal competition. We have to work together. Times are changing. Fast. Smart phones, smarter people. Cameras everywhere, the old ways gone. We need to come up with new ways, and I've got a few ideas, but we also need to remember the old values. We need to protect and grow our families. Those that act against us need to be taught to leave us alone or work with us. We need to keep the peace and let business move."

I looked Khemkaeng directly in the eyes, holding them. "I want you to be my district head for your father's territory of Bang Bo. I hope you and I enjoy the same long, good relationship they did. Damrong, you'll have to move across the river to Phra Samut Chedi, you'll be taking over Aroon's district."

He looked pleased, a small grin on his face. He glanced at his brother to see his reaction. It was a generous gift.

Aroon was the slipperiest of all the 'Godfathers', but he was no slouch at making a baht out of a salung.

Damrong's hard, crafty eyes narrowed. The thought flitted in that he might be going for it. "Why now? Why take them out?" It was a fair question.

"We don't know if Aroon or Chainarong are guilty of anything, at this point, but that's beside the point. The point is we invited them to lunch to discuss the situation of our war with you. Neither of them responded. That's enough guilt. Your brother, Supot – where does he stand in all of this?"

Khemkaeng spat on the ground. "He didn't have the stomach for it."

"Did he say why?"

Khemkaeng looked out towards the main airport building and sighed. "He wants out. He wants to be a clothes designer. He's quite a sensitive kind of guy…" He flicked his eyes, shrugged his shoulders, and sighed again.

"Oh."

"Yeah."

"Shit."

"Yeah."

I sucked the last bit of life out of the Marlboro. "Well. That leaves Chainarong's territory open. I've got a guy. A good guy. Been with us a long time, Uncle Tong – remember him?"

"Yeah, I remember him."

"What do you say we put him in and split the profits five ways?" Again this was generous, I could have kept it all for our family, but I didn't just want peace – I wanted allies.

"That'll work," Khemkaeng said.

"Damrong, what do you think?"

"It works for me, Khun Oh."

"Okay, I propose that we move on Chainarong and Aroon first thing tomorrow morning. Crack of dawn. Keep the preparation low profile. Only count on those you can totally trust," I said, flashing on Tum and Somboon, "and Somboon, I want him."

"We don't have him. He came to us about the Ferrari with the dead body, but he never gave us the car. If he had, we probably would have used it by now." The 'probably' was superfluous but polite.

"Any idea where he is?"

"No, but of course, if we find him, we'll hand him over and the car."

I believed him, cursing myself for not paying more attention to these two. Business is business, and a large part of business is who you're going to work with to make it work. Ignore that, and I had, at your peril.

"Okay. I suggest, strongly, that we let Mere Joom coordinate tomorrow's action – she's had much more experience than any of us, and she has her war room set up."

"We heard rumors about that. So it's real?"

"As real as you are," I said. "I'll show you it, later tonight."

It was over an hour later that we left the airport. We'd spent it talking through details of the pre-planning stage. Taking out two district heads on the same day is no small undertaking, please forgive the pun.

I called Mother.

"Chance, how was it?"

"It went well as far as I can tell. Have to wait to see if they're really with us, but I'd bet my bottom baht on it and…"

"I know you're not a gambling man, Chance, I'd be extremely disappointed if you were. I heard from Por. He's on his way back. He sounded pleased with the results of his new leg."

"Did he say which way he was coming in?"

Mother chuckled. "You know him. He didn't say anything on the phone; he just doesn't trust them. I've tried to explain our system to him, but he prefers talking in someone's ear. Usually close enough to stick his tongue in."

"The brothers agreed that you'll run tomorrow's show."

"Of course they did. Their mother was a smart woman; she went too early, sad. None of this need have happened."

"I know, Mother. I've got to go. We're on our way to hand over the first tranche of the payment. I'll call you when we're done."

She hung up. From here on in she'd focus on setting up the day to come. Khemkaeng and Damrong were about to get a whole new perspective on taking orders. Thing is, I could trust Mother to do it with grace and a total awareness of their needs – a rare skill.

We had to deliver eleven million United States dollars to the trio that had met us in Fuji. They obviously didn't trust each other enough to nominate a mutual bag man, so it had to be all three. We were headed to my house in Prachachuen and then the parking lot of the Chao Phraya

River Hotel on Ratchadapisek.

There hadn't been a reaction to the press conference from either Sankit or his wife. I had thought there would have been. Doubt niggles at a decision made like a tailor at a first fitting. Push on, don't let doubt second-guess you. It's the road to hell.

The Prachuen house is one of eight I have around the city under different names. Each stocked with food, spare clothing, weapons, and false I.D. Usually a spare vehicle parked in the garage, cars or vans from Mother's business. We'd left the Vito here from the morning and decided to use it again. We took Nat with us to stay in the van while we did the deal. If anything happened he could dial it back to Mother.

The three of them stood at the rear of a 7 Series BMW. Judging by the stickers in the window, it was the cop's car. The monthly salary for a national deputy police chief is about five thousand dollars. A 7 Series BMW costs at retail two hundred and fifty thousand dollars – you do the math.

Wired for sound, a Dr. Tom cocktail of speed and pain suppressant winding through my veins, I stepped out of the van. Behind me, hidden from view in the van, Nat filmed everything with a news-footage-quality camcorder. Chai carried two of the holdalls, and I had one, three point six million per bag. We'd switched to USD and seeded the pile with marked and fake bills, ten per cent of the total. Saved a million, and if or when the bills showed up, we'd know where the money came from. The bags for the prosecutor and the lawyer contained all real and marked money; the bag for the cop all the fake. It was a risk, but a calculated one.

"You're late," the cop said, showing us his heavily jeweled Rolex. The lawyer glanced at the cop, an annoyed frown on his face. Push buttons time.

"Can't you keep him under control?" I said to the lawyer. The cop's tan went dark purple.

"Let's just get this over with," the lawyer said, but he gave the cop another look.

"Yeah, the sooner the better, but keep him on a leash," I said. Inferring that anyone is a dog, I think is an insult in just about every country in the world – we're no exception. The cop, stupid though he was, did not miss the insult and now resembled a volcano about to erupt.

We put the bags in the trunk and unzipped them. The prosecutor picked up a money-counting machine. It had two little lights in its face, green and red, one of the more modern machines that could detect fake notes. We figured they'd use one – we would – and we went with psychology to beat them. Most times you line three things up and let people choose, they will very seldom choose the middle, almost always selecting either end.

The prosecutor dipped his hand in the bag nearest him and pulled out two bundles. We were standing in a U around the trunk, shielding it from prying eyes. Cop, lawyer, me, Chai, prosecutor. The prosecutor leaned over the little machine whirring away in the trunk counting a ten-thousand-dollar bundle in the time it takes to say ten thousand. He reached for the middle bag, looked at me, and dug his hand in deep, pulling a bundle out. If he'd taken one off the top, I'd be sweating. The little red light stayed off. Whirr of paper and that was it. He looked up at the other two, grabbed the first holdall and walked away. I reached in, grabbed the bag on the right, and handed it to the lawyer.

"Pleasure doing business with you, and remember, one word of our agreement getting out and the deal's off – then you'll be delivering this back to me – got it?" He didn't look happy. The cop, as I thought he might, took his chance.

"You watch who you're talking to," he said, spittle flying out the corners of his clenched lips.

"Go fuck yourself," I said and walked off, Chai walking backwards with me, keeping an eye on them. We made it to the van and jumped in. I lifted the lid on the notebook, the bug in the base of the holdall in the trunk of the cop's car working perfectly.

"As soon as we get the last bag of money, I'm killing that fucking farang lizard."

"You need to calm down. We don't need any more publicity than we've already got. The big guy hasn't forgotten whose idea it was to store the cash with Sankit in the first place."

"You don't tell me what to do, and don't worry about publicity. Whatever happens I'll deal with it, but that farang shit has got a bullet coming to him and soon."

The bug was only good for a range of up to fifty meters, and as we were pulling out of the car park, it started to fade, then picked up again but slightly delayed. I was getting the feed from the Honda Jazz with Beer in it, parked three cars down from the cop's BMW. Outside the Chao Phraya hotel as if waiting for customers, another three taxis lined up, all with receivers for the bug.

I heard the sound of the trunk closing and then a car door. A lot of banging, sounded like a fist on wood, I lowered the volume a little on the speakers. "… fucking farang talk to me like that. Who the fuck does he think he is? I will cut his lips off before I kill the little fuck." I thought he might be talking to the lawyer, but a separate channel opened up for him as he got into his car. The cop was talking to himself, screaming actually. 'How to Make Enemies and Influence People', move over Dale Carnegie.

Chai handed me a phone, mouthing, 'Moo-cop' at me.

"Moo, hi, everything okay?"

"I got the phone. Is twenty thousand okay? I got to pay the sergeant fifteen." I'd bet it was five.

"Moo, I'm coming to pick it up. I've got fifty for you. Good job."

yaa feuun faawy haa dta khep – Don't scratch in the rubbish to find a centipede

MOONLIGHT SONATA

Saraburi, Thursday, 3 November 2011 10:35PM

Coming down from Dr. Tom's cocktail, like an addict, I was mentally ticking off how many minutes it should be before I could have another and still maintain a perception of normality. If anything in my life could be called normal.

Coincidence happens all the time, but the 'coincidence' of Damrong saying Tum had slept with Chainarong's sister was not exactly the same as two guys turning up to a meeting wearing the same color shirt. Chainarong's sister was a lesbian, a 'Tom', bound breasts, boy's boots, and a man's watch kind of Tom. I wondered why Damrong would lie about that. Wondered what it might have to do with his very pretty second wife, Som. Uncle Mike had once told me, many years ago, ninety-nine times out of a hundred, a woman, directly or indirectly, would be the root cause of the problem. That didn't mean Uncle Mike did not like women, far from it, he loved them; what he meant was, in Thailand women always play an integral role in any plot. Ignore this advice at your peril.

Chainarong loved his sister and vice versa. Thinking of them at my wedding: Chang Noi drunk, his sister, Mai, with a pout and genuine concern on her face. His sister, I was guessing, had somehow pissed Damrong off, and this was his way of repaying the favor. I hoped Here Leng's phone, currently being dissected by Mother, would give me some answers.

Somehow it was all connected. Dot to connected dot, lust to betrayal, betrayal to greed, greed to deceit, deceit to revenge, revenge to retribution, and that's painting it with a broad brush. Within the broad brush strokes, finer details of slight, loss of face, delusions of grandeur, naïveté, guilt, envy, jealousy, and innocence lost.

"Are you stoned?" Chai said, looking straight ahead. He was driving, and it was pitch black with only the scythe of the headlights to show that we weren't driving in the belly of some big black hole. About fifty meters in front of us a police BMW with red and blue lights flashing added to the surreal moment. We were on Route 1, the 'Friendship Highway', which in a year probably kills more people than cancer.

"A little," I said and stifled a yawn. "Tom, how long before you can give me another shot?" I'd brought Doctor Tom along; he'd volunteered, just in case.

"Not within another forty-five minutes."

I turned around in the front seat of the van and looked

at him.

"Tom, Chai's current speed is two hundred and twenty kilometers per hour. We are approximately eighty kilometers from our target. We don't have forty-five minutes."

Tom's face was a ghostly white in the light of his iPad as he absorbed this latest news. "How long before we're there?"

"About twenty minutes, depends on traffic out of Saraburi, but it shouldn't be bad at this time of night."

"Then I'll give you a shot just before you reach the destination." I think he was regretting volunteering.

"I'm an idiot," he said.

"No arguments from me," I said, giving him a smile. He didn't smile back. I turned back to watch imminent disaster. We were reaching the mountains, the road twisting up, slow trucks in the far left lane, intimidated by the flashing lights and siren of the cop car not to come out into the middle lane as we swept up a steep incline.

Chatree and his mother had been up this same road two hours earlier. They'd first gone to a four-bedroom house in an exclusive moobaan, gated community to you farang, and then after staying there for two hours and Chatree's mother making a number of phone calls, all to the same number, they'd left and gone to a private house within walled grounds about ten kilometers from the house in the moobaan.

I was guessing, but I thought she'd gone to visit Sankit, to claim her cut of the money she thought he had. She thought he had the money because she got the same story from two separate, and at least to her knowledge, reliable sources. The first was Chatree; told by the cops he could go home because Sankit had the money and all was forgiven; the second source was Khun Preecha's contact, who had planted the seed of Chatree's robbery in the first place. The contact, a close personal friend of Chatree's mother, had succumbed to the lure of another three hundred thousand baht, cash, of course. I felt sorry for Chatree's mother. She'd been betrayed by everyone, and her luck wasn't about to improve.

A few hundred heart-stopping brushes with death later, Chai parked under a tree next to a high wall. No cameras on the wall as far as we could see. The cop car had peeled off just after Muak Lek. I had brought only Nat and Beer with us and Dr. Tom, of course, but he'd stay with the van until I called for him. I hoped he wouldn't be necessary.

He gave the rubber band around the bicep of my right arm a twist and released the flow of blood for the needle he had jabbed in the crook of my arm. Pain dulled immediately, and a fiery need for action moved through my body.

The moon shone brightly behind us, turning the landscape a gun-metal gray. We had no plans of the house, just a grainy image taken off Google Earth. Our plan was simple – gain entry, take down anyone who pointed a gun at us or who resisted, and subdue the rest.

The house was built on top of a small hill. The wall surrounding the property was at least five hundred meters from the house. Lawns ran from the front of the house to the wall, dissected by a straight driveway, which ended in a large metal gate. Using a leg-up from Chai, I scrambled onto the roof of the Vito. Nat, already on the roof of the van, draped a large rubber mat over the wall and slid an aluminum ladder between us and it. Chai passed up a plank, and Nat laid the plank on top of the ladder. That's how much use, barbed wire, glass and spikes are when put on top of a wall.

I walked across the plank and jumped down onto the lawn, moving to the right, staying in the shadows of the wall. The lights were on, first and second floors of the house. I could hear music, 'Big Band', cha cha cha Thai-style music. Chai dropped soundlessly and immediately took off at a silent run straight up the lawn. I followed Nat as he sprinted after Chai; adrenalin's a great painkiller. Beer had remained on top of the van, rifle aimed at the house.

The music a lot louder, I crossed the driveway in a crouch and ran to the wall of the house. I peeked in a window, the curtains open. Empty room, well lit, looked like a family room. Chai with hand signals went left, and I went right, inching my way up the wall towards the front door. No cameras as far I could tell. On the other side of the front door, large wooden-framed French windows, curtains closed, light appearing around the edges. I edged closer, keeping low, listening, but hearing nothing except the cha cha cha music. The air cool enough that there'd be a mist in the morning. I looked at the time on my cell, 11:13pm.

A door in the side of the house. As agreed I stopped by the door.

"Nine at door right side of house." We each had numbers, Chai's was seven, Nat's was eight, and Beer's was ten.

Over my earphones, "Eight, door left side of house," and, "Seven, window, rear."

I placed a small shaped charge next to the handle and retreated back about four meters. Listening.

"On three," Chai said, "three."

I pressed a button and covered my ears, five seconds. The blast blew the windows on the garage opposite me, and it had taken the door off its hinges. My hearing still ringing with the effect of the blast, I went into the house pointing an MP5, suitable for this type of situation, down the hallway. The music stopped. I froze. Listening. Nothing. A piano, faint, getting louder, Beethoven's Moonlight Sonata, creepy. I forced the chill out of my spine and mind. Focus. At the end of the hallway were two doors, one in front of me and one to the left. The room with the French windows and the lights on was down here somewhere to my left.

Pointing the gun with my right hand, I eased the door handle down with my left. It gave, and the door opened. I gave it a little shove, a dark room behind it. Kneeling by the door, I reached up and found the light switch, squinted my eyes, and flicked it on. A pantry, an empty one, Mother Hubbard popped into my head. Focus. I eased the handle down on the other door. Gave it a shove. Another hallway, open door on the left and then what looked like the front entrance of the house, stairway opposite. Chai was kneeling at the bottom of the stairs, his Uzi pointed up them, Nat behind him with a pump-action shotgun now pointed at the ground. As soon as he'd seen me it had dropped. Good, he was calm.

I poked my head around the doorway of the room. Chatree was in the middle of it. His blood covered the floor nearly to where I was standing. No need to check if he was dead. I could see by his eyes he was long gone. It would have taken a while for the blood to seep out this far. Around the edges it was a darker shade where it had congealed, with bubbles in it. He was lying face down, a large portion of his back missing. Looked like large-caliber exit wounds, maybe magnum rounds from a shotgun up close.

I backed out of the room. Chai moved to the first landing of the stairs. At the top of the stairs a hallway went left and right, the music was coming from the room at the end of the corridor. With Chai next to me, we walked slowly down it, weapons pointed at the door. Nat took up position at the top of the stairs guarding our rear. I eased the door open with my foot.

Chatree's mother sat up in bed, on top of the covers, fully dressed – a bullet hole in her forehead the only indication she wasn't waiting to take a bath, a black phone on the pillow next to her. I walked into the room and around the bed. Someone had shot her up close, powder burns around the entry wound, and she did have a surprised look on her face. The latter just an observation; I'm not a forensics expert. I picked up the phone. Five missed calls. All from the same number.

I called Mother.

"Mother, I'm about to call a number 089-8077048. I need to know where it is located."

"Wait five minutes. I have to call first and check which company it is." She hung up.

Chai appeared in the doorway. "I've cleared the house." He lifted his chin towards Chatree's mother. "There's no one here but this one and the one downstairs."

I noticed Moonlight Sonata had ended, waited, nothing else came on. The only sounds were my breathing and the hum of the air-conditioning. Chai left the room.

My cell rang.

"Yes, Mother?"

"The number has just left Sakeo, heading east, fast, on the road to Aranyaprathet, maybe Poipet." She hung up again.

I hit 'Call'. The boost from Dr. Tom and the stalled adrenalin rush hit like a heavy rock dropped in a deep well, slipping down into the constrained depths.

It connected on the third ring. I didn't say anything. I could hear breathing and background noise. I couldn't make out what it was, maybe just the sound of the road.

"Hello," I said. The silence had stretched enough. "Hello."

"Chance, I'm glad it's you. It makes it easier," Suchada said.

"If she's harmed in any way…"

"Don't, Chance, just don't. I'm not in the mood. As you no doubt know, I've had a trying day, and I'm still not finished with it. Pim is alive, and she will remain so provided you do exactly what I order you to do. Do you understand?"

"Yes."

"Good. I want the billion baht and Khun Preecha, and I want them by tomorrow evening. You will deliver Preecha and the money to me at an address I will give you.

Then I'll give you Pim. Before 8pm tomorrow, no later. By now you should understand how serious I am about this situation, so you understand that I will not hesitate to kill her. I've never liked her, not from the minute Sankit brought her home, and I like her less now, so just do what you're ordered."

"Yes, I understand."

She hung up. Chai was back in the doorway.

"Suchada?" he said.

"Yes, Suchada." I exhaled, hard, it was that or I'd burst. "She is an evil fucking bitch, I give her that."

"She will die badly and in great pain," Chai said. He was stating it as fact.

"Yes, she will, Chai. Yes, she will."

thaawt khiaao thaawt lep – Remove fangs, remove claws

A SIAMESE FEMALE

Bangkok, Friday, 4 November 2011 01:45AM

The tricky part of any deal is the handover. In a kidnapping, because there's a, hopefully, live body involved, it's doubly tricky. When there's an exchange of bodies and money, well, I'm sure you get the picture. I hadn't received any further calls from Suchada. Didn't expect to until, at the earliest, dawn. Whichever scenario I worked out for delivering the money and Preecha for Pim, they all worked out bad. The money wasn't the issue, didn't care about it. I just couldn't see Suchada putting herself in a position where I could get at her, and that meant she could kill all of us. If she could kill Preecha, then she could kill the rest of us.

We dropped Dr. Tom back at the house. I'd stayed off his cocktails for the trip home, dozed most of the way.

He left a few of them with Chai. It was shaping up to be another long night and day. In these circumstances you snatch sleep when you can.

We didn't have a billion in cash. We had seven hundred million but everything else, including Uncle Mike's money, was tied up until Monday. Counterfeit wouldn't cut it. That meant we had to borrow or steal three hundred million baht, about ten million United States dollars, and deliver it to Aranyaprathet within the next nineteen hours.

I knew exactly where to get the ten million, but it would derail, in a major way, Por's return to Thailand. If I stole the money back from the cop, the lawyer and the prosecutor, Por would have his murder charge moved up the court schedule. Everything down that path only got worse.

If, on the other hand, I could get them to give it back to me, then I'd have the ten million and Por would be free and clear. Drugs will do that to you, but I had a wispy vision of an outline, of something that in an optimistic moment you might say resembled something vaguely like a plan.

In parallel we were engineering the hostile takeover of two long-standing district heads, kicking off in about another three hours' time. Some things cannot be delayed. We still didn't know if Aroon or Chainarong were guilty of anything at this point; that was beside the point.

I had Moo's family, the corrupt cop from Phra Pradaeng not Mother's bodyguard, in mind for taking over the Phrapadaeng district. In the week since Here Leng's shooting, he'd shown an enterprising nature for graft; that coupled with his inside knowledge and network of cops made him and his wife a natural fit. Apart from getting us Here Leng's phone, Moo had been feeding us the Phra Pradaeng station chief's schedule on a daily basis. Who he met, where he went, all of that. He'd positioned some choice electronics (also not from Panthip) in the station chief's office and tipped a kilo of sugar in the chief's car's gas tank, causing the car to be replaced with a temporary one; naturally supplied by yours truly. Like I said, Moo was enterprising.

Via the wired car, we knew that the chief was in a short-time hotel. He and his date having both consumed a nice dinner by the flooded river, 'rim naam' and a bottle of Chivas. Both had also consumed enough Rohypnol, known as the 'Date Rape Drug' or 'roofies', to put an elephant down for a day. Actually, that's a bit of an exaggeration; the chief was due to wake up in about twenty-five minutes. We were nearly there.

I was thinking about what I had to say to Khun Preecha in the morning. Delivering a death sentence, no matter the cause, is pause for thought. I had no doubt that Suchada would kill him. My best guess was she'd do it in front of Pim, and I didn't have a plan about that yet.

The short-time motel was at the back of a row of shop-houses, near the river, just off Charoenkrung. Access was through a short alley just wide enough for our van to fit through, which opened to two rows of vinyl-curtained parking spaces, ten per side. The Phra Pradaeng police chief's car was fourth from the entrance on the left. We pulled into the next room's empty space, ignoring the boy with the flashlight indicating to park opposite. As he came around the van, Nat opened the door and stuck a gun in his face, putting a finger to his lips. In the same hand he held a hood. Once the parking attendant had his hood on, the rest of us got out. Nat cable-tied the attendant and carried him into the room. Better for him that way, to be a victim rather than someone assuming he'd been in on the snatch.

I parted the curtain for the chief's room and skirted around his Benz. Chai sprung the door with a crowbar. The chief was still in his uniform, and his date still in her uniform. His, the mud brown of a police uniform; hers, very short black skirt, two sizes too small white blouse, standard university outfit nationwide. She lay sprawled on her back across the chief's legs. His belt was undone, and his shoes were by the door, but that's as far as he'd got.

Nat and Beer carried the croc in, a Siamese female (Crocodylus siamensis) with a recently hatched brood. They'd left the brood back at the farm, and she wasn't happy about it. Rubber bands kept her feet tucked in and her jaws shut. They put the croc on the bed with the chief and picked the girl up, carrying her out to the van. They'd take her back to her apartment, nearby on Charoenkrung Road, while Chai and I had a chat with the chief.

We pulled the chief's clothes off, left his boxers on, got to leave a man a little dignity, and gaffer taped the croc to the chief, belly to belly. The croc's snout ended just under the chief's jaw. I had a look at the time, 2:10am. He should be waking up any moment now. Chai took up position by the door. I settled for a bench seat opposite the chief.

I noticed an ashtray on the dresser. Pavlov's dog, I lit

up, reached over, and put the ashtray on the seat beside me. The croc hadn't settled down yet. The chief's smell in her nostrils, she wriggled. The gaffer tape held but only just.

The chief moaned.

Chai stepped forward and got the bands off the croc's nose. She opened her jaws wide, blocking my view of the chief's face, and then closed them with a snap. The chief's face was still there.

He moaned again. We'd left his arms free and mouth open, just taped his feet together. If he lifted his arm, there was a good chance the croc would take it off. I was paying attention; I didn't want him dead. His eyes blinked open. His tongue licked his lips, and he reached for a bottle of water on the side table. Only the bedside lamps were on. He hadn't seen us or the croc yet, his eyes focused on the water. I realized he'd have to twist the top off to drink it.

His other arm moved and hit the croc, his head turned, and he screamed. His screaming set the croc off, and she was fighting with everything she had to get free of the tape. I had to put my hands over my ears. Chai stepped out of the room in case we needed crowd control. I got up and switched the main overhead lights on and sat down on the bench seat again.

"It's best if you stay calm. They get excited when you yell," I said, stealing another drag on the Marlboro. His head twisted as far away from the croc's jaws as his arched back would allow, and he stopped screaming. I moved sideways on the seat so he could see me better.

"How's it going?" I said, smiling.

He didn't reply and didn't smile back. He did a lot of

blinking.

"You see, we've got a problem, you and me. You've got a Siamese female crocodile strapped to you; me, I've got a father with a murder charge strapped to him. Now before we begin, there's something I have to tell you about the crocodile you're strapped to. She's no ordinary croc. She's a lie detector. We've used her on many occasions, and she's never steered us wrong yet – kind of like that octopus at the last World Cup – so if you tell me a lie, she'll know, and she's got just enough lunge room to take your face off. Do you understand?"

He gave the tiniest of nods, which under the circumstances was a reasonable response.

"Good. So the way I see it, you either swear on your life and those of all your family that you will work with me to solve the problem I've got or I walk out of here. Which will it be?"

He nodded his head.

"I'm sorry, I didn't hear that."

"I swear on my family's life and my own that I will work with you."

Chai came in, a little shake of his head, all quiet outside. Loud screams in short-time motels are best ignored.

"Chai, the chief has decided to work with us. Could you please untie the croc?"

Six cuts of Chai's Ka-Bar later, the croc was free. The chief fainted. Chai put his hand on top of the croc's snout, rubber bands around his wrist. He tapped the croc three times on the nose. As she'd been trained, she shut her jaws. He slipped the rubber bands over her snout and picked her up in his arms. He gave her belly a stroke, crocs are fond of that, most of us are.

I walked over to the side table and picked up the bottle of water the chief had been going for before he met Wanda, that's the croc's name by the way, not the chief's date. I twisted the top off and upended it over the chief's face. He came around.

"Sorry, Colonel, I really am. I hate for our relationship to start like this, but I'm short of time and long on problems. Would you like some coffee?"

"Just water." Now that the croc was gone, there was a bit of color in his voice.

I walked around back to the other side of the room and got another bottle of water from the top of the refrigerator, twisted the top off, and handed it to him. He gulped like a man who'd just walked out of a desert. In a way he had.

***

The deputy national police chief had not let the bag of money, our holdall, leave his side. He slept with it, which meant, courtesy of the bug in the bag, I was subjected to listening to him snore while the phone in the background rang. Opposite me, in our van, the Phra Pradaeng police colonel was holding the phone that was calling. Chai had his Uzi, suppressor on, loosely pointed in the direction of the cop's belly. He was sharing his seat with Wanda. The phone was answered on the fifth ring. We were on Sathorn headed for Ploenchit Road.

"What?"

"You gave me up."

"Who the fuck is this?"

"The police colonel you sold out for ninety million

baht."

"Who? I don't know what you're talking about…"

"You know exactly what I'm talking about. I've got you on tape talking about it."

"Who is this?"

"Meet me at Mahatun Plaza, on Ploenchit, second-floor car park in an hour or the Fuji restaurant meeting will be on Our Home This Morning today." There was a long pause.

"All right, make it an hour and a half. I've got to take a shower."

"One hour, you stink already; a shower won't make any difference."

I was beginning to warm to the Phra Pradaeng colonel. He hung up.

"Shit, that farang thinks he can play with me." The voice over the notebook's speakers was harsh, filled with venom. The beeped tones of a number being dialed.

I had two of our boys parked in a taxi on the street outside the deputy chief's house. They had a signal jammer with them and were on two-way radio with me.

"Jam now," I said into the radio. The signal jammers you can buy off the web, they're illegal in Thailand, but are for sale in Panthip, just not on display.

"Fucking thing." More dialing, heavy breathing. The deputy was no slim Jim; he was carrying a paunch you could feed a small nation of cannibals on. I hoped he wouldn't have a heart attack with all this stress I was handing him, not yet anyway.

"Fuck, fuck, fuck. Fucking thing." A loud bang, sounded like the phone being thrown on something. A banged door, coat hangers being slid along a rail, a loud thump on the bed, a heavy sigh, footsteps, a gun being racked, keys, footsteps, a door banged, footsteps walking away, fading, silence, footsteps coming back, "fucking money" muttered, footsteps, door slammed, loud footsteps going downstairs... he was taking the money and our bug with him. I smiled and took the headphones off.

"He's coming out. Stay on him, and keep his phone jammed all the way. He's going to Mahatun Plaza on Ploenchit, you know it? Over."

"We know it. Over."

"Nine, out." It would take the deputy police chief at least forty-five minutes to reach Ploenchit. We'd be there in another ten minutes or so, depending on traffic coming out of Sukhumvit. We were lucky on Sathorn, green lights all the way in light traffic. We kept going up Wireless Road, past Lumpini Park, my thoughts filled with Pim. All I wanted was to find her and get the hell out of all of this, but it seemed like every step forward pushed me two steps back. Focus. Do this thing, then the next, and the next until you get done doing what you thought needed doing; then you relax for a bit and do it all again – Uncle Mike talking about life. We turned onto Ruam Ruedi. Focus.

Beer parked the colonel's Benz on the second floor. We let the colonel out and waited for him to get in it. Beer closed the colonel's car door, walked over and got in our van, and went up to and parked on the third, roughly opposite to where the colonel was parked on the floor below us. Nat rigged a camera on a thin piece of PVC pipe and taped it onto the large red water pipes that ran down the outside of the building. I played with the zoom until I could read the brand on the colonel's eyeglasses. Then we sat back and waited.

The advantage of Mahatun Plaza is that to reach the entrance to the car park, you have to drive around the whole building. Beer kept watch on the guard hut with its pole barrier, a Nikon D7000 in his hands.

All that remained now was for the Phra Pradaeng police colonel to play his part. We'd had a good chat in the motel. He got a raise from what brother Dragon had been paying him. A monthly stipend that would keep him in pretty girls, fattening food and expensive alcohol for the rest of his days. He also got a signing-on bonus of ten million and the promise that I'd see if I could get him a promotion. I got his agreement to drop the murder charge against Por and play a role in the little drama that was about to unfold.

The cameras in the colonel's car showed he was sweating. It wasn't that hot outside. I stepped out of the van and lit another Marlboro. If the colonel betrayed us, we'd have little option but to kill him and the deputy national police chief. Not something you can bribe your way out of easily, if at all. The only benefit to that scenario was a death sentence as opposed to life in prison.

"Boss, the chief just turned onto Sukhumvit. He's five hundred meters from the entrance."

"Tell the guys in the taxi to stay on him but not to enter Mahatun. Circle round the block, and park in the taxi rank."

Nat repeated my instructions to the guys in the taxi. I took a last drag off the Marlboro and dropped the butt on the floor. I stepped on it, giving it a good grind. Showtime.

yorn pheuuak raawn – Throw a hot potato

THE LAWYER

Bangkok, Friday, 4 November 2011, 5:45AM

It had taken two hours to get the sound and images to where we wanted them. Reversing a piece of film and then splicing it in so it appears the reverse happened just takes time. The guy doing the work usually works for Hollywood studios for up to five hundred dollars a day. The rate for a couple of hours for this freelance stuff was a lot higher, but it was seamless.

The flood hadn't gone anywhere, it had stopped moving, but it still surrounded three-quarters of Bangkok. Slowly draining out to the gulf, east and west of the city. A bloated, muddy brown mess of stagnant effluent, polluted and toxic, similar to the contents of the DVD in my hand; the national deputy chief of police handing over a DVD for a fat envelope filled with money. The part where he rifled his thumb over the money in the envelope and licked his lips, that hadn't been altered, that was real.

The lawyer lived in a condominium on Ratchadapisek. I'd called him five minutes earlier, and he'd agreed to meet. When I told him I was in his lobby, he said to come on up.

The elevator doors opened, and he stood by an open door, gun in hand. Short, with a healthy paunch, in a white terry-cloth bathrobe and carrying a Magnum .44, his eyes owl-like behind round spectacles. I've seen better things before breakfast.

I had my hands clearly visible by my sides. I smiled. Seemed like a smart thing to do.

"Relax, Counselor, I've come to talk. We've got a bit of a problem, and I need your advice."

He pointed the gun inside his condo. "Come in. Would you like some coffee?"

"I could murder for a cup of coffee."

He glanced back at me as he headed for the kitchen. "You've got a strange choice of words, Khun Oh." He rolled his eyeballs at me, shook his head, tut-tutted, and put the gun on the counter.

"How's Mere Joom?" he said.

"She's fine," I said. "Working too hard as usual. I keep trying to get her to take a holiday with Por or just with her friends, but she always says she's too busy."

He poured me a mug of coffee and slid the sugar bowl over, sitting down on one of the stools around the counter. "So what's the problem?"

"Your cop has been telling tales."

"Who's he been talking to?"

"The cop who I was going to talk to."

"Ah."

"Yes, ah."

He took a sip of his coffee, eyeing me over the rim of the mug, wondering if I was making one of him. "And how did this information find its way to you?"

"A contact in NACC (National Anti-Corruption Commission)."

"Ah ha. Hmm."

I waited. Less is more. As NACC sunk in, his eyes widened a little, but he was good at keeping his emotions in check.

"And what information does NACC have?"

"The clips I was shown are the parts where you guys indicated that I could take care of the cop in Phra Pradaeng, personally, and without interference from you. But I was told they have the whole meeting. Also I was shown the chief handing the DVD of the meeting over to the colonel from Phra Pradaeng. Have you got a DVD player, a notebook?"

He got off his stool and collected a notebook from the sofa, put it on the counter in front me, and flipped open the lid. I popped the DVD in.

"Who in NACC has this?" he said.

"Don't know? Our friend is a secretary. She was asked to pass on a message."

"What message?"

"They want one-third, or they move forward with what they have."

"Oh."

"Yes."

"So what do you want me to do?"

257

"Call the prosecutor and the cop. Tell them to bring the money back here to you. Big Man's orders." I watched him for the confirmation. His eyebrows flicked up; his gaze focused on the DVD.

"Good. We give the eleven million to NACC…"

"You said a third."

"Yes, a third of a billion baht is roughly eleven million dollars. Sorry, I was talking US, not baht."

"What do I tell the cop and the prosecutor?"

"You show them the DVD and tell them, 'Big Man's orders.' That should work, shouldn't it?"

"The prosecutor is not going to be happy with it. He won't buy it. No way."

"I understand. It's a lot of money."

"What about the rest of Sankit's money?"

"Off the table. You guys broke the deal. The guy with the money's gone."

"You don't have it?"

"No. Strap me to a lie detector, ask the same question, you'll get the same answer."

"Hmm, I believe you."

More sipping of coffee. It was good coffee, I needed it, the couple hours I'd snatched while the computer guy did his thing had worn off fast.

"It's the prosecutor's choice. If he wants to be seen on video agreeing to pervert the course of justice, all power to him." I raised the mug in salute.

"I'll talk to him. Wait here." He took his cell from the counter and started walking towards what I guessed was his bedroom. I sipped more coffee. The whole NACC thing was bullshit, of course, but it was such a huge bluff, given the circumstances, it lent credence to the story. When you're out of options, you take what you're given.

There was a bowl of croissants on the table, smelled like they were fresh out of the oven. I was starving, but he hadn't invited me to breakfast, just coffee. Eating one of them would be rude. I felt a little light-headed. I got off the stool and stood, swaying a little. I'd stiffened up, my joints felt like they were made of mismatched rusty metal parts that hadn't been lubricated for a while. I walked across his living room. The view over the balcony was east. A fat, deep orange ball of sun hung on the horizon of skyscrapers, behind the Cultural Center, the sky above a dark blue, clear, no clouds. East. Somewhere out there, Pim.

"The prosecutor has agreed," he said, as he walked over and sat down on the sofa. I sat down on an easy chair opposite him. It felt better than standing up.

"Are you all right?"

"Yeah, I'm fine, just haven't had much sleep lately."

"This thing with NACC. You sure you can bury it? I mean really sure?"

"Mere Joom's handling it."

"Ah. Okay."

"Can you handle the cop?"

"Between the prosecutor and me I think we can come up with a case, yes."

"Okay then. Would you mind if I send one of my guys to pick up the money. I could use some sleep, and I've got a long drive ahead of me."

"No problem, the only other thing would be my fee."

"Your fee?"

"Yes, Chance, my fee. You honestly don't think I believe any of this crap you fed me this morning, do you?"

I didn't answer that. I figured whichever answer I gave would make me look like an idiot.

He leaned forward, knees together, elbows on knees, hands clasped, a polite little smile on his face.

"You're lucky, Khun Oh. The cop's a known yellow-shirt sympathizer overdue for a transfer to an inactive post for the duration. We're moving someone else in. This is a bit earlier than we had planned, but we can use it anyway. I'm not worried about being on the tape. I'm a lawyer, people expect me to do shit like that – with that advertising I'll increase my rates." The polite smile wasn't so little anymore.

"How much?"

"Five million."

I didn't insult him by asking baht or dollars. "Done. But I can only settle with you on Monday evening, and you have to hand over all of the cash this morning."

"Done." He reached over, and we shook on it. I stood up. Saw bright little pinpricks of light dancing in my eyes, it was an effort to draw a breath.

"You know, Khun Oh, you really don't look good. You're sort of a gray color." He looked pink, but I wasn't going to tell him that.

"One other thing, check the cop didn't slip any counterfeit into the mix. Our friends over at the NACC have the most modern counting machines in the country. I'll send my guy at noon."

He walked me out to the elevator and waited while it arrived. I got in, final smiles, the doors closed. I put a hand against the wall of the elevator for support. It was very difficult to breathe. The doors opened to the lobby. I pushed myself off the wall and walked out. Each step felt like someone was stabbing me in the ribs with a blunt hot knife. I made it to the forecourt.

Chai pulled up with the Vito, the auto door opening. I started a step, but my leg wouldn't cooperate. I was wondering about it when the road reached up and hit me in the face.

***

The first thing I thought of when I woke up was that I'd missed the appointment with Suchada. Cold sweat doesn't get close to describing the feeling. Freefall into a dark void filled with hideously grotesque gargoyle-like creatures screaming and laughing all the way down, closer but still too heartwarming. I grabbed my cell off the bedside table. 10:40AM 4-11-11. A machine beside me might have been responsible for the sounds of screaming in my waking thoughts.

Dr. Tom came rushing in and went directly to the machine, glancing at me as he twiddled knobs and flicked his eyes back and forth over a printout.

"You're awake, good. Are you feeling any pain?"

"No."

"Good, and how is the breathing, easier?"

I took a deep breath, easing it in slowly, anticipating the pain, but it didn't hurt. I was impressed. I tried another.

"Yes, much easier, no pain."

"I'd be disappointed if there was. You've got enough codeine and muscle relaxant in you to sedate a diva."

"Are divas hard to sedate?"

He gave me a look. "Obviously your mental faculties are normal, and your vital signs are only mildly in the red."

"What happened?"

"A hybrid spontaneous tension pneumothorax."

"Tom, please."

"Collapsed lung from a fractured rib splinter, from what I can tell with the equipment here." Doctors always talk with disclaimers attached.

"Tom, I've got to be able to move around for another twelve hours at least. After that it doesn't matter. I should be able to rest. Can you do that for me?"

He stepped back, hands on the bed, head hanging down, almost like he was going to do a push up. He raised his head; his glasses slipped down his nose, which he wrinkled to push his glasses to where he could see me properly. He looked ridiculous and deadly serious.

"Chance, I should operate immediately. Would have done so already, but Chai stopped me. I've had a look for the splinter but couldn't find it. I did find the hole in your lung. Judging from the size of that hole, the splinter is quite large, perhaps over two centimeters, or it could be inside your lung. Without an x-ray I can't tell. Chai tells me a trip to the hospital is out of the question, so no x-ray. The short answer is I can kill the pain and put enough speed in you for you to operate at a reasonable level of coherent thought; however, you could drop dead at any moment." A definitive disclaimer delivered.

"And you can't smoke anymore."

That last one really hurt. I reached out and put my hand on his shoulder, giving it a good squeeze. I understand.

"Fair enough. Tom, I need you to get on with what you need to do to get me up and running."

My cell flashed. An SMS from the lawyer – your guy can come over – brown v.angry @55 money – be careful. I am sure he had my best interests in mind and not his five million dollar payday. Five in Thai is 'ha', so 55 means haha, haha means funny – translation – the cop was pissed at the counterfeit found in his bag – I was sure the lawyer and the prosecutor would be on him to replace it with the good stuff. Shit happens.

"Is Chai around?"

"He's on the porch. I'll get him."

"Thanks, Tom, and give me a moment alone with Chai, please."

He walked out into the living room. I was in the guest house in Paknam. Beckham stuck his head around the door.

"How you feeling?"

"Good. How are you getting on?"

"Not bad," he said in English and grinned. 'Not bad' translated literally into Thai means 'Not not bad', it was an old joke deserving of a grin for the moment chosen to replay it.

"How's the takeover going."

"Everything under control. Not a shot fired, and we've taken over sixty percent of their known people off the streets. We've taken over eighty percent of their businesses. We'll have the rest of their businesses later today. Aroon and Chainarong are holed up at their homes, surrounded by their hardcore guys. Everyone else is either locked up at the warehouse or running." I could hear Mother's voice in the summary.

Chai appeared in the doorway.

"The lawyer's got the money. Can you pick it up?"

His eyebrows flicked up, and he left.

"Got to get back. Mother's hourly briefing in ten. I have to get ready," Beckham said, the fear of screwing up at one of Mother's executive briefings palpable in his voice. Worth another grin. Everyone was terrified of Mother. Funny thing is, she's never raised her voice at anyone that I can remember, not once.

Dr. Tom slipped a needle into the top of my hand. Needle connected to a valve, connected to a female plug. Four injections into the female plug later, he handed me a small leather case, looked like a diary.

"One every four hours."

"Got it and, Tom?"

"Yes?"

"Thanks."

He gave me a hard look, as hard as a Cambridge-educated, overweight doctor who's also a friend can. I smiled at him, trying to make him believe I was coming back alive, Aunt Dao's voice in my head.

I had a shower. A long, hot shower. Got dressed in casual combat gear, hot under the body armor, and went to tell Khun Preecha, my real father-in-law, his death sentence. He was sitting out by the pool, under the sala drinking iced-tea. I had made love to his daughter in that sala one night. I gave him a wai.

"Oh, sit down and join me in a glass of this excellent tea."

"Por krub, yesterday I confirmed that Suchada has

Pim. She wants a billion baht and you delivered to her before eight this evening." Straight at it is the only way.

"Did she say dead or alive?"

"No."

"Wants to do it herself, and Sankit?"

"Still no word from him or about him, but I did briefly speak to Pim."

"Good, that's very good. Oh, your mother is a wonderful hostess. Both Noot and I have enjoyed our time here. Please pass on my heartfelt thanks to her and tell her that I hope to have the opportunity to host Por and her soon at my house in the mountains."

"I will, Por."

"What time do we leave?"

"I'm waiting for Chai to get back, and then we go."

"All right, then. If you'll excuse me, I must spend some time talking with Noot about things."

"Of course, Por." I raised my hands again in a wai. This man who'd never killed anyone and only had good thoughts about his fellow man had taken the news of his impending death with a calm that even the most cynical mean-spirited person would have to respect.

Mother's team had whittled the list of phone numbers on Here Leng's phone down to the number that had called him informing him that Goong had raped Michael Sullivan's son. Supot, Virote's middle son, had made the call. Supot, who according to Khemkaeng, was out of our business and going to be a fashion designer. More questions than answers came from the information, as is usually the case.

ohm phra bpra thaan maa phuut gaaw mai cheuua – Hold a Buddha in your mouth, speak, I will still not believe

LAST CHANCE RESORT

Aranyaprathet, Friday, 4 November 2011, 3:15PM

Three black Mercedes-Benz Vitos, all with black-tinted windows and the same number plate, are something that every cop in Thailand will ignore. The more adventurous among them might make a call to a superior, who most likely will reprimand him for being an idiot. None will stop such a caravan if it is preceded by a police car. We had made Aran in record time.

According to Mother's source in crime suppression, the mobile phone in Aran had stayed on and hadn't moved. Beer and Nat had been dispatched to Aran by Chai while I was sleeping. According to base station position and the phone's signal, the address was a resort called Last Chance Resort, I know, but truth is stranger than fiction. I'm sure the owners meant it was the last resort before Cambodia, but it didn't inspire me, let's leave it at that.

Still, a last chance is better than no chance. Work with what you have. It was a small resort set in about ten acres, twenty rai, out of the city on Route 3446. A feature of the property was its location, the back ending in Cambodia. According to the man who'd answered the call to the landline in reception, they were closed for renovations.

The driveway had a faded red-striped metal pole across it, tied off with a chain, padlock attached. Nat got out with the bolt cutters. I flashed on Chai cutting the padlock on Sankit's gate when we snatched the Berlin Wall art. Almost a week since I was supposed to leave on a honeymoon with my new bride. Just a week, it felt like a lifetime.

I drove slowly, Khun Preecha in the seat beside me, and nine holdalls with the thirty-three million dollars split between them – all clean money – in the back of the van. On the middle seat, armed for war, Chai, Nat and Beer.

The red-orange colored dirt road that passed for a driveway had deep ruts the Vito could get stuck in. On either side were Eucalyptus trees, bamboo, and scrub with glimpses of paddy field between them. I focused on driving, keeping one set of wheels on the hard verge and the other on the middle of the road. The road curved around to the right and opened to a clearing with a large tree in the middle of it, a single-storey, half-concrete and half-wooden house with a single door off to the left. The road continued straight ahead. A sign above the door said 'Reception' in Thai, of course. The door was open.

I stopped the van between the tree and the house and waited, counting off three hundred, slowly scanning the view in front of me.

Nothing happened.

"I'm going to take a look. Please, stay in the van." I got out slowly and sprinted for the window of the house. Getting behind the wall, I peeked in. It was empty. I skirted around to the back of the building, nothing behind it but some trash and dried scrub. I went back around to the front, signaling Preecha to stay in the van.

The room was cool inside. On the table, a phone on top of a typed note – Call me when you get this. I checked the contact list. No contacts or phone numbers in the phone. Clever. I pressed call.

It rang twice. I was trying to stop my heart beating so hard, thinking about the splinter, had to get this job done.

"Hello, this is Oh."

"Chance, how nice of you to call. Please pass the phone to Preecha."

"He's outside in the van guarding the money. Where's Pim?"

"I believe I said I wanted to talk with Preecha."

"I'll get him." I went back out to the van and walked around to Preecha's side. He lowered the window.

"She wants to talk to you." I handed the phone up, careful not to accidently disconnect. He took it and held it to his ear.

"Yes," he said and frowned. "Blue, her favorite color was blue." He paused, said, "All right," and handed the phone back to me.

"Yes."

"Drive up the road about three hundred meters. You'll come to a fork. Take the left fork, and drive for another hundred meters. Stop when you reach the big tree on the hill."

"I want to talk to Pim now."

"That's not possible. She's waiting for you at the tree. I'm watching her through the sights of a very powerful rifle. If you don't do what I say, I will start shooting."

"I'm leaving now."

"Take the phone, and call me when you get to the tree on the hill."

"Understood."

I put the van in 'Drive' and eased out of the clearing, keeping the speed at twenty kilometers per hour. The road climbed when I took the left fork and climbed sharper after that. Fifty meters further I saw the tree she was talking about. I pulled to a stop next to it. The road continued around and then down the hill, which sloped gently down for about eight hundred meters. In front of the tree was rice paddy, full grown, golden, ready to be harvested. At the bottom where the hill rose again a single tree stood in the middle of the rice paddies. A tall thin tree, something strange about it, I grabbed the glasses and focused in. Pim, moving her body around, trying to get free of the rope around her. I zoomed in closer. Definitely Pim.

I called Suchada, putting the phone on speaker.

"Happy now? If you stay calm, then everything will be fine. Preecha will drive the van down the road. You walk to the girl, untie her, and make your way back uphill. I have two expert snipers on you, and I know how to shoot just as well as your mother does. If Preecha turns back or you interfere in any way, I'll shoot her first and then you. Do you understand?" There was more than a hint of 'shrill' in her tone. I'd suspected on the first call, but I knew listening to this she'd lost it, gone over the edge, loco, nuts, looped de loop, or in Thai, 'ba'. Crazy. Bad news, smart and crazy, worst kind of enemy.

"I understand. I will tell Khun Preecha and start down the hill."

I sat there for a moment. I looked at him, he at me, I waied and got down from the van.

The rice may have been golden in color, but it looked sparse. I made my way over the hard-packed earth that separated one paddy from another. I heard the van move back onto the gravel dirt road. It came into view slowly over my left shoulder, keeping pace with me, the view partially blocked by strands of eucalyptus on the edge of the road.

The sun was at my back, an advantage depending on where the shooters were. I'd been scanning the opposite hill, as well as you can when you're walking down one, but hadn't seen anything yet. Keeping an even pace, steady without running. Didn't want anyone too excited, not with so many fingers on triggers.

As I closed the gap to Pim, I wondered how far Chai had got. He had bailed out just before we took the left fork. I started looking on the right for places we could take cover. Chai would be coming down and in from the right as fast as he could. Nat and Beer were somewhere over on my left, keeping comms to a minimum; we didn't know what kind of scanners they might have.

The elevation of the opposite hill made cover difficult. The best thing we'd be able to do would be to run for the jungle on either side of the paddy. They'd have thought the same thing when they planned this and expect me to go for the jungle on my right, it was slightly closer. If it was me, I'd put a man in there. I'd give us time to reach the jungle and then take us out by silenced weapon. I was relying on it.

Pim stood up straight, chin in the air, only a few hundred meters between us. Her eyes on me all the way down. It was hard not to speed up, but I had to give Chai time. She looked strong.

"Seven – right clear – tango neutralized." Timing is everything. The phone rang. I was a hundred meters from Pim.

"Tell Preecha to speed up. If he doesn't speed up, I will start shooting. And you slow down."

"Khun Suchada, I cannot tell Khun Preecha anything. He's in the van. We're following your instructions exactly. If you start shooting, he'll turn around. Please stay calm."

"I am calm. I'm watching you right now, ready to pull the trigger. Tell Preecha to speed up, or she dies right now."

The van off my shoulder speeded up, reaching the bottom of the hill before I did, and continued up the hill, red brown dust billowing out behind it.

"Khun Suchada, do you see? The van is moving fast. Do you see?" She hung up. Khun Preecha had about a six-hundred-meter drive to the top of the opposite hill. I walked faster. Each step closer notched the tension up. The tree was thin enough that a large section of Pim's back would be an easy target from up the hill. Any moment I expected her chest to explode. Raw fear, true dread, all life, all hope, ripped away in an instant.

I reached her. She was tied by her throat, under her

armpits, around her thighs and her ankles. It wasn't rope, it was white electrical cord like the kind you use to wire a house. I stood behind her, the phone rang, and I ignored it, busy with the wire cutters at Pim's throat.

"Pim, listen to me very carefully, okay?"

She nodded her head.

"After I've cut you free, I'm going to put my body armor over you, and then I want you to immediately start walking fast to your left. No hugs or hellos, okay, just move fast towards the jungle. Chai's in there, so it's safe. Okay?" One curt nod, eyes focused, looking pissed off. If she wasn't gagged, she'd be swearing a docker into embarrassment.

The last wire around her ankles gave. I dropped the cutters and took off the body armor I was wearing. Standing up, moving between Pim and the tree, I got her arms in it.

"Okay, go, walk fast, but don't run. Stay on the top of the paddy." The phone in my hand rang again. I answered it.

"Walk back up the hill. If you go closer to the jungle, I will shoot."

"One approaching target in twenty meters," Preecha said in my earphone, "two vehicles. I can see her talking to you. There's a shooter on top of one of the vehicles."

"Khun Suchada, please stay calm. Khun Preecha is arriving now. You see?" The line went dead. It was about sixty meters to the edge of the jungle. I couldn't see Chai, but he'd be there. We kept moving sideways, walking fast.

"One – Suchada is pointing a shotgun at me, and I think she's just told…"

"Run, run, run now," I shouted, and Pim took off.

Pim couldn't just run, she could fly. She'd been a two-hundred-meter hurdler at university; a dry rice paddy with earth dykes didn't faze her one bit. She took off like she meant it, head down, arms pumping, leg straight out as she hurdled the dykes. No way I could keep up with her. She crashed through a space between a clump of eucalyptus trees. I could hear her, but she'd disappeared. A bullet smacked into the tree in front of me, cutting a branch off. Big bullets, the crack echoing in the valley as I dived for cover in the jungle.

"Behind you."

I turned around, and Chai sat next to Pim behind a tree about four meters away. Shooting further up the hill was fierce. Chai leading, Pim in the middle, I brought up the rear, and we went further into the jungle. The undergrowth was like the rice, sparse, easy for moving in, hard to live on. As we ran, I noticed a body wearing camouflage, face down, almost hidden under a bush. Pim hadn't seen it. We'd guessed right.

I wasn't worried about the shooting I could hear up the hill, explosions were another matter, but I hadn't heard any yet. The shooting increased – sounded like at least three weapons.

"One. This is nine. Can you hear me?" Silence. Chai started digging a foxhole. "One, this is nine. Can you hear me?" I repeated it a few times more, but the result was the same. The shooting up the hill stopped.

According to the images we'd seen on Google Earth, a track ran from the right fork of the road we'd been on. It went all the way to the border with Cambodia roughly four hundred feet from where we were. I was watching the track. Preecha should be coming down it at any moment. At least that had been the plan. Losing comms wasn't part of the plan, but shit happens, particularly when you least need it to.

But we'd done it. I looked at her. She didn't look scared. She looked pissed off. She looked beautiful. Focus. Keep on the move. Keep thinking, when people are shooting at you, it's the difference between living and dying, excluding plain bad luck. Nothing moved on the track. I expected the second Vito with Beckham and ten of our guys in it to come in from the dirt road at any moment with Dr. Tom behind it in the third Vito.

"Nine? Nine?" It was Preecha.

"Nine, this is one. Sorry I knocked the comms off. They've left. Tell your mother I want one of these vans."

I laughed. Chai gave me a sharp look. I grinned at him, got a grin back, and then he resumed position, Uzi pointed up the track.

I love it when a plan comes together.

***

Never discount luck, good or bad, it's going to want a part in the play. Luck had played a huge part in what we'd pulled off, and we knew it. I'd called Mother before leaving Aran and shared the good news. The move against Aroon and Chainarong was going better than planned, most of their boys under guard at two warehouses, one in Bang Phli and one in Klong Toey. Between them, Aroon and Chainarong could put about sixty decent guys into the field. We had just over a hundred, and Virote's boys, my new allies, Khemkaeng and Damrong, about sixty between them.

Mother's plan had been simple. Grab as many 'hard-core' guys from either Aroon or Chainarong as possible. Do it fast. Tagged numbers and locations. Get in, get out, bag and tag. Drop them off at the warehouses. All mobiles collected, cross-reference numbers, select more targets, rinse and repeat. Simple, but highly effective. It had just passed five in the evening. We were on the motorway heading into Bangkok. It had been twelve hours since Mother had kicked off the early morning raids. Twelve hours later, we had fifty-three of Aroon's and Chainarong's people under guard one for one with our guys.

Their businesses shut down, holed up in their homes with twenty of our guys waiting outside, reality for the old guard. How to take them down without too much bloodshed was the next step. Most likely we'd find a Brutus, a Judas, someone willing to stab a knife in a back for peace and a piece of the action. But that was tomorrow. Tonight was to celebrate.

We'd won.

mat lek gap thoong meuu gam ma yee – Cover the iron with a glove made of velvet

A Promise Kept

Paknam, Friday, 4 November 2011, 7:15PM

I shot up another one of Dr. Tom's cocktails and went back into the bedroom. Running around a rice paddy hadn't done my ribs any good. No bitching from me, though, Pim was lying on the bed, watching me towel my hair. I had her back, and that's all that mattered. I lay down beside her. She snuggled in, head on my chest.

"Did you smoke while I wasn't here?"

I just knew she was going to ask me that. "Yes."

She slapped me on the stomach. I didn't feel a thing. "It doesn't matter anyway, but I wish you'd quit."

"What do you mean it doesn't matter anymore?"

"I'm pregnant."

"For sure?" I leaned forward and kissed the top of her head.

"Sure, I haven't had Dr. Tom check yet, I'll ask him later if he's still up, but I missed my period last week, and I feel different. I'm sure." She sat up to look at me, one hand on the bed, the other on my heart.

"What happened won't happen again. I'll never go anywhere again without leaving you and our child in safe hands."

"I had a lot of time to think in that room. I expected my period the day we were flying to London. When it hadn't come by the second day I knew I was going to have your baby. All I could think about was how to protect him." I noticed the 'him'; she'd sworn to deliver a son. I didn't doubt her word.

"I've got a bit more business that has to be taken care of, and then I've got to spend a few days in hospital."

Her eyes widened.

"It's okay, I didn't want to tell you earlier, but it's been a hard week. I'll bore you with all the details some time, but after I come out of hospital, we'll take off. I've got a nice safe place in mind, down south, in Thailand, and it should be cool for a few months yet. There's something else I have to tell you." I had asked Preecha for time alone with Pim, to tell her the news that the people who she had thought of as parents were the people who had stolen her as a child. He'd agreed with me that it would be better.

"This is hard to say, so I'm just going to give it to you straight. Suchada and Sankit were not your real mother and father." I waited, watching her face.

Her eyes hardened. "Where are my parents?"

"Your mother was killed when you were a baby, and your father is alive. I've met him. Did you hear Suchada talking about 'Preecha'?"

"Yes, but only when we were driving to Aran."

"He's your father," I said and leaned forward, my eyes centimeters from hers, stroking her hair. "He's a great guy. He put his life on the line for yours today. I like him a lot, and you will too. You have a sister, Noot, and she's a wonderful, smart lady, older than you, in her early thirties. Your father is downstairs with Mother, and he's looking forward to meeting you very much."

A tear rolled down her cheek.

"Don't cry, baby."

She shook her head, sniffed. "I'm okay. I've always wondered why she hated me so much. Now I know. It's better. Would you mind if I see him now?"

"No, it'd make me happy. I've got some urgent business that needs dealing with, but it should only take a few hours. I'll be back before midnight. Your father and you have a lot to talk about, take whatever time you need."

***

"Hey, great job," I said. I was on the phone to Khemkaeng, the line had just connected.

"Credit to Mere Joom. She is one smart woman."

"Well, she told me that you and Damrong were smart guys, so I guess that makes a great team. I've got a seafood barbeque and enough pretty waitresses that you wouldn't want to bring your wife waiting for us over at Big Tiger's – in a couple of hours, okay? I'll SMS you when I am on the way."

"Sure, can do, Damrong?"

"Of course, I was going to call him next. Is he with you?"

"Yes, and he says, 'Great.' See you in a couple of hours."

I disconnected.

The Maserati, fully restored to its pre-bus-encounter condition, throbbed. I sat listening to it for a little. I'd missed the sound.

Supot was staying at a condo in Soi Maha Lek Luang 2, on the twelfth floor. The route there was dry, and inner city traffic still light.

There were four condo units per floor. Supot was in 12C. I rang the bell. Looked inside the peephole, nothing but a curved corridor. I rang the doorbell again and knocked. Chai took out a shaped charge, the kind we'd used in Khao Yai. He tore the adhesive off the back, stuck it on the door next to the lock, and the elevator pinged. Supot walked out, head down looking at the keys in his hand. He looked up and saw me. He stopped, mouth open, like he was going to say something. He looked at the door, Chai, back at me, and ran for the stairs.

"Supot, stop. We're not here to kill you."

He stopped by the door to the stairs.

"Really, I just want to know what the hell's been going on, that's all."

"How did you find me," he said. He hadn't moved from the exit door to the stairs, still had it cracked open like he might bolt any moment. I felt like a hostage negotiator guy, talking someone off a ledge.

"Your phone, base stations, picacells, you know." I shrugged.

"From the SMS?" he said.

"No, from the calls."

He looked confused. "But I never called you."

"You called Here Leng, though. Hey, can we have this conversation in your condo? I just want to talk, but I'm under doctor's orders to take it easy, stay off my feet as much as possible. Can we do that?" I smiled. He walked across from the door. Chai removed the charge as Supot put the key in the lock.

"Sure, sorry, Chance, come in. I understand you've made peace with my brothers? Come in, please." We took our shoes off and went in.

Supot played with dimmers and lit the room up with soft tones, standing by the switch with an expectant look on his face.

It was a comfortable two-bedroom condo with a living room large enough to swing a cat, one with a long tail. A pink sofa ran along the wall of the living room. Scarlet and orange cushions rested on it. Pop art covered lacquered cement walls, and more than one earthen jar had twigs in it; high-end haute couture with five-star hotel bar overtones, a cliché of designs. I wondered if that was the point, and maybe I was missing something.

"Do you like it?"

"Yes, it works. This your place?"

"My home away from home. Please sit down. Would you like some tea?"

"I'd prefer a single malt or a cognac if you've got one." I sat down on the sofa, it was comfortable enough. Chai stood by the hallway to the door. Supot was by the counter next to what I guessed was a small kitchen.

"On the rocks or straight up?"

"If it's malt, one rock, cognac straight up. Why did

you call Here Leng?"

He didn't say anything, but walked around the counter with a balloon of cognac in one hand and a diet coke in the other. He handed me the cognac. "Cheers, congratulations on your wedding. Sorry I couldn't be there."

"No problem and thank you. Why did you call Here Leng? It was two days before my wedding, you called him. Why?"

He sat down opposite me, forearms on his knees, diet coke cupped in his hands. "I was angry with Goong. He caused me a lot of problems. I called Here Leng because I was angry with David being raped."

"So you know that Goong raped David?"

"No, Goong didn't rape David. I told you that already."

"So you sent me those SMS's?"

"Yes, who else did you think it might be?"

"I didn't know. I was just kind of pissed off wondering why someone who called themself my friend wouldn't just pick up a phone and give me a call instead of sending me cryptic fucking SMS's."

"Sorry, I was scared."

"Apology accepted, and I understand. You were right to be scared, but I've got to know the whole story."

"Wow. Okay. Um, so you know I'm gay, right, but while Dad was alive I was in the closet…"

I realized he was waiting for me to confirm that I understood he was gay. "Got it, you're gay. How does that fit into what's been going on?"

"Michael Sullivan and I were having an affair. We'd been seeing each other for a while. Back home with Dad

I was middle son, voice of reason between my brothers. But living here I was free of all of that. I met Michael over a year ago. It was at some charity event for one of his companies. Anyway, we hit it off, and one thing led to another. We were very discreet, but sometimes we went out together. Most of the time we stayed here." He shrugged and sighed. "We had a good time together, a lot of laughing and fun." He seemed to drift away, thinking, and took a sip of diet coke.

"Goong?"

"One night Goong was out with his boys. I was staging the launch of a new collection of mine. Susan, Michael's wife, was away visiting her brother and had taken David with her. Michael was there with me. Anyway, Goong and his boys ruined the show, laughing and making rude comments at the models and the designs. It made me mad, so I called Here Leng and told him what Goong had done to the sheriff's son. Damrong got mad with me about something. Some small thing, it happened all the time. Petty things. Anyway, Damrong told Goong that I had ratted him out to his father. This all happened before Songkran."

"What did Goong do?"

"Nothing for a while and then Michael did something very stupid. Michael didn't know Goong, didn't know what had happened, and I didn't try to explain. He could never understand our world. He went to Goong's massage parlor. Purely an accident. God, of all the gay massage parlors in Bangkok and he had to choose Goong's. Goong recognized him and had him videotaped."

"Goong was blackmailing Michael?"

"No. Goong didn't think that far. Goong sent me the video of Michael getting extras from one of his rent boys. He sent it to me hand delivery at Dad's house. It was late, just before midnight. It came with a red rose and a note, 'With Love...' written on it. I put it in the DVD and saw Michael with another man. At the end it cut to Goong lying on his back laughing. He broke my heart. We'd been talking about living together when Dad died. When I saw Goong laughing, I lost it. I got in my car and drove as far away as I could."

"Which of your brothers found the video?"

"Khemkaeng. Actually, it was his wife. She turned on the television, and there it was. She told Khemkaeng I had left gay porno on the television, and he called me. I was very down, angry and bitter. I hope you understand me, Chance. I told him it wasn't porn, it was a blackmail tape from Goong, a threat against our family." Supot looked at the floor between his feet. "Khemkaeng watched the tape and called Goong. Goong told him who Sullivan was and what he was to me. I denied it, if I could take that back, I would, but I denied it." His voice cracked. He coughed, cleared his throat.

"Anyway, Khemkaeng found out that Michael was signatory, advisor, and auditor at a number of large, publicly listed companies and that Michael was married. Khemkaeng blackmailed Michael, told me he was doing it. I didn't call Michael or see him. I changed my phone numbers and stayed with Dad while he was dying. It was funny. One day while I was bathing him, he said make sure you only wash what you need to. I asked him what he meant, and he replied he was just joking, he knew I was gay, and he didn't mind. He understood that I wanted out."

"Your father was special. I don't say that to bullshit you. He really was."

"Yes, he was. I miss him, and I'm free at last. It's a weird feeling."

"What happened with David?"

A tear rolled down his cheek. "Michael came to see me here. He told me he was going to stop paying and helping Khemkaeng, he was coming out to his wife and son. He said he was living a lie and he wanted to live with me. We spent the night together. Early the next morning he got a call from Susan, she was at Bumrungrad Hospital with David. I think you know the rest."

"What was it that Damrong got mad at you for?"

"Sorry...?"

"You said Damrong told Goong you had ratted him out because you did something to him. What was it?"

"You remember the wedding of the sheriff in Chorakhe Yai?"

"Yes, Damrong mentioned it the other day as well. He said Tum left with Chang Noi's sister, implying Chang Noi might have been the one to turn Tum against us. I didn't stay long at the wedding, so I don't know."

"Damrong was there with his first wife, Penny, you know her. His second wife, Som, showed up. Damrong was mad, slapped her, and told her to go home. She went off with Mai." The raised eyebrows, tilt of his head and hands spread wide told the rest of the story of Mai and Som. I looked at the time on my cell phone. 9:15pm.

I stood up. He stayed seated, looking up at me.

"I've got to go. Go to Milan, Khun Supot. Change your name, live your dream, you're free now. Thanks for the drink. Do me a favor and don't call or message anyone tonight. Stay here. It's a matter of a life and death."

He blinked when I said death, knowing from my face I was talking about him.

I walked out, put my shoes on. Chai and I didn't talk on the way down to the car. That was normal. I knew what he was thinking, and I think he knew what I was thinking. We got in the car; he started the engine.

"Let's go get some seafood over at Big Tiger's," I said.

Big Tiger's is a seafood restaurant out in Bang Pu by the sea. Located at the end of a long concrete pier that you can drive a truck down, it used to belong to, unsurprisingly, a guy called 'Big Tiger'. He died last year during the riots. Chai parked on the pier in front of the restaurant.

I was dressed casually in a light cotton shirt and trousers. This was pleasure, blow off a bit of steam, get to know Khemkaeng and Damrong better. For them a little reward for a job well done. Got to keep people motivated. I hadn't told anyone about Pim being pregnant, but I reckoned that cat would be out of the doctor's bag as soon as Pim confirmed with Dr. Tom. He'd be too scared to keep something like that from Mother.

Big Tiger's is a five-storey restaurant you could comfortably hold several Olympic events in, were you of a mind. We'd sectioned off an area on the third floor balcony and closed that floor to everyone but staff and our party.

The balcony at the rear of the restaurant looks out to the gulf. Below was a small concrete landing for fishing boats to pull up and deliver the catch to the restaurant. A reputation for fresh seafood is an important thing in Thailand, I guess anywhere. The landing was empty, brown sea sloshing calmly, a pleasant slip, slap, slop slip, slap melody to the salt air.

I moved away from the barbeque, the heat coming off it in waves moved along by the soft breeze. It was a perfect night. Not a hint of rain, a deep blue sky, stars shining bright, still waiting for a moon, and a dark ocean in front. Like the world ended at this balcony.

I got a beer from the cool box and leaned over the balcony, my back to the room. I heard their entry but pretended not to, show them my back, that I trusted them with it.

"Hey, Khun Oh, we're here."

I turned and smiled, arms spread on the balcony rail, hands empty except for the bottle of Singh. They were both wearing suits.

"Khun Khemkaeng, Khun Damrong, welcome. What are you drinking?" I raised the Singh I was sipping on.

"Sure, beer's good, and Khun Oh, please call me Ken, and my brother's nickname is Dan."

I flashed on Dan slumped over the steering wheel of the taxi as the klong lit up around him. These two had caused that.

"Cool, Ken. Dan." We shook hands, a new generation 'inter' kind of thing. I handed them each a beer.

"Chai not joining us?" Dan – Damrong said.

"No, he's got some stuff to take care of for Mere Joom, but he might drop by later if we're still here."

"And where are all these pretty waitresses you

mentioned," he said, winking at Ken.

"They'll be along, when we've eaten. I thought we could eat, drink and talk ourselves a bit first, and then later we'll invite some guests of the female persuasion to soften the company. Work?"

"Works – sounds good. This seafood looks delicious. Shall we start? I could eat a horse."

"Sure, get some of that shrimp on there. We'll do the squid and the fish on the other side. Here, I got it." I started putting shrimp, squid and fish on the barbeque.

"So what's the day's tally? How many of them did you get, Ken?" I said.

"At the last briefing from Mother and count from the warehouses, we've taken in all but fifteen. Ten from Aroon and five from Chainarong remaining. We have solid information that those few are with them at their houses. We've cut the phone lines, electricity and water to their homes. They won't last more than a couple of days. Already two of Aroon's guys quit. Mother said they asked to switch gangs."

"That's excellent. How's the situation out at the warehouses?"

"Not a problem. Completely under control. I have my guys on them one for one and same with Dan over at the Klong Toey warehouse. Their people aren't going anywhere. Maybe you should turn that shrimp over. It looks like it's nearly done on that side."

"I think you're right. Shit, it's hot. You any good with these things," I said, waving the tongs at Ken. I took another swig of the ice-cold Singh beer. It was delicious, perfect with seafood.

"Sure am, give me those things."

I gave Ken the tongs and smiled, thinking I wish he'd chosen another name, I hate being reminded of the people I've killed.

"Dan, how's your beer?"

"Yeah, I could use another," he said, waggling the bottle at me. I grinned. Just three normal guys having a barbeque.

I'd chosen a 9mm Beretta 92FS with a Gemtech suppressor for this job. Reliable, accurate, relatively low recoil. It's a combat proven weapon, and this particular one had been stripped, oiled, and assembled by me – it wouldn't jam when I needed it.

I fished out a couple of bottles of Singh.

"How's that shrimp coming?" I said and handed him one beer and the other to Dan. The moon rose fat and yellow out over the gulf.

"Good, nearly there, maybe another minute," Ken said. He was doing a good job; the fat long river prawns, size of lobsters, grilled to perfection.

I went back to fetch myself a beer. Walked back over and stood next to Dan.

"Cheers," I said, raising my beer. He raised his beer bottle to mine, and the necks clinked as I brought the Beretta up with my right and shot him in his left temple. As he fell, I took a step forward. Ken still hadn't realized his brother had been shot, focused on the shrimp. I shot him just behind the ear. He fell forward onto the barbeque. I pulled him off, the acrid smell of burnt hair mixing with the smell of the roasting shrimp.

I sat down at the table we'd prepared, twisted the top

off a bottle of Hennessy Cognac XO, and filled half a glass with it. I put the gun on the table. Chai, Nat and Beer came out of the restaurant, Nat and Beer carrying body bags. I took a long swallow of the cognac. Chai poured himself one and held the glass out. I lifted mine, and we touched glasses.

Nat and Beer had the first body bag unfurled next to Dan. He died happy, with a full beer in his hand, looking forward to tasty seafood and a night of debauchery with pretty women. There're worse ways to go.

"Wait." Beer was about to close the bag.

I took my iPhone from my pocket and walked over. Zoomed in to show just the floor, the body bag, and the face. I took a few pictures, my hand still shaking with the killing, but I needed at least one clear shot to keep a promise.

"Okay, you can take them away. Drive carefully."

Nat and Beer each grabbed a bag and dragged them into the restaurant.

I checked the photos. At least three were clear. Good technology the iPhone.

I took another long swallow, enjoying the burn. Chai slid across a packet of Marlboro. I thought about Dr. Tom. Fuck it.

It tasted great, and I didn't die.

naam loht dtaaw phoot – When the tide goes out, the stumps speak

NEAT AND TIDY

It would be nice to have everything wrapped up with a neat little bow. But life doesn't come with neat little bows. It's messy, unpredictable, full of unresolved issues, within and without, looking for a conclusion. Suchada and Sankit had disappeared. Somboon had disappeared. I didn't know, I had guesses, but I didn't know why Tum had betrayed us. Khemkaeng and Damrong had disappeared, known dead. Pichit had disappeared, presumed dead. The floods were receding. Life was getting back to normal.

Aroon and Chainarong had come for lunch when we'd asked. It had taken three hours while we laid out the plan we had. They'd agreed to pull back and not react. The people that Mother had 'pulled' off the street were paid ten thousand baht each. The list of 'hard-core' guys had been made up of street vendors, hawkers and construction workers. A day of sitting with a hood over your head and tape over your mouth, worthy of the price and then some.

Ken and Dan's guys were disarmed without a shot at the warehouses. A standard shift change, each guard relieved by one of ours, "take a break, go have a shower." Walking into a room, a guy behind the door with a shotgun. No one was harmed, everyone had their photo taken, and after the barbeque at Big Tiger's, everyone was sent home.

The rape of David Sullivan was the culmination of a series of events that happened way before they hit my radar. Ken had David raped. David had been on his way home after watching a movie with friends and climbed into a taxi. Damrong had been driving the taxi. Ken figured it would keep Sullivan on track.

Supot was pissed at Goong for creating the mess he'd put Sullivan in, and David's brutal rape was the last straw. He called Here Leng and told him that Goong had done it again, this time to a farang. Here Leng had called Por, knowing the old man would take a firm and final line on Goong. Here Leng had pleaded for a second chance for his only son, and Por had relented.

Speedy Gonzalez was one of Ken's guys. When Ken heard that we'd taken Speedy from in front of the hospital and Tum was shipping Sullivan out of the country on our behalf, Ken assumed we knew what he'd done. No matter who you are, there are limits to what is acceptable behavior. Even in our world raping children is a long way off the mark. These details and others we picked up from Ken's people when we questioned them at the warehouse.

We didn't tell anyone the brothers were dead. We didn't talk about them in the past tense.

Around the time Por and Mother were sliding lit tapers of fire to the pyre surrounding Loong Virote's dead body at the temple, his will was being rewritten, leaving everything to Supot. The wives of the brothers complained, of course, but Supot set up bank accounts to make monthly payments to Khemkaeng's and Damrong's families from a not-so-small trust. All was settled within the week. Supot left Thailand and went to open a design studio in Milan. We talked a fair bit before he left; he visited me in hospital.

On the table beside me, the *Thai Rath* newspaper, front page, was a picture of the national deputy chief of police. The winds of fortune had blown his way in the last week, and the hot word on the street was he was about to become the national chief of police. I had some mending of burnt bridges to attend to, but that could wait to cool down a bit.

I had received a clipping from Mother, also from *Thai Rath*, two days previously, on page five, about a car crash in Saraburi in which a mother and her son were killed. It named Chatree and his mother.

Loyalty is about closing ranks against a threat, no matter the reason for the threat. Cop loyalty anywhere in the world is a strong force. Thailand is no different in this regard; the police were closing ranks on anything to do with Sankit. They knew who Chatree's mother was and to whom the land on which the house was built belonged. They saw the 'prison room'. They had a statement from Pim.

Just another deal. We keep quiet about what he did, and you keep quiet about the money and our role. Preecha's case and previous conviction 'disappeared' from the records in return for ten million. Dollars, of course. We'd practically drained Bangkok of American cash during the hours we'd converted Sankit's billion into dollars; we spent a lot of the last week putting it back in play.

The five million got paid to the lawyer on time. There are some people that you shouldn't screw with – he was one of them, his boss was another.

We put five million into the fund that Supot had set up for the families, I put half a million aside for Sullivan's kid, the remaining twelve and half Khun Preecha gave Pim and I as a wedding present. We gave half to Noot, the rest we gave to Mother to give to charity. We didn't want any part of it. It was 'bad luck' money. Use it for good things through as many hands as possible to wash the evil karma off it.

I checked the time on the cell. I had a flight to catch.

***

It was past one in the morning when I landed in Melbourne. I was traveling on a legitimate passport, just not mine. In less than fifteen minutes I was out of the airport, in a cab headed toward the city. The guy who'd picked me up, driving a Mercedes-Benz diesel, came from Hua Hin. The gun he gave me came from Russia. The money was from us via our tailor to another tailor in Melbourne and then picked up by this guy. No money moved on wires. Five kilometers from Tullamarine I dropped him off so he could get a cab home. He would pick up the car later in the day from the airport. I wouldn't be staying long.

Sullivan's wife had a brother who lived near Kalimna, in the seaside town of Lakes Entrance, east of the airport by about three hundred kilometers. An easy four-hour drive, staying within the speed limits. The brother ran a four-bedroom bed and breakfast just off Marine Parade. Michael, his wife, and their son, David, had been photographed there by a detective agency I'd hired through a friend of mine in Singapore earlier in the week. The agency had been keeping a discreet watch on the place for the last forty-eight hours. We'd pulled them off at midnight, just before I landed, or so I hoped.

Aussie cops aren't immune to a bit of graft, and it had cost less than a second-hand Holden to get photos of the brother meeting them in Darwin when Tom dropped them off and they disappeared. The same cop pulled the license number of the car they got into at the car park. With a name and address and a story about an embezzling accountant, the agency had taken less than eight hours to produce the photos of the family at her brother's B&B in Lakes Entrance.

I stopped once for a pee by the side of the road, but otherwise I drove until I saw a small café open early on Marine Parade in Lakes Entrance. The bed and breakfast place was just around the corner on Laura Avenue. I bought a cup of coffee, got back in the Benz, and drove around the corner, parking opposite but about two hundred meters down from the B&B. The coffee, a 'long black' in Aussie parlance, was good – strong and sweet.

Sullivan, as he had for the last two days, came out of the B&B at 5:30am. I let him do his warm-up and then start his jog toward the beach. I gave him a couple of hundred meters start, then slipped the Benz in drive and followed him. About a kilometer later, just as he was hitting stride, I lowered the window and pulled alongside him.

"Sullivan."

He looked over his shoulder, slowed, and recognized me, immediately averting his eyes from mine, jogging on as if pretending not to hear. I heard him gasp, it could have been a groan, as he looked for a place to run, slack-jawed mouth open, visibly shocked. The horror of the nightmare in Bangkok brought to the morning jog along the beach in Australia.

"Don't run. If I wanted you dead, you'd be dead already. Get in the car. I want to talk to you."

He looked up and down the road. An automated street-cleaning machine, a couple of early morning fishermen carrying long rods walking down to the seas edge and a lot of seagulls; I could see what he could.

He came around the car and got in, looked straight ahead, didn't look at me.

"Look at me."

He turned to face me. He looked older despite his new tan. He still looked tired and not from jogging, he'd hardly broken a sweat.

"Reach into the backseat, and grab the backpack. Take a look inside." He did as I asked.

"Why?" he asked.

"It's not for you. If you spend one cent on yourself, start looking over your shoulder because that's where I'll come from, and next time I won't call out your name. The money's for your son. Half a million doesn't go as far as it used to, but you know that, you're an accountant. Here." I handed him an iPhone open to the photos of Damrong. "That's for you, as I promised."

"Who is this man?"

"Why do you want to know? So you can explain to your son why he was raped? That it wasn't a random accident. That, although not directly responsible, his father had a hand in what happened? Is that why you want to know?"

"He doesn't know. My wife knows. I told her everything. We agreed not to tell him, not now anyway, maybe when he's older. She's divorcing me, but not until David is fully recovered."

"I'm glad to hear that he'll recover fully, but it isn't the physical wounds, although I'm sure they hurt like hell. Supot says hello – wants you to know that he has no bad feelings towards you and your family. He's sorry for what happened."

"I loved him, you know."

"Well, maybe when you're divorced and your son is in a safe place you can find him. He's in Milan. He said to tell you that too."

"Why are you doing this?" That was a big question with a long answer.

"Don't come back to Thailand. Don't ever talk about any of this to anyone, including your son and wife. It's done, move on, regret is a waste of time. Don't look back, look forward. Leave the phone on the dashboard, take the backpack, and get out of the car, please."

I watched in the rear-view mirror as he put the backpack on and started running back the way he'd come. I had a long drive back to Tullamarine, but I pulled over another two kilometers further up the road. A little grass lawn park, called Esplanade Reserve according to the sign at the entrance, led down to the water, across from that, about two hundred meters away, sand dunes and then the ocean, Bass Strait, to be precise.

I took my shoes and socks off and sat cross-legged looking east, out over the dunes in front of me. The time on the phone read 5:51am. I looked at Damrong. I'd liked him, found it hard to imagine him doing what he'd done. These were the only photos of his last moments. I deleted them, took the SIM out of the phone, wiggled it back and forth until it snapped and threw the pieces into the water.

The top of the sun rose above the dunes. A new day. Behind me I heard a shriek of joy. A couple and a young child, a boy. The father, I guessed, kicked a ball into the park. The boy, couldn't be more than three, ran after it, laughing and giggling all the way. The mother glanced at me and looked away, a frown crossing her face, maternal instinct I guess.

I turned back to face the sun, sat up straighter, put a hand, palm up, on each knee, made an 'O' with thumb and forefinger on each hand, shut my eyes, breathed in deep, and when I couldn't breathe in anymore, I let the breath go. Let the thoughts come, let the thoughts go, let the breath come, let the breath go.

It was a good way to start the day.

gam dai khrai gaaw gam nan yaawm sanaawng – Who sins, that sin will come around.

TILL DEATH DO US PART

Bangkok, Friday, 11 November 2011 8:45PM

I spoke to Chai while I walked through immigration and then arrivals. Weaving through people traffic, I made my way up to exit 5 on the departures level. Chai was waiting to pick me up in one of the Vitos. Pim was at Mother's house with her father, Noot, Por, Mother, and Uncle Mike. I spoke to her while the plane was taxiing to the gate. Dr. Tom had confirmed Pim was pregnant. Pim told him she would personally cut his balls off if he told anyone, especially Mother, before Pim. So far, according to Pim, no one knew, and tonight was the night we'd share the news.

Every time I thought of the baby I smiled, but I had some hard truths to lay down to the family tonight. Things I'd been thinking on for a long time. The family could have me, did have me, but they weren't going to have my child. I'd be the boss, I'd do what needed getting done, but my child would grow up free. If they could accept that, and I still didn't know what it meant in terms of our life moving forward, then I'd stay and take over from Por. I knew they'd agree, they loved me, and I them.

Chai was waiting next to the Vito, its hazard lights flashing. As soon as he saw me, he crossed the road.

"How's everything?" I said.

"Good, all quiet. Everything's settled down. A few of Khemkaeng's guys got a bit rowdy in a karaoke bar early this morning. Uncle Tong handled it, no one got shot, they're all in hospital. We're picking up the tab."

"Any news of Sankit or Suchada?"

"Nothing."

"I don't like the thought of them being around."

We got in the van. An airport cop pickup truck parked next to us and flashed its lights. We moved on slowly. I looked in the side mirror, couldn't see who was in the truck, but it looked like at least two cops. The headlights flashed again.

"What do you want to do?" Chai said, as he turned the hazards off.

"Keep going. Slowly pull into the far lane."

The cop's pickup followed us into the far lane, flashed its lights again.

"Shit. All right, pull over, and let's see what they want."

Chai pulled over, and we sat in the van waiting. I was watching the passenger-side mirror. A cop, youngish looking, got out, straightened his uniform, straightened his cap, tugged the peak lower, and started walking towards me. You can tell when someone is going to be a pain in the ass just by their actions. He knocked on the window. I lowered it.

He was a captain, roi tamruat ek in Thai, according to the pips on his epaulettes.

"How can I help you, Officer?"

"Could you step out of the vehicle, please?"

"Why, Officer?"

"I was asked by my new boss to introduce myself to you."

"I see, and who might your new boss be?"

"Please step out of the vehicle so that we may speak properly, sir." He put a little bite in his voice and stepped back from the van a pace. I glanced at Chai and nodded. He got out, walked around the front of the van, and then I got out.

"Thank you. So allow me to introduce myself. I am Roi Tamruat Ek Sompong Leeswattanaasawahame, recently transferred from Special Branch, reporting directly to the national police chief, in charge of a new operational unit." He'd clicked his heels together when he said his rank.

"Nice to meet you, Captain Sompong." I smiled; it seemed the polite thing to do.

He took a step closer, getting in my face. "No need to introduce yourself, Khun Oh, I know who you are. I know a lot about you. I didn't tell you what operational unit I'm running, did I? No, I forgot to mention that. It's got a nickname already; I'm quite proud of it. Do you know what the nickname is? No, of course you don't. It's 'The Untouchables'..."

"Wasn't that a movie with Sean Connery in it?"

"Yes…"

"Where he helps Jesus in a leper's colony?"

He smiled, a thin mean look that didn't get anywhere near his eyes, and dead fish sprang to mind when you looked at them. "I'm going to put you away, and when I do, you're never coming out…"

"Could you step back a bit? Your breath stinks."

He hit me. A hard, low jab, with his body weight behind it. I held up a hand towards Chai; he was going for it. Bent over, I was trying to find air to put back in my lungs. I got it sorted and straightened up.

"Nice punch, a low blow, but I get the message. You're coming for me, you're a hard case, but before you do, make sure you know what you're being told is right, or are you just an attack dog, blindly following orders?"

Six guys, all hard looking, wearing camouflage overalls, had materialized out of the back of the pickup truck.

"That's my team," Sompong said. "I wanted them all to get a good look at you."

"Are we done here?"

"Yeah, we're finished here. Be seeing you soon, Chance." He turned, almost like he was on a parade ground, and marched back to the pickup. The six guys did their own disappearing act into the pickup, and Sompong gave me a little two-fingered salute as he climbed in. They drove off.

"He's going to be a problem."

"I'll start finding out what I can. Do you want a smoke?" Chai said, holding out a packet of Marlboro red. I grinned.

"You're a bad influence, but you know me better than

anyone else. Thanks." I took one out, Chai lit it, and I leaned against the Vito, watching planes take off. After nine hours ten minutes in the air and a punch from a cop on arrival I figured I was due a smoke.

My phone buzzed. An SMS from Aunt Dao – 'Had a new dream about you, Pim and a baby? All okay, call me.' I smiled, cool.

I dropped the butt on the road, ground it out, and got back in the van.

"Let's go home."

We took the backstreets home, cutting through sois we'd been running over since we were kids, learning the gangster trade. Back here is suburbia, quiet at nine thirty on the backstreets, population heavy on the frontage roads. Food vendors, motorcycle taxis, mothers walking home after being at the factory or office all day, people waiting for crowded busses. Just another part of Bangkok's eighteen million going about their life. Forty kilometers away, Don Muang, the old airport, was still under a meter of water, the final death toll for floods over eight hundred and climbing.

We pulled into our soi and stopped at the gate in front of the property. Chai pressed the remote, but nothing happened. I flashed on the remote failing in the trunk of the Benz, how could I have thought that Mother would have allowed a faulty remote? The subject hadn't come up, but it would.

"I'll get it." The gate had been playing up for a couple of days. The rain had got into everything. I'd meant to mention it to the old guy who looks after the place but forgot. I got out and walked over to the control box.

Entered the code on the little box, and nothing happened. Normally it beeps. I looked underneath it; the wires coming into it were cut.

My first thought was Pim, Suchada, and something hit me hard in the back. I heard a shot. Everything went slow motion. I turned.

From across the soi, walking out from behind the trees that give us shade in the summer, Muscle Boy, screaming something at me, arm extended, gun in hand. It flashed, and I felt another hit in my chest, right side. Chai exploded out of the Vito, Uzi in the air above the door. Chai came over the roof of the Vito, the Uzi ripping out a burst. I tried to get out of the firing line. I could see the firing line, could see the muzzle of the pistol, watched it flash again, and felt the hit in my belly, left side.

A group of holes appeared in Muscle Boy's chest and worked their way up his throat until he fell, I went with him. Down on my knees, I knew I'd been shot. There's a part of your brain operating normally, having a casual chat with you. Telling you, in a matter-of-fact way, you've been shot, it's serious, but being calm about it. There's another part of your thought controlled by what you're looking at and feeling. Blood pumped out of the hole in my belly. I put my hands over it, but the pressure and amount was huge, it squirted out in pulses around my fingers.

Chai took me by the shoulders, only time I've ever seen him freaked out, and I knew I was dying.

I wanted to say a lot of things, but something was blocking my throat. I coughed, and Chai was covered in blood.

"Don't let Pim see…" I couldn't say anything more,

my throat was blocked again, and the line between my mouth and my brain temporarily out of order. I realized what Muscle Boy had been screaming, "I loved him, I loved him, you killed my love." Fair enough, he was right.

The tarmac felt warm on my cheek; it hadn't rained today. I looked over and saw Muscle Boy's cowboy boots – second time lucky. I felt bad that I was doing this to Pim on what should be her happy day. Aunt Dao's dream was…

BANGKOK WET

CPSIA information can be obtained
at www.ICGtesting.com
Printed in the USA
FSHW021309070721
83019FS